HAIL MARY DUET #2

RED
Zone

C.A. RENE

Copyright © 2022 C.A. Rene

www.careneauthor.com

This book is a work of fiction, and any resemblance to any person, living or dead, is purely coincidental, the characters and story lines are created by the author's imagination and are used fictitiously.

No copyright infringement intended.

No claims have been made over songs and/or lyrics written. All credit goes to the original owner.

Cover by: Black Widow Designs Co

Edited by: Kim BookJunkie

www.KimBookJunkie.com

PLAYLIST

Legends Are Made - Sam Tinnesz (Red Zone Theme Song)

Petty Too - Lil Durk ft Future

City of Gods - Fivio Foreign/Kanye West/Alicia Keys

Diet Coke - Pusha T

Gospel - Dr.Dre/Eminem

Rumors - Gucci Mane/Lil Durk

G Lock - Digga D/Moneybagg Yo

I Wish - Kodak Black

Tell The Vision - Pop Smoke/Kanye West/Pusha T

Champions - Ty Dolla $ign/Wiz Khalifa

Marvins Room - Drake

Ruff Ryders' Anthem - DMX

DEDICATION

For Michelle Ann

Thank you for stepping in and helping me when I needed it.
Your friendship is so appreciated!

"We're a team that's fighting for **RESPECT**. Sometimes you earn it. Sometimes you **TAKE IT**."

– *Anthony 'Boobie' Dixon, Buffalo Bills.*

PROLOGUE

Sebastian

Her head snapped back with the force of that bullet, spraying her blood all over the cabinets, stealing the life I valued more than my own. The moment I watched the light vacate her eyes, I changed.

I began to lose the man I'd fought to be, the one who kept his rotten core hidden, and my life became a series of reels. I watched the lives I'd taken much the same way, the nights I'd spent coked out of my mind, then always coming back to Dixon. Only to start all over again.

All on an endless loop.

All my life's choices culminated that night, and when she died… I died with her. The football career, being a father, running the streets all faded into the background. My head blanked, and I forced myself to watch each mistake on that reel, over and over. Just to make sure I understood who's truly at fault here.

I'd let my wants overshadow my needs… I'd become a fucking pussy. The guys would take me out with a shot to my own fucking head if they knew the shit I'd been up to.

I fucked up.

It's all good, though. I won't be held down for long, and when I come back, it'll be like it was before the rookie showed up. I've given him too much, softened too much, and now I'm fucking suffering for it.

I won't lose sight again, and I won't ever find myself in this spot, where I'm questioning how everything happened. It happened because I didn't think of the consequences of my actions. The effects of my choices.

There's only one way to fix it all, and that's to harden every bit of me that's gone soft, letting nothing penetrate. It's back to the streets, back to the life I've always known.

Dixon North will be nothing but a distant memory.

CHAPTER ONE

He's been gone for three months, suspended off the team pending the results of the police investigation, and I can't get a hold of him. That last phone call still echoes throughout my mind, and sometimes it's the last thing I hear before my mind gives over to sleep.

"Dixon!" His voice reverberates out of my phone's speaker. "Everything I did was to protect you!"

"Seb, where are you?" My voice shakes as worry clutches at my chest. "What is that noise?"

I can faintly hear sirens, like an ambulance or cop cars.

"I can't go to jail," he whispers, his voice drowning out.

"Seb!" I yell. "Do I hear cops?"

"I just needed to make sure you were kept out of shit, that you were safe."

Jameson and Ortiz have been tight-lipped. I don't know if it's because they were told to keep their mouths shut or because they haven't heard from him either, despite them being his boys.

It's been all over the news. Home invasion, dirty cops, murder. His wife was shot in the head, a cop was shot next to her, the whole story sounds like something out of a gruesome, true-crime documentary.

His wife is dead, probably killed in front of him, and no one has heard from him. He's suffering alone, probably wallowing in self-pity, but in true Sebastian form, he's refusing to ask for help.

It's the off-season, and we're preparing for the upcoming season, making sure this time we get that ring on our fingers. But the team is shrouded in worry as one of our own is going through something terrible, it's always there in the back of our minds.

We closed the season sitting in fourth place in the conference, not bad considering the shit we dealt with. Like having a player benched for the most crucial games. The boys pulled through, though, and Zeal was given the MVP award. Most deserved.

I've been working with my physical rehabilitation, trying to get my knee back into top shape. It's been hard, and I can't deny that I've been taking Toroidal off and on. I'm not abusing it like I did during the on-season, but I use it when I need that extra boost. I can't be completely useless, sitting on the sidelines, watching my team achieve greatness without me.

I need to feel like I am contributing to it. I want to do that in my brother's memory.

If I fuck this career up, then I may as well join him. I neglected him to get to this point, and it would be like spitting on his grave if I fail.

Danny was my sole motivation to succeed… Now his spirit is my reason to continue.

The gym is quiet as we all train today, the air around us heavy with concern, making the mood dark and brooding.

"He's been given the greenlight to come back to Buffalo," I hear Ortiz mutter to Jameson, causing my heart to stutter in my chest.

"He called you?" Jameson asks, his voice hushed to match Ortiz's.

They're standing behind me, working the dumbbells as I use the leg press on the lowest weight possible.

"Nah," Ortiz huffs. "I heard Coach say something on the phone."

"I've been calling him non-stop. It's been three fucking months, man," Jameson whines. I can't help but sympathize with him.

"I was talking to my boy, and he said when he was under investigation, the police took his phone."

I perk up at that. That makes sense; they did the same to Ma and me when they were investigating Danny's death.

"Avando has like four fucking phones. If he wanted to talk to us, he would," Jameson snaps, making me deflate once again.

"He's just keeping us out of the mess," Ortiz tries to sooth the rejection. "You know how it is."

They stop talking after that, and when my knee begins to protest the machine, I reluctantly leave them to hit the weight bench. I find Zeal there, spotting Dex as he pumps an obscene amount of iron.

"How's the knee?" Zeal asks without taking his eyes off Dex.

"Frustrating," I growl. "This healing process is taking forever."

"Don't overwork it," Dex warns. "It'll only take longer."

"Take your time with it," Zeal advises. "We have months until the next season."

"I'll be put on second string," I snap.

"So what if you are?" Dex drops the bar back into the holder then sits up. "Better than never playing again."

They're right, I know that. But I'm still so fucking frustrated.

"You've been working hard," Zeal slaps my back. "What do you say we hit up Sky Lounge?"

"Zeal goes home in a few days to spend some time with his mommy," Dex snorts, pulling a smile out of me. "Let's send him off right."

"Sounds good," I nod. It does sound good, regardless of the memories it unearths.

"Did someone say Sky Lounge?" Ortiz comes up beside me, wrapping his arm around my shoulders.

If this was five months ago, I would've knocked his fucking lights out, but things have changed. I can never forgive their part in the attack, but if I can forgive and fuck my rapist, why should I hold a grudge against the men who helped?

"Zeal wants to party before he goes home to Mommy," I snicker, making the guys all laugh.

"I'm down for some drinks and titties." Jameson appears on my other side. "Maybe we can convince a chick to take Zeal's virginity."

"Man, fuck you guys," Zeal chuckles as he grabs up his towel. "I lost my virginity when I was thirteen."

"Your cousin doesn't count," Dex chimes in, and we all lose it to raucous laughter.

"Har, har." Zeal claps a hand on Dex's shoulder. "I'm still a virgin in the back, big man, if you want to have a go?"

My stomach drops into my stomach as they all laugh around me. I can't even summon up a smile. This conversation has taken a turn onto a road I have a hard time entertaining. I know it's jokes and laughs, but all I can think about is Seb.

Everyone files out, the air filled with excitement, yet I'm the one sore spot as I continue to let Seb stew in my thoughts.

"North." Coach's voice hits me, pulling me from my contemplation. "Can I see you in my office?"

I nod, paying close attention to the older man's face. It's lined with stress, the crease between his brows a constant feature these days, and his usually ruddy face has lost its color.

He closes the door behind us, alerting me to the fact that this will be an important, *private* conversation. I can't help but think of Danielle.

"I had a conversation with Dani," he begins as I chew into the flesh of my cheek to keep from blurting anything out. "She's been to the doctor recently, and the results are alarming."

Please tell me she has kidney stones or something.

"She told me she had spoken to you a few months back about

her situation."

"Coach," I lean forward, making sure to meet his eyes. "I am not the father of the child she's carrying."

The office fills with thick tension as I stiffen, preparing for a fight.

"I know you two were tight for a while there," he pauses to run his fingers along his forehead. "But I won't hold it against you until the child is born. I suspect you'll want a DNA test?"

"Yes, sir," I nod.

"She's adamant she was seeing no one else." His eyes narrow as his head tips forward.

"I understand, sir, but with all due respect, I don't want to lay out in detail what I witnessed that makes her claim incorrect."

He nods briefly, his eyes closing then his mouth curving downward. I bet he knows all about his daughter and her penchant for fucking his team.

"Okay, thank you, North."

The dismissal is heavy in tone, so I stand with a nod before heading out of the office, my stomach twisting with apprehension. She really is pregnant. There was a part of me that was hoping it was all a ruse to lock one of us down permanently, but now all I can see is Seb plowing into her while his hand held her head to the desk her father is currently sitting at.

Could he be the father?

I'll fucking kill him if that's the case.

His dumb ass was trying to teach me a fucking lesson, and he did it raw inside of the woman who's been taking turns with his teammates like a fucking carousel ride. The only saving grace is he came in my mouth instead of inside of her.

"Dawg," Ortiz says as I come into the locker room. "Take a fucking shower, you smell like death and desperation."

"That's a big word for you," I grin as I rip my hoodie over my head. "Did you read the dictionary this week?"

"Yeah, your mother gets off on it." He thrusts his hips, motioning like he's fucking my mother, making me fight hard to keep the smile off my face.

"She did say you had trouble with pronunciations," I sneer as I grab a towel. "Hooked on Phonics is always available."

"Fuck you!" he calls as I head for the showers, hearing the guys laugh at our banter.

It's been different without Seb here. I don't know if it's because he's not here or if the team has finally accepted me wholeheartedly. It was no secret that Sebastian hated me the moment I arrived, and it bled through to a few of the team members. But he changed, we both did. We went from bitter enemies to something I can't describe. We still hate each other, we just express it differently.

The images of how we express it floods my mind, making me fall against the tiled stall, my cock hardening and my throat closing with emotion.

Where is he?

Three shots in, and I find myself in the bathroom, staring at my reflection in the mirror. My skin is no longer vibrant with color, it's dulled, the undertone giving me a sick appearance. The bags under my eyes are dark with lack of sleep, making my brown eyes look lifeless.

I finally cut my hair, the fade looking fresh, but whatever I lost on my head, I've gained on my face. The beard started through pure laziness while I was home recovering and worrying about someone who couldn't give a fuck about me. Now it's staying because I like the look.

My eyes skip to the stalls behind me, remembering the last time I was in here with Seb. My throat clogs, and I try to swallow it down, my heart pounding in my chest.

I just want to see him.

The way I long for my one-time rapist and tormentor is not fucking healthy, but I can't stop it. It's like he's doing it on purpose, taunting me by acting like I don't exist. Ignoring me was always his go-to choice for torturing me, and it worked every fucking time.

I long for him like a lover, and the thought no longer twists my stomach into knots. He *was* my lover.

I dry my hands as I curse, knowing I've been in here longer than it requires to take a piss, and I can only imagine the flack I'll catch for it from the guys. I pull open the door, shoving all thoughts of Seb down, promising myself to enjoy the night.

"Fuck, North!" Dex exclaims from the bar. "Glad to have you back. I thought maybe you had a female in there with you."

I can hear his words, but the sight in front of me has stolen my ability to speak. He's there, facing the bartender, looking thicker with muscle, his head completely shaved. But I know it's him. His terracotta skin shines under the fluorescent light, highlighting the dimple in his cheek as he leans in to order his drink.

A new tattoo crawls along his neck, just under his jaw. *Paola.* The sight makes my chest tighten with sympathy. Or maybe it's jealousy.

That must be his wife's name.

His dead wife.

Murdered wife.

"Look who's back!" Zeal throws an arm around my shoulders. "And he decided to come see me off."

Seb turns slowly, those thick, black brows drawn together, eyes glowing as his mouth turns down into a serious scowl.

Fuck, he looks so good.

"Just for one drink." His voice drips with honey, making my cock swell instantly.

He turns back to the bar, never acknowledging me, not even a single glance, and I swallow down the urge to scream his name. It wouldn't be out of place for Sebastian Avando to ignore my presence, the team is more than aware of his disdain for me, but my heart is breaking from his brush off.

Well, I'm about to make this real uncomfortable.

Those three shots in my stomach begin to burn—giving me the courage I would never possess otherwise—as I shoulder my way between him and Dex, slapping my hand to the bar top.

"This calls for a celebration," I exclaim, making Dex roar with appreciation. "Let's get another round of shots."

I stare at the side of his face, willing him to look at me. Instead, I'm met with the tightening of his jaw. So what? He's been gone for months, and all of a sudden he's over us? He doesn't even want to be near me now when he was all too eager to fuck me not too long ago?

The bartender approaches us, dropping shot glasses to the bar then grabbing the Grey Goose from the shelf. She gives me a sweet look, her eyes squinting from the force of her smile. She brushes her dark, brown hair behind her shoulder, and her honey skin glows with a creeping blush.

"You grew out your beard!" she calls over the music, loud enough for everyone to hear. "I like it."

Dex whistles, but Seb stiffens, his reaction telling me he's not immune to me.

"Oh, yeah?" I lean forward, bringing my face closer to hers. "How much do you like it?"

Her brown eyes widen then darken immediately with suggestion. "Enough that I'll get fired if I show you."

His hand fists on top of the bar, and I feel like a fucking addict, doing everything I can for his small reactions. So I take it even further. My hand reaches out, wrapping around the back of her head, bringing her in closer so our noses touch.

"I think I could speak to your manager about it." My tongue dips out, brushing along her lip, making her moan.

It does nothing for me, but Seb shoving back from the counter, and stalking off to the bathroom does, making my stomach swirl with excitement.

I pull back from her and watch as she pours our drinks. I want to follow him so badly, but I refuse to be his fucking puppy dog. We take the shots, the guys all scream Zeal's name, then I watch as they all head out to the main area in search of women.

Seb is still in the bathroom, and I can't help but think he's waiting for me. Or else he's sniffing enough coke to down an elephant. I head to the bathroom when I'm sure no one will notice my absence and try to tamp down the feelings inside of me. I'm nervous, excited, but fucking angry.

A Molotov cocktail.

I shove open the door with more force than I intended, making it bounce off the doorstop with a loud thud before it closes slowly behind me.

The first thing I notice is the smashed mirror over the sinks, the shards looking like a menacing spider's web, some covered in blood. I swallow down my trepidation as I follow the drops of blood along the floor to the first stall.

"Seb?"

"Get the fuck out of here, you fucking pussy."

Yep, back to square one.

I know his words are nothing to smile about, but he's fucking talking to me.

"I figured you were waiting in here for me," I taunt. "What made you so angry you needed to bust in the mirror?"

"I was imagining it was your fucking face," he snarls from behind the stall door.

"You're the fucking pussy," I retort. "Hiding in there."

He flies out of the stall, consumed by anger as his bleeding fist grabs the material of my shirt, shoving my back to the wall. His face is contorted and looking demonic as he gets in mine.

"Fuck you, you homo bitch." His words are like sharpened knives, stabbing through my ribcage. "Stay the fuck away from me."

I'm momentarily shocked by the vitriol spewing from his mouth, his hatred a little more potent than what I expected. I stare into those amber eyes, trying to decipher his reaction.

He was there when my brother was murdered, he watched me grieve, and I never once thought this is what I would get in return. I want to be here for him, but I can't do that if he's back to hating me. I need to know why.

"What the fuck did I do?" I can't help the shocked tone of my voice or the trembling of my limbs. "Why are you being like this?"

"Fuck you." He releases me, his face a mask of disgust. "I don't want to ever touch you or speak to you again."

His words explode in my chest, burning me as my heart incinerates.

He heads to the sinks and turns one on, dousing his bleeding knuckles under the water. I watch as the stream slowly turns from red to pink, and when he still hasn't acknowledged me, I know he means every hateful word he's said.

"Fine," I swallow down my feelings, turning for the door. "I'm sorry about your wife."

"You should be," he growls as I pull the door open. "It's your fucking fault it happened."

CHAPTER TWO

Sebastian

Being back here feels like a waste of my fucking time. I want to be back in Rochester, working with my boys to find out everything we can about those dirty fucking cops. But I can't be affiliated with gangs while I'm still being watched. I was given the go-ahead to come back to Buffalo because the cops couldn't pin anything on me, and I won't let them find a single thing to latch on to.

The walk up to the stadium is like fucking torture when all I want to do is walk the streets, knocking a bullet into anyone who looks my way. This anger is fucking getting the best of me, making it harder to control myself.

I clench my busted knuckles, relishing in the pain as it shoots up my arm. The sting reminds me of my confrontation with North, and it takes everything in me not to soften. I hated how hurt he looked, but I can't deny that my accusations were fucking accurate. If I wasn't out trying to find revenge for his gangbanger of a brother, my wife would still be alive.

Carla would still have her mother.

I know it was my choice, he still doesn't know exactly what I've done to avenge his baby brother's death, and he can't know. It doesn't help the animosity that runs through me with every fucking thought of him, though. And I think about him often.

The only way this will work, the only way I'll stay out of jail, is to make sure I hate the fucker and he hates me just as much. I can't fold for him, no matter how much I want to.

Just watching him flirt with that bartender last night made me nearly homicidal, wanting to reach for my piece and shoot her head open. I took it out on the bathroom mirror instead.

I can't go out with them anymore, I can't chill and hangout if Dixon is going to be there. I need to keep myself clean. That's the hardest fucking part. I can't numb myself while I have eyes on me, so no coke or weed until the heat is off, and that means I'm fucking nuclear in the meantime.

I pull open the door and take a deep breath. Regardless of how I'm feeling about football, this place feels like home. I head down the corridor that leads to the locker room, stopping in my tracks when I see Dani walking out of her father's office.

Dani with a baby bump.

Her hazel eyes collide with mine, and a nasty smirk begins to line her lips as her hand rests on the slight swell of her stomach. I breathe, I fucking count to ten, then I do it all over again.

"Welcome back," she says, her hand rubbing circles onto her stomach. "I'm sorry about your wife."

My teeth crack as she speaks, and my jaw is so fucking tight, I worry it'll stay that way.

"Whose is it?" I sneer.

"Dixon's, of course." Her eyes narrow. "Maybe you can convince him to be a man about it."

I take a menacing step forward then stop, reminding myself that anything Dixon related is not my fucking problem.

"Good luck with that," I snarl as I continue by her, holding my breath to avoid her stinking perfume. "That's what happens when you fuck boys."

I push open the double doors to the locker room, finding Dixon in deep conversation with Dex.

"Avando!" Dex stands and strides forward. "Fuck, it's good to have you back."

I give him a nod and clasp his hand, moving past him without a word, grateful he hasn't brought up anything about my wife's murder. I don't know how much the team knows.

Jameson and Ortiz aren't here yet, and they weren't at the club last night. Dex said they were supposed to go but never showed. It's not unlike them… They probably found blow and pussy elsewhere.

Cravings for the white powder course through me as I feel the beginnings of a headache forming. Since my last concussion, these headaches have been frequent, and now that I can't numb the pain, life is about to get brutal.

"Jameson and Ortiz have been fucking lost without you," Dex chuckles as I step up to my locker, feeling the heat of Dixon's stare on my face.

"That's because they're bitches." I toss a grin over my shoulder at him as he laughs.

"Is that our boy?!" Jameson hollers from the locker room entrance as I turn toward him with a grin. Ortiz is there too, and seeing them both alleviates some of the tension in the room.

"You guys miss your daddy?" I taunt as they rush forward, clasping me in their arms.

"We're sorry about Paola, man," Jameson says quietly.

"We tried to contact you," Ortiz adds.

"Yeah, I know. I just wasn't in the right mindset."

The heat of Dixon's stare is starting to get to me as I yank off my sweater, tossing it in my locker.

"Gym?" I ask Jameson and Ortiz. They both nod, following me out of the locker room.

This is going to be harder than I fucking thought.

Being back in the gym at the stadium almost feels like no time has passed, almost like my wife and daughter are home, waiting to watch me every Sunday night.

Almost.

The thought has my chest seizing and my lungs stalling on my next breath. Paola. She didn't deserve what happened to her, but she stayed loyal, right to the very end. I wish I could've been the man she deserved, the one who didn't fuck around on her and did more than just provide her with the material shit in life.

At least she knew I loved her in my own way.

"What have I missed?" I ask when I can finally suck in a lungful of air.

"Coach is cracking down on partying and piss tests. Last week he sprung a surprise one, no one fucking knew," Jameson spits out.

"You all passed, though," I shrug. "Who cares?"

"North didn't," Ortiz snickers, and I freeze on the spot.

"He failed a drug test?" My mouth dries out as I stare at Ortiz, shock lining my muscles.

"It was a false positive," Jameson says as he sits at the leg press. "Toroidal does that. He's lucky Coach gave him another right after, then he passed."

"He's still shooting up his leg?" My voice sounds like fucking gravel, filled with anger.

"Not as often," Jameson's brow raises. "Just every now and then when his knee acts up."

"You will not give him another syringe, am I fucking clear?" I point my index finger at him, the look in my eye making him sheepish.

"Yeah, sure."

"What's the big deal?" Ortiz interjects. "What do you care what the rookie does?"

"I don't give a fuck about him," I snarl, turning on him quickly. "What the fuck do you think will happen when he does test positive? Who do you think the pussy will rat out?"

Jameson swallows thickly. "I don't think North would do that."

"Then you're a bigger idiot than I thought," I snap. "Do not give him anymore."

Jameson nods as he begins his leg routine, but Ortiz stays rooted at the dumbbells, his eyes inspecting me closely. He's not as fucking stupid, and I can see the wheels in his head turning. He's wondering why I fucking care so much.

"Eyes are on me, and if you guys go down, I may get caught up," I explain as I grab a dumbbell.

"I thought you were cleared." Ortiz begins his repetitions with me.

"Only because they couldn't connect me with more than self-defense."

They don't ask any more questions, knowing I won't give them much more than that. They know only a miniscule bit of what I do back home, and that's all they'll ever get.

The sauna light is on when I get back from the gym, making my teeth grind when I think of him being in there. I was the last one to leave the gym because it's been a while since I worked out, and I needed to forget, just for a short time. But knowing he and I are here by ourselves is setting my fucking blood to boil.

He's still taking Toroidal.

Without much thought, I storm toward the wooden door, yanking it open as the hot steam hits my face.

"Are you seriously still hitting up *my boy* for your fucking drugs?" It comes out louder than I mean for it, and I can only hope Coach isn't here in his office.

Dixon sits up straight on the bench, his eyes wide with shock then flaring with anger.

"Mind your fucking business."

"Mind my what?" I grit out as I stride to him, my hand shooting out and gripping the ridiculous beard on his chin. "It is my fucking business."

"Why do you all of a sudden give a fuck?" He slaps my hand away, his grin growing like he fucking caught me in my feelings.

So I do what I do best… I crush his feelings. "I don't give a shit about you, but if you test positive again, my boy could get dragged into your fucking drama. Kind of like my fucking wife."

He stands abruptly, getting in my face, and as soon as his scent washes over me, I harden.

"Why do you keep saying that?" His voice is low. "What does your wife's death have to do with me?"

The rapid rise and fall of his chest relays his anger. When I don't answer right away, he shoves me backward.

"Answer me!"

I lock my jaw and turn my back, opening the sauna door. "I wasted my time when I was needed elsewhere." I toss over my shoulder as I leave.

I need him to hate me.

31

C.A. RENE

Chapter Three

Dixon

I fucking hate him.

This is worse than when I first joined the team, his hatred came from nothing but jealousy back then, not bothering to give himself the chance to get to know me. Now he's been *inside* me, so his hatred burns my very soul.

I was a waste of his time.

The thought has my head pounding as I pull up to my gate, slamming my finger to the keypad as I punch in the gate code. How dare he think he can control what I do with my life? It's bad enough I have to deal with Dani, but to add his shit to the mix makes me want to fucking lose it.

My tires burn as I accelerate up the driveway then shove it into park, my anger boiling over. I grab my bag, my fists locking as I consider my options. I only have two syringes left. There's no point going back to Jameson, he's always been Seb's fucking bitch.

I get to my front door and look up at the red light in the corner, remembering a night not too long ago when Seb did the same then stole my breath in front of it. With each memory that's unearthed, my stomach twists more. I'm not only grieving my brother but also the man who made me doubt everything.

As soon as I step in the house, the smell of roasting chicken greets me, making my stomach grumble with hunger. I forgot to make a shake today, and I didn't touch the protein bar in my bag.

"Ma!" I call out, hearing her answer from the kitchen.

When I walk in, I see she's busy at the stove as I take a deep breath, inhaling the scent of mashed potatoes.

"Shit, that smells good."

"You watch your mouth," she points a spoon at me. "How was practice today?"

"Fine," I shrug. Dani once again filters through my thoughts, but I will her away. I don't ever want to tell my mother I knocked a girl up.

"The news was broadcasting at the stadium today, saying your teammate was back. Why didn't you tell me it was the young man who visited you in the hospital?"

"What does it matter?" I ask as I take a seat at the kitchen island.

"Because he was more than a teammate, Dixon. I could see you were close friends."

Her words send chills down my spine. Panic begins to swell inside me as I stare at her, trying to figure out what she knows.

"He was there when I was hit on the field," I explain. "That's why he came to the hospital."

"I see," she hums, turning back to the stove. "You should invite him over for dinner one night. We have this big home and no one to fill it."

"Ma, you wouldn't want the team over here," I shake my head. "You can't even handle me saying *shit*."

"I know how much ruckus grown men can cause, Dixon," she tuts at me. "I just remind you to be a gentleman because you're mine."

"All right," I smile at her.

"It would be nice to cook for a full house," she muses as she goes back to the gravy.

"Sure, Ma," I concede. "I'll see about having a poker night."

"Poker?" Her eyes widen as she looks at me. "You're going to host illegal gambling in our home?"

"Ma," I roll my eyes with a chuckle. "See?"

"Fine," she waves me off. "Make sure your friend comes by," she looks at me over her shoulder. "It looks like he needs a friend now, and he was there for you."

Again, my stomach twists at her words. "What do you know about it?"

"As much as the news tells me." She pulls the chicken out of the large, industrial-sized oven. "His wife was killed in a home invasion."

"Yeah," I mumble as she dishes out a plate of chicken, potatoes, and green beans for me.

"That's rough." She places the food in front of me. Suddenly, my hunger transforms into something close to nausea. I don't want to discuss Seb.

Thankfully, that's all she says as she washes her hands and excuses herself, leaving me alone to stew in her words.

I don't want to feel the pity collecting in my stomach for the man who used me. I can't sympathize with him because he won't let it happen. He'll fight me tooth and nail, and I just might find myself at his mercy once again.

I don't think I could handle it.

It's not mandatory to come to the stadium every day during the off-season, but I still like to run the track. Some days it's just me, while on others, Coach or a few of the guys come by. Football has always been an integral part of my life I don't know what I would do with myself without it.

This morning I'm left to face the one person who loves to break me for sport.

He's taping his hands up when I walk in, causing my feet to falter as his shoulder muscles bunch with the motion. He doesn't look up, as if he knows it's me, starting the whole heartbreaking process over again. It hurts that he can't even stand to look at me.

I swallow down the lump in my throat and open my locker, pushing my sweater inside. He's not the only one who can force himself to shut down.

"North!" Jameson booms as he comes into the locker room. "Man, you practically live here."

"Yeah," I nod. "I need this knee in top form this season."

"Do it without using," Seb grumbles behind me.

"I'm gonna go run some laps," I say to Jameson, squeezing his shoulder as I pass.

"All right, Avando." He claps his hands. "You called me here at the ass crack of dawn to spot you, so let's get this shit started."

I leave them behind, their voices becoming hushed as soon as the doors shut, and I force my feet to take me up the ramp to the field. My knee begins to burn the second I begin to run, making me grit my teeth to stop from screaming. It's so fucking frustrating. It shouldn't take this long to heal.

Seven fucking laps, and I can't put my full weight on my foot. My knee is radiating with agony. I stop, staring at the field under my feet, the colors beginning to blur as moisture collects in my eyes. My hands fist the material of my shirt at my waist as I bite into my tongue until the iron taste of blood coats my mouth.

Will I ever be a hundred percent again?

I exhale through my teeth as I begin the slow, hobbling trek back to the locker room. With each soft step of my foot on the concrete, pain shoots up to my groin, making me huff out the breaths I'm holding.

"You're not following PT, are you?" I startle to a stop, my bad knee catching my stumble, forcing a scream from my throat.

Seb rushes forward and grabs me before I hit the ground, the heat of his body penetrating my skin.

"Fuck, North," he snaps. "This isn't good."

"No shit, asshole." I shrug him off before my heart remembers what those hands felt like in other places.

"You've stunted your recovery with the fucking Toroidal."

"Fuck you, Avando!" I rebuke. "You don't know what it's been like." Again, his features contort as my fucking eyes fill.

"I know what it's like to be injured. I know what it's like to watch your teammates struggle to do what they can usually do easily," he says quietly, his hands shooting out when I begin to hobble by him.

"Don't touch me," I bark as the first tear hits my cheek. I swipe it away angrily, growling at the fucking weakness I'm showing him.

Seb of all fucking people.

He doesn't move to help me again, he just stays rooted to that spot, watching me slowly make my way back to the locker room. I breathe out a sigh of relief when I find it empty, then I slowly strip off my clothes, grabbing a towel to wrap around my waist. I hobble to the sauna, knowing the heat will increase the swelling but also soothe the pain. It's a double edged sword, but I choose to dull the pain, seeing as pain relief will be harder to come by now.

I sit in the fucking sauna, letting the tears loose while all the pain I've held in these past few days rushes from my chest in choked sobs. There's a part of me that wishes the door would open then the steam would cascade around him as he stepped inside, like the many times before. Then there's another part of me that hopes he never sees me like this. It would just be ammunition, and I always find myself on the wrong side of his weapon.

Like a desperate target begging for the pain he inflicts.

Sebastian

The second I saw the agony shining through his eyes, I knew I would fucking soften, and I did. I was like a pile of mush at his feet, and if he would've let me, I would've had him in my arms in a heartbeat. Not giving a fuck who saw.

So fucking weak.

I don't know what it is about Dixon North, but he came into my fucking life and turned it upside down. He grabbed a hold of a piece of me, claiming it for himself. He has no idea, the power he holds.

I can't ever let him know.

My phone vibrates on the table beside the bag of blow I've been eyeing for the last hour. I came home, needing a fucking outlet for all this pent up shit inside of me, and that was the first thing I thought of. I just can't bring myself to fuck up, not with Paola's memory coloring everything I do, not with our daughter depending on me.

Carla has been staying with Paola's parents, and she's been a wreck since the day I told her Mommy went to heaven. I will never forget how her little face fell. It was then I made the unbreakable promise to bring down the crooked cops who decided to play with the big boys.

I swipe open my phone to see a text from Ortiz. He's telling me Dixon is having a get together at his place tomorrow night, and the guys are going. I shut the phone without responding, pressing my finger into the plastic covered powder.

There's no way in hell I can go to his place, not after everything that went down in that house, that went down in his *room*. My cock hardens painfully, jerking as I look at my gun resting on the table. I groan into my fist as memories flood my mind. The shit I did to him with my fucking piece.

The shit I still want to do to him with my fucking cock.

I grab myself through my pants, gritting my teeth because not even the prospect of pussy pulls me out of my thoughts of Dixon anymore. Nothing does. The only time I feel alive is when I'm hard and thinking of him.

I fucking hate it.

He's still the only thing I crave more than the powder my finger is currently swirling in. Dixon North is my fucking vice, a drug I won't ever see the bottom of.

I told myself I wouldn't go. I woke up at five a.m., ready to head to the stadium, knowing he'd be there and wanting to make sure he was okay. I was nearly out of bed when I forced myself to lie back down, enduring the withdrawals from Dixon North. He's the reason I'm feeling so fucking alone.

I promised myself I would lounge at home, drink a beer or two then watch a movie. The guys could go hang out at his house, but I wasn't fucking stepping foot near his front door.

Ortiz and Jameson texted me when they got there, talking about how his mother made a feast, and they were playing poker.

It sounds like a fucking teenage slumber party, all they need is to put on some blurred out porn and giggle over the noises. It solidified my decision about keeping my ass on my couch ... until I found myself in the shower.

Didn't mean I was going anywhere.

Next I'm in my closet, imagining I'm grabbing my sweats and a tee. Instead, I'm dressing in fucking jeans and a black V-neck. My hand hits my jaw, feeling the stubble that's beginning to grow in. *If* I was going somewhere, I'd shave that shit. But I'm not, so who gives a fuck?

I stand in front of my open fridge, groaning when I see I'm down to five beers. That's just pitiful. If Jameson or Ortiz show up, how hospitable would that be? Not very. At least my addict of a mother taught me that much.

Always have booze and drugs for your besties.

I grab my keys off the table and my leather jacket off the chair, shrugging it on slowly. I could go to the convenience store up the street, but they only sell beer, and I know I need a bottle of Hennessy.

I'll have to pass by Dixon's house, but honestly, I need to have liquor in the house.

Hospitality and all that.

His street is up at the next intersection. I can turn right to go to the liquor store or left to see what this party is all about. It's not like I'm going to stop in, I just want to make sure the guys aren't drinking and driving. I shouldn't see any vehicles in the drive, and it's Dixon's responsibility to make sure they call an Uber.

I sound like a fucking female.

When did I ever give a fuck about who drove from my fucking house?

I press on the gas, speeding down his street while his gate passes in my periphery with a blur. I need to let him go, he's not mine.

That's what I'm telling myself as I pull a U-turn at the end of the street, making my way back toward his house.

Okay, I'm fucking curious, and a whole lot pissed off that I wasn't invited. I'm a part of this team—an integral part—and he's just going to gloss over me on the fucking guestlist?

Hell nah.

I think it's time I remind this rookie bitch who runs the fucking show. Maybe he needs to be reminded of where the fuck he belongs.

Under me.

The gates are open when I pull up to the house, and it's oddly quiet for a party. I don't hear music, no one is spilling out onto the porch, and the lights are all on.

This really is some pussy shit. Are they painting each other's nails?

I get out of the Hummer then slam the door, hoping the noise startles the house full of nanas inside. Maybe they're playing a game of Bridge and drinking boxed wine. I stride up to the door, my steps faltering when I look up at the small red light in the corner as more memories flood my mind.

The overwhelming need to taste him, to feel his lips on mine rushes through me. I long to reach inside of him, just to grasp anything left belonging to me in there.

Fuck.

My fist hits the door in a quick rap, hoping I won't have to hit the doorbell and bring myself an audience. The uninvited teammate, the one hated by the host, is begging to be let in.

I ain't begging for shit, though.

The door opens, revealing Dixon's mother standing in front of me. Her graying hair is pulled back into a bun as she peers at me, the look of kindness giving me pause. Her dark brown eyes scan over me from head to toe, but when they collide back to mine, her mouth curls upward.

"You're a little late."

"Sorry, ma'am." I suddenly feel guilty under her penetrating glare. "I wasn't sure if I should bring something—"

"Come on in, son." Her hand grabs onto my arm, hauling me inside with more strength than she looks like she possesses. "Are you hungry?"

My stomach rumbles as I bite my lip to hold in a groan.

"Poor thing," she mumbles as she drags me toward the kitchen. "I told Dixon to make sure you were being fed."

"I am, ma'am. I'm eating."

"Marian," she tsks. "Call me Marian."

I force myself to swallow, the attention not something I'm used to and the motherly affection hitting me deep inside. I don't like how it's forcing me to face the neglect I had growing up, and it's giving me another reason to feel envious of the fucking rookie.

She bustles around the kitchen while I stand off to the side watching her pile a plate with food, then she turns to look at me.

"Well? Come sit here and eat."

"Yes, ma—" She throws me a warning look, and I swallow down the rest of the word. "Marian."

"Would you like a soda?" she offers as she opens the fridge, grabbing a Pepsi without bothering to wait for an answer from me. "Eat." She snaps her fingers, pointing at the plate.

I listen to the woman because even though she's small, she's fucking scary. She has this hardened look in her eyes that reminds me a hell of a lot of her boy.

The food is good, making me moan around a large spoonful of creamed corn. Damn, Dixon has it too good at home.

My eyes flick up, watching as she leans on the counter, her chin in her hand as she watches me eat. She has a small smile playing around her mouth, the mischievous twinkle in her eye almost making me choke on the yams.

"Um," I clear my throat, sounding like a fucking child. "Where is everyone else?"

"In the basement." Her smile widens. "It's the only soundproofed place in the house." She gives me a fucking *wink*.

Does it make me uncomfortable? Hell yes.

Does it also make me want to join in on the teasing? Another hell yes.

"Did you test that out before we all came over here tonight, Marian?" My head dips as my eyebrow quirks upward.

"Oh, gosh!" She tips her face back, letting out a hearty laugh as her eyes light up with glee. "I can see why he likes you."

The statement catches me off guard because I know who she's talking about. I also know how much he's trying to dislike me right now.

"Ma?"

His voice is like a missile to my heart, obliterating the organ and eliminating me on the spot.

"Look, Dixon." Marian smiles at me. "Sebastian came by after all."

"Seb," Dixon looks at me with confusion.

Seb.

The way he says my name makes me want to swoon like a bitch in heat but throttle him all at the same time.

"Hey." I don't meet his eyes as I stuff my mouth with some food.

"I'm going to go get ready for bed, I have an early service tomorrow." Marian reaches out and places her hand on mine. "It was nice to see you again, Sebastian."

"You as well, Marian. Make sure you say a little prayer for me tomorrow."

"Oh, dear." Her hand settles on my cheek, and I feel myself curving into it. "I already have, and I plan on saying more."

Her words strike a chord inside of me. When she walks away, I continues staring at the spot she vacated.

"What are you doing here?" Dixon asks, crossing his arms over his muscular chest.

"I gotta go." I shove up out of my seat, the food I just ate threatening to come up as my heart beats in my throat.

This is the moment my grief decides to come, kicking me in the ass in front of the man I love to hate. All because someone paid me some fucking attention for once. How fucking pathetic.

I rush to the door, but I should've known how fast Dixon is, especially when it's something he wants.

"Seb." He grabs my arm, and suddenly everything zones out.

No noise penetrates the space around my head, and all I can see is him, his face right there in front of mine. I grab his shirt, throwing him against the wall as I suck in a deep breath, letting his scent stab me in the chest.

"Don't touch me," I grit out. "Forget I even came."

His mouth curves upward in a sneer, that ridiculous beard

moving with the motion.

"Can't do that with you all up in my face." He grins as his hand slips under my leather jacket to grip my hip.

He hauls me into his body, and that's when I smell the beer on his breath. "Are you drunk?"

"Nah." His glassy eyes focus on mine. "I'm nice."

His other hand winds around the back of my head, and like a foolish fucking fool, I let him pull me into him. His hard, muscular chest hits mine. I let our breaths mingle, then I let his lips graze mine because no matter how angry I am, my black, tarnished soul belongs to Dixon North.

I just can't ever let him know it.

My lips open over his, then my teeth sink into his bottom lip, biting hard enough to draw blood. Hearing him hiss from the pain only leaves me aching to hurt him more. I want him to go back downstairs to our teammates with my teeth marks on his mouth.

His tongue brushes along my upper lip as I push off him, knowing if I let this continue it won't stop.

I lick my lips. "You still taste the same, rookie." I back up a few paces. "Full of daddy issues and desperation."

I watch as his face falls, his eyes drop, and his mouth sets. Finally, he wants to act like a man.

"Get out," he grinds out, his eyes narrowed in anger.

"Glady," I scoff.

I yank open the door and step outside, only to feel my heart sink down into my stomach. I know I need to keep my distance, but at the same time, I can feel this man was made to battle my toxic fucking energy.

I turn to say *something* just as the fucking door slams in my face, effectively shutting me up. I snicker, shaking my head as I look at the black lacquered door.

His balls finally dropped.

CHAPTER FOUR

Dixon

The room spins when I finally fall onto my bed.

Dex was the last to leave, and when I called him an Uber, he was sucking back the rest of my Johnny Walker Black Label. I don't know where he puts it, impressed when he walked out to the waiting car without a stumble in his step.

I had seven beers, and I'm wishing the fucking ceiling would stop rotating.

The only thing that's staying with me from this whole night is the way my mother and Seb were interacting. She was treating him like another son, and the way he was teasing her reminded me of Daniel, back when he enjoyed being a part of our family.

My chest grows tight, my throat sealing up as my eyes give away to that telltale burn. I want my brother back, I want to have meaning again, but more than anything, I want to see my mother smile like she did tonight.

When I heard her laugh, I almost fell over. She hasn't laughed like that in a long time. I didn't realize how much I missed the sound.

I turn over in my bed, grabbing my pillow and letting the tears finally flow. Time does nothing to ease pain, it only proves to make it more unbearable, and the worst part? You can never get time back.

Once those sand grains fall, they stay rooted to where they land. And in the end, time is nothing but a bitter enemy.

When I finally roll out of bed, my head feels like it's been hit by a truck, and my mouth feels like cotton. Not even going to talk about the smell of my breath.

"Fucking hate guys' night," I mumble as I stumble into the bathroom.

I look in the mirror, finding my face looking a little worse for wear, but it's the deep indents in my lips that make me lean in for a closer look.

"That piece of shit," I growl as I run my finger over the marks, hissing when they smart.

He really bit me that fucking hard.

After my shower, I glance at the time, seeing it's well past noon. Not my usual routine, but I've given myself the day off. It'll help my knee to rest since it's been flaring up more lately.

I'm trying not to push the recovery too hard, but I can't help the frustration when I feel like it's back to square one. Seb is right… Taking Toroidal isn't smart, so that's why I've cut down a lot. I still need it on days when I can barely bend the joint.

As I head down the stairs, I stop mid-way and clutch the banister in a death grip. My mother is laughing while talking to someone downstairs, and I know exactly who it is. Is it wrong when my ass hits the step, and I sit there, listening to her melodic lilt as she laughs again? Is it wrong when envy burns its way through my stomach, making me wish she would laugh for me like that?

I remind her of the boy she lost.

The one she blames herself for.

I think she blames me too.

My forehead hits the wooden spindle as I listen to her tell a story about the church ladies back in Baltimore, making him laugh as I sink deeper into this pit of despair I've created for myself.

"It was nice of you to come over and check on Dixon," Ma says. "Are you sure you don't want me to wake him?"

"Nah," Seb replies. "I was just a bit worried when he didn't show up at the stadium for training. I'm glad to hear it was just a hangover and not his knee."

Is this all a show for my mother?

Why does he care how she feels about him? He hates me.

"You're welcome to sit here and wait for him." I hear keys jingle, hoping it's him leaving. "I need to grab fish down at the market before they sell out."

"Thank you, Marian," he says, his voice soaked and dripping with honey.

"You're welcome, dear. Come by again, okay?"

When the door shuts behind her, his voice calls out in a taunting sneer. "Come on down, North. You're creeping me the fuck out."

How the fuck?

I stand and bound down the rest of the steps, turning the corner into the kitchen. He's sitting there in his leather jacket, short-cropped hair, and twinkling amber eyes. He takes a sip of coffee then places *my* favorite mug on the counter.

"Why are you here again?" I let the irritation bleed through my words.

"Your gate was left open all night, the camera facing the garage is out, and the security light on your porch was flickering. I have someone coming by to check the place out." He stands like the conversation is over as I fly around the counter to quickly grab his arm.

"What the fuck do you mean you have someone coming over? Didn't I tell you to mind your business?"

"Your brother was murdered in cold blood because he reneged on an initiation he agreed to. Are you comfortable with Marian dying next?" His words are sharpened points driving through me. "I'm not."

"I was getting them fixed." I say quietly, making his face soften a bit.

"Not quick enough. There are people watching you don't even know about, and it's not something I would want your mother hauled in to."

"Who's watching me?" I ask, my hand grabbing his sleeve.

"I don't know, North." He shrugs my hand off. "Just be prepared for people to be watching you. There's an active investigation for your brother, and cops are sniffing around the Baltimore gang scene. Be smart."

"You sound awfully concerned for someone who said they don't give a fuck," I snort, crossing my arms over my chest.

"It's for your mom," he quips as he strides to the front door.

For my mom, my ass. I chuckle as the door slams shut behind him, and I grab the coffee that's sitting in the machine.

He still cares. I need to find out what happened to his family and just how it is I was involved.

Sebastian

When I sat outside his house after leaving last night, I grew more and more irritated at his lack of security, especially after what happened to Little North. The final straw was watching all the lights in the house go out and the fucking gate staying open. All I need are these crooked cops coming to scope him out, knowing this all started with me taking out their runners for killing Daniel North.

This fucker has no sense of self-preservation.

That's how I know he didn't grow up hardened by the streets. He grew up with ambition and a mommy who supported him every step of the way. He and his mother need a proper man in that house to take care of them, but it can't be me. I can only do it from the outside.

I'll ensure they're safe, all while ensuring he still hates me.

The drive back to my house is long as my mind keeps wandering to the man who's ruined my life. Not that he meant to, but he did. He ruined everything I thought I knew about myself. He took my carefully built character then smashed it to pieces. No matter how hard I try, I will never be the man I once was.

What hurts the most?

Paola saw through me. She saw the moment I changed, begging me to trust her with the secret that would ruin my whole life. Now all I can do is let the regret transform into guilt, let it sink down throughout my soul, only to have it manifest into hatred for the man I know I could never truly hate.

My head begins to throb at the same moment my phone shrills with a call through the Hummer's Bluetooth. I hit the accept button on the screen as I squint from the pain radiating through my skull.

"'Sup?"

"Avando," Delano's voice ricochets around in my head. "We might have a problem."

"Bro, we always have problems."

"We have a few more bodies," he continues. "A couple of low runners, but still, it's a message."

I turn onto my driveway, clenching my teeth at the fucking words pouring out of his mouth. He knows not to say this much over the line.

"I gotta go," I snarl, hoping he hears my tone. "I'll reach out next week."

I hit end on the screen before he can say anything else, punching my fist into the wheel. How is he slipping up now? When the heat is at an all-time high?

The next thing that sets my blood to boil is the fact that these crooked assholes are making their way into my turf and taking out my people. I reach into my sweater pocket, pulling out my wallet then flipping it open. Right there in the clear sleeve is Little North's bus pass, his angry face glaring back at me.

I don't regret doing what I did to avenge his death, I just regret letting my guard down when it came to my family. I was absorbed in Dixon, all while deeming myself untouchable, a big man on the streets of Rochester. I wasn't prepared for Baltimore, and that's on me.

No matter how much I try not to, I blame the man I crave like the air I breathe.

My head begins to really pound as I get out of the Hummer, and when I push myself through my front door, it's worked its way behind my eyes.

"Fuck," I fist my forehead as I fall back against the door.

Something is really wrong, I know this is more than a fucking headache. But I can't go see a doctor, and telling Coach would only pull me from the team, landing me on medical leave.

My eyes land on the bag filled with merciful relief, still sitting on my table.

"Fuck it." I stride over to it, sitting in the chair then pulling open the bag.

A small mound sits on my table as I reach into my wallet, grabbing my Amex and cutting the powder up into two thick lines. Just this once. I need it now because there's too much going on, and I need to be able to cope without pain clouding all of my thoughts.

I roll a one hundred dollar bill, the smooth paper slipping through my fingers like butter. The bill hits the line just as my phone pings, making me groan in frustration. My eyes move to the screen sitting on the table, the surface dotted with white specks, and I see his name.

I sit up, the powder long forgotten as I swipe it open.

North: Thanks.

Even as my fingers tap out a message, I know I should continue to ignore him, yet all I think about is him. How do you ignore the one person you think of all day then dream of at night? I'm trying, but it's getting harder and harder to do.

Me: Yeah.

I sit there staring at the phone screen, praying those dots

appear. Because right now, this is the only thing keeping me from sinking into a chemical bliss and forgetting every fucking thing I promised my wife's ghost.

North: Are you ever going to talk to me?

Me: My head's been hurting a lot lately. I can't sleep.

Why the fuck did I tell him that?

My fingers end up in my mouth, my teeth sinking into my nail as my heart flies a mile a minute. I haven't bitten my nails since fucking high school.

Those three dots appear, then they disappear, making me question what the fuck I'm doing. As the seconds roll into minutes, my jaw tightens, and my forehead draws closer together, making me instantly regret everything.

I lock the screen, cursing as I wallow in self-deprecation again. I'm the fucking pussy now. I was a fucking goner from the moment I heard his voice at the fucking club. All the self-berating, trying to be strong … to hate him. It all disappeared.

He fucking owns me.

The bill hits the first line as I begin to snort, just as my phone pings with a message.

"Is this really fucking happening right now?"

I pop back up again, scrubbing my nose with my sleeve, the white powder dusting along my sweater's surface. My screen darkens again, taking away the notification as I continue to stare at my phone, wondering where the fuck my balls went.

My finger runs along the screen, opening to my home page which shows that my messages app has a little, red *3* beside it.

Three?

I hit the message icon before I can change my mind, seeing they're all from Dixon.

North: After Danny died… I didn't sleep for days.

North: I punished myself for his death. I didn't do enough.

North: Is that how you feel?

My fingers itch to fly over the keyboard, to tell him everything, hoping it'll relieve the agony that's pressing on my soul. It's always easier over text, not having to see the person or witness their true feelings as you pour your soul out.

Because that's what I'm about to do.

Me: I watched her die, every second of it, and now it's all I see when I shut my eyes.

"Fuck!" I stand from the table, pacing the floor as my vision slowly blurs from the onset of tears. Tears I've held back this whole time. "I won't give in now."

But I already have … many times with him. I just keep on giving in.

I have the screen open and in front of my face before the ping resonates through the speaker of the phone.

North: I see his body laying on that gurney every night.

I can still remember the scream that wrenched from his throat that night, the sound echoing around me in that stifling hallway as I fought the urge to run to him.

Me: How do you get past it?

I know he's not snorting coke to get over the images that break his skull apart, lighting a flame of torture through his head.

North: I try to remember all the things I promised him. I tell myself I can't give up until I've achieved them all.

I made promises too, the type I knew I wouldn't fulfill, the worst being my wedding vows. The ceremony may have been a sham, but Paola was my soul's companion. Just not the one who can cast an inferno with only a single touch.

It makes me feel disgraced… So guilty.

Talking to him in any capacity is dangerous, but texting him, telling him my deepest aches and regrets, feels like I'm bending the rules but not breaking them. I need him in some way, so if it's pouring my heart into a fucking text message, then so be it.

Me: I broke all my promises the day I met you.

CHAPTER FIVE

It's a rough fucking morning when I get to the stadium. I've barely slept because I didn't know how to respond to Seb's text. Now I have to see Dani and deal with her fucking attitude.

I can see her standing there at her father's door, her arms crossed, resting on the slight swell of her stomach. My own stomach churns at the sight, knowing what I did with her, but also knowing there's really no chance it's mine.

With my eyes averted, I push through the locker room doors, coming face-to-face with Seb. He's sitting on the bench again, taping his hands while keeping his head down, not bothering to acknowledge me.

I want to apologize for not answering him last night, but I don't know what to say, and it feels like what's said over text stays there. So I keep my head down and open my locker door, throwing my bag inside then sitting beside him to put on my knee brace.

"How's the knee?" His voice is quiet, the words mumbled and unclear.

"Shit," I answer honestly. It's been aching a lot recently, and it gives me anxiety, knowing our season is fast approaching.

"The force of your weight combined with the bend while

running is fucking up your recovery," he continues to murmur. "Light jog or light weight training is the best, pushing for more reps every day."

I stare at the side of his face, his profile studying the tape as he wraps it around and around, his jaw tensing with restraint. I want him to look at me, to show me he still feels *us*, that this is still me and him.

He's stoic, though. His will is like steel, and I can do nothing but wait for it to bend.

My finger lightly trails over the bulge in his jaw, making him sink his teeth into his bottom lip at my touch, trying to lock in the sound I know wants to escape.

"Stop fighting me," I murmur.

"I can't," he answers, sounding strained and tortured.

"Look at me," I demand, my finger sliding under his chin, the scruff there pricking my skin.

I force his head to turn, to make him look me in the eyes, and when those amber irises rise, I nearly fall off my seat with want. Desire and despair rage in their golden depths, telling me everything I suspected. Seb still wants me, but what happened with his wife is holding him back.

My forehead hits his, and we stay like that, our breaths mingling. I want to tell him to talk to me, but I can't break this moment, not when we're giving in, letting our feelings show. Just for a small moment in time.

His nose grazes mine as I lean in a little more, needing to absorb every touch. His hand lands on my thigh then drags it upward toward my achingly swollen cock. His nose continues to drag along mine, his hand traveling at a torturously slow speed and my heart threatening to fucking explode.

A throat clears, and we both stiffen, our proximities leaving little to the imagination. I pull away from him, ready to toss excuses, hoping to God I can justify everything. I stand quickly and look around, gripping the locker door for support.

"It's your pregnant girl at the door," Seb growls, getting to his feet. "I'm sure she wants to share her recent craving or how swollen her fucking feet are."

Then he's gone, disappearing around the row of lockers toward the gym. I watch him leave, and when he reaches Dani at the door, I see the longing for him in her dark orbs.

Bitch.

"What's up?" I call out to her, making sure she knows I saw everything.

"Can we talk?"

"You have DNA results or something?" I cross my arms over my chest.

"That's what I want to talk to you about." She gives me an exasperated look, making my heart sink into my stomach.

It's not fucking yours, I remind myself.

I humor her, striding forward to stand in front of her. Thank fuck she's not allowed to come into the locker room because I don't know what I would've done if she'd seen Seb and me earlier.

"What's up?"

"I'm waiting until our baby is born to get the test done." She lifts her chin. "The process of getting a DNA test while in utero is dangerous."

"Okay," I shrug. "It doesn't matter to me because I know it's not mine."

"We had sex, Dixon," she huffs. "I wasn't imagining anything."

"I never once came in you," I finally admit. "I could barely get through it, to be honest. I'm sorry to tell you like this, but I can't be held down by a child who's not mine."

"I don't believe you," she smiles, the curve of her lips looking sinister. "And I would keep that to yourself, if I were you. Admitting to not being able to come in a girl sounds awfully suggestive."

She turns without noticing the effect her words have on me, her strong, cloying perfume hitting my face.

Awfully suggestive?

She's saying I'm gay? She's threatening to expose my sexuality?

I stumble back into the locker room, and the backs of my knees hit the bench, making me sit with a heavy thud. She can't know anything, it's an empty threat. What I said was harsh, and that was her retaliation. That has to be it.

No one knows about me and Seb.

Once I have my breathing under control and my heart calmed, I shake off the lingering fear from her words. Seb seemed unaffected, so that can only mean she knows nothing.

She has to know nothing because I fear the consequences if she does. This is Seb we're talking about.

I get to the gym and see him pounding into the punching bag, his fists hitting it with such force, I'm afraid he'll split it open. I hope he's not imagining my fucking face there.

The leg press looks formidable this morning as I set my usual low weight then sit in the leather seat. The first push against the plate has my knee burning with pain, and I grit out a curse. I feel like I'm getting weaker by the day. Shouldn't it be the other way around?

I get to the third rep when his shadow falls over me, the loud tsk through his teeth sounding over my loud pants of pain.

"Too much weight, rookie." He walks behind the machine, dropping the weight to a fraction of what it was. "Do twenty of those and call it a day."

"What?" I sit up, staring at the weight blocks in shock. "That's not enough, Seb—"

His hand hits the side of my head as a vicious growl rips from his throat. "You're fucking up the team with the way you're rehabilitating your-fucking-self."

"No, I'm not—"

Another slap to the head has my vision bleeding red.

"Do as I say, or I'll tell Coach you weren't given enough rehab time. I bet you flew through that on Toroidal, huh?"

I bite into my cheek to stop my retort and fall back in the seat, ignoring his presence as he watches me. I do the reps he asked, and when I try to do more, he grabs my fucking beard, yanking it hard.

"What the fuck did I say?"

I should be pissed at him, not getting hard at the look of anger in his eyes and the fiery tone of his voice.

He sees my reaction because his eyes widen, then his mouth opens, his tongue snaking along his lower lip.

"How's the knee?" Dani calls from the door.

I struggle to free myself from his grip, but Seb does nothing to change our positions, only glancing over his shoulder at her.

"About as strong as your claim on that fetus's parentage," he jibes, turning back to me.

I'm blocked from her view by his body, so she can't see how he's tightening his hold on me as I struggle. But she must see how close we're standing, and it's sending my anxiety through the fucking roof.

"Fuck you, Sebastian," she growls.

"Bet!" he calls as her heels click along the tile in the corridor, the sound fading as she leaves.

"Are you crazy?" I stare up at him, his grip still firmly wrapped around my beard. "She could've seen us!"

"Seen us what?" His black brows lift. "Arguing over your training? Me treating you like the bitch you're acting? So what?"

My mouth drops open at the abuse spilling from his lips.

"If I had let you pull away from me and jump off this machine—looking like a naughty boy with his hand in the cookie jar— what do you think she would've thought then?"

I grind my jaw and twist my head, trying desperately to get out of his hold, but he shocks me further, yanking me forward into his face.

I open my mouth to tell him to fuck off, but my words are smothered by his lips and tongue. He's like an angry tidal wave, pouring everything into me then watching as I have no other choice but to flounder under him.

And I do, I fucking *drown*.

Our tongues tangle in a war neither of us really wants to win. I'm willing to lose for the rest of my life if it means this is the punishment, and fuck, I really want his punishment.

My hand grabs his cock through his track pants, and the groan he releases into my mouth is swallowed up, sealed inside of me, my very own piece of the man who's claimed me completely.

I only wish I could claim him in return. I've only ever hungered for football, but now I can say I want someone more than my aspirations and dreams.

He tears himself away, shoving me back with a brutal force and cursing as he strides over to the punching bag.

"I want to hate you, Rookie." His teeth are gritted, and spittle flies at the force of his words. "Why do you fuck with my head?"

It's on the tip of my tongue to apologize, to beg him to forgive me for caring so fucking much, but at the last second, I bite my tongue. Fuck that. No one should apologize for caring about another, it's the most selfless thing you can ever do.

I get off the leg press and grab a towel, moving toward the door. I feel his eyes on me, but I can't give in now. He can't take the purity of what I feel for him and muddy it with the anger he's feeling toward himself.

I don't deserve it.

"North." My name leaves his mouth in a strangled cry, but I continue walking right out of the door and back down the corridor to the locker room.

It's not easy, I leave behind my heart that's nestled in his hands, and it feels like I'm splitting in two. But I can't let him volley my feelings back and forth, I'm not a fucking game.

Sebastian Avando is an athlete, through and through.

I should shower, I should sink into the warmth of the sauna, but I want none of it as long as he's in the building there's an urgent need inside of me to escape him. So I hurry through changing then book it out of the stadium, leaving behind a broken man who's dead set on breaking me right along with him.

Sebastian

He ran like I was contagious.

Everything turns sour inside my stomach as I wrap an arm around the bag. I can still taste him on my lips, and his scent has invaded my senses, rendering me unable to absorb another.

"Fuck!" I shout as my fist hits the leather of the bag.

What the fuck do I do now?

I give myself five minutes to pull it together then head back to the locker room. If he's in that sauna, I don't give a fuck, I'll fuck him right into those wooden seats, giving up this whole ruse. I can't control what my heart is yearning for, and I don't think Paola would want that either.

Just the thought of her chastising me for denying myself the life she felt I deserved is enough to send me to tears.

"You look like someone stole your candy," Dani sneers from her father's office.

Hot, molten lava courses through me as I stride into the office, my face so close to hers, our noses brush. I kick the door shut, and her eyes widen with delicious fear.

"What else you got to say, whore?" I grind out. "Who's the father of your baby, hmm? Do you even know?"

She swallows thickly. "Get out."

"*Get out*," I mock her. "Tell me who the real father is. Save yourself the inevitable embarrassment."

"Me? My embarrassment? Why don't you tell me why you care so much? Why is it a problem that Dixon is the father?" I see the slight uptick in the corner of her mouth and match her with one of my own.

I lean in, letting my mouth graze her ear. "Because when he was struggling to fuck your loose pussy, he was fantasizing about sucking my dick." I pull back, smiling wider at the look of shock in her eyes. "Swallowed everything I gave him too, like a good boy."

"I knew something was going on," she whispers, and I nod emphatically.

"That something was my big cock in his ass. You remember how that feels, don't you? Well, he fucking loved it too."

Just speaking the words and seeing the shock register on her face has me hard and throbbing. I brush it against her swollen belly and smirk.

"I'll tell everyone," she whispers, taking a step back. "It will be a huge scandal."

"Perhaps," I shrug. "But they might be more interested in a coach's daughter who sleeps with every fucking team member and needs Maury to tell her who the daddy is. Don't you think?"

The deep olive tone of her skin pales as the words absorb, and her hands begin to shake. "Get out."

"You got it," I nod, stepping back. "But you watch yourself, yeah?"

I step out of the office, whistling as I walk back to the locker room. Was that smart? No. Most things I do are spontaneous as fuck, and most of it is impulsive, but fuck it, I'll deal with shit any way I have to. That woman just makes me fucking burn with rage.

The locker room is empty, and the sauna is unoccupied, making my heart clench in my chest. He used to sit in that sauna to taunt me, to make me see the color red as bright as the occupied light by the door. But now he's stopped.

Why the fuck am I here, crying over it like a pussy?

This is what I wanted.

I rip off my clothes as I head to the showers. Maybe I'll go by his house and see what Marian is up to. I like to think that she and I have become friends, and friends don't avoid each other for too long.

Maybe she needs a friend to hear about the service she went to the other day, or maybe someone to talk to about Danny. I know she finds it hard keeping it all inside, and she doesn't want to worry Dixon while he's busy with his career.

I can be that friend for her.

"Are those lemon tarts?" Marian gasps as she steps back, letting me into the house.

"There are raspberry too. I figured not everyone loves lemon, but if you hate raspberry too then there's a problem."

Her head tips back on a loud laugh. "You got that right, young man. Luckily for me, I love them both."

"I knew we were friends for a reason." I wink at her as I walk to the kitchen. I know my way around the place now.

"How has training been?" she asks as she takes the pastry box from my hands to set on the counter. "Dixon doesn't tell me much, and I worry about his knee."

"Don't worry," I give her a sure nod. "I'm watching him."

"That's reassuring," she says, and I nearly snort. It's really not. "When he first came out here, he didn't sound like himself, and I was worried he wasn't getting along with his teammates."

"How could anyone hate Dixon?" I give her a wide-eyed look, making her chuckle.

"My sentiment exactly. He's a good boy. He's always putting others first, so I worry he's not living the life he truly wants."

I make a mental note to ask Dixon what life he wants to live and if he's living it. His mother should see him happy, and if she's saying all this, he's probably fucking miserable. She can sense it.

"I think he's okay," I shrug. "As good as he can be, anyway."

"Yes," she gives me a sad smile. "We're all coping in our own ways."

I nod because we are.

Loud, heavy thuds hit the stairs as I cover my grin with my hand. He probably heard most of that conversation, and I can't wait to see him try to act like he's not fucking livid with me right now.

"Sebastian." My name is terse coming from his mouth.

Sebastian.

"Hey, North." I give him a sweet smile, all toothy and wide. "How's the knee?"

"Fine," he grumbles, opening the fridge to grab a Gatorade.

"Sebastian brought us some tarts." His mother opens the box to show him.

"What kind?" He looks in, crinkling his nose.

"Lemon and raspberry," I say then bite my cheek when his lip curls upward in disgust.

"No, thanks," he mumbles.

Marian and I give each other knowing looks, then in a matter of seconds, both of us erupt into raucous laughter. He looks at her with shock, then his eyes narrow on me, angry tears lining his brown eyes.

"Enjoy those, then," he says quietly, storming out of the kitchen.

I go to follow him but stop and look at Marian. "I'm just going to…" I point in the direction of where he went as she gives me a reassuring nod.

He's pacing in front of the patio door outside in the backyard, his hand on his head and his fingers gripping into his hair. I can feel his frustration from here, I'm just not sure what it's about. I know it has something to do with me, but what exactly is what I want to find out.

I open the door, sticking my head out. "Did I say you could walk laps on that knee today, rookie?"

"What the fuck are you trying to prove with my mother?" he snaps, catching me off guard. "That you can make her happy and I can't? Just another thing this rookie bitch is failing at?"

"Whoa." I step outside, closing the door behind me. "I honestly just like your mom, and maybe it gives me an excuse to be here."

"I don't want you here," he barks, his face contorting with anger.

"I know that." I lean against the door, slipping my hands in my pockets. "I just don't give a fuck."

"I can't take your back and forth bullshit." He finally stops pacing to look at me. "It's confusing."

"Rookie, I just brought your mother some fucking pastries because she's sad. I'm not back and forthing about anything." *Fucking liar.*

"You're a liar." He points in my face.

One point to the rookie.

"Why'd you get so pissed in there? And don't say because I'm here," I warn him.

"She laughs with you like she did with Danny, and every time I hear it … it's stupid." He turns away from me, but I grab his arm.

"Tell me."

"I forget he's gone, and it's like he's here with us, like he was always meant to be." His eyes fill with tears, and I struggle not to join him.

"Have you even tried to hang out with her? Talk about something other than your fucking knee or your career?"

"Fuck you, Avando," he snarls as I tighten my lips to stop myself from exploding on him. I get how bad that sounds.

"Have you tried to connect with her?" I try again.

"She's my mother." He raises a brow.

"And?" I shrug. "Being your mother doesn't mean you know her. Go out for dinner and fucking talk about things she likes. Like the ladies at church who look down on her for living in the rich area with the rich, athlete son. Or about the minister who stinks like garlic she has to stand two feet away from when she speaks to him."

I can see he's shocked by what I know about his mother, but truth be told, I really do like the woman, and I like the kind of mother she is. I wish I had one like her. Maybe I would be in a different place in life.

"Just talk to her, and ask her how her day was." I push off the door to grab the front of his shirt, dragging him in closer to me. "That's what I did."

His breath is on my face, his eyes are darkening, and I'm so fucking hard, it's torture.

"This is the back and forth shit I'm talking about." He shrugs me off. "Stop coming around here, Avando. We're not friends."

"You're fucking right we're not friends." I snarl as I turn, opening the patio door. "Not even close."

CHAPTER SIX

Sebastian

Friends.

He's on some next level shit.

I'm still fuming a day later and ready to rip into the grass of the field outside. He really thought we were friends? The fuck is he on?

My head pounds as I sit on the bench, letting it fall forward with a groan. The pain's been pretty constant for the last few days, so I'm dreading when I actually have to put on a helmet. The weight and confined space are only going to amplify it.

The doors swing open, and in walks my ex-*friend*, his jaw setting when he sees me, his hand automatically forming a fist.

He's still a little bitch.

"Did you talk to your mom?"

"Do you ever shut the fuck up?" he barks back, making me snarl in response. Deep inside, I'm reveling in his new backbone.

"She's missing Danny because they had a connection from being together more often. Now that she's living with you here, you can form the same bond, you dumb fuck." I shove his shoulder, the pain in my head making me more irritable.

"I know that," he quietly admits while he opens his locker door. "I don't know how to do it, though. I've always been training for football."

"Bro, if I can befriend your mom, so the fuck can you."

"What are you doing here today?" He turns to look at me. I let my eyes travel down his form slowly.

Dixon still maintained his muscle, even while being laid up with his injury, and I can see it in the way they're rippling under my perusal. His hair may be cut short now, but that beard on his face is starting to grow on me, giving him a bit of mystery while not obscuring those sexy ass lips.

"Can you stop?" He shifts as my eyes drop to his shorts, watching as he hardens before my eyes.

Jesus.

I stand, opening my locker door then throwing my bag inside just to give myself a moment to get it together.

"Let's jog the field," I say as I shut the door, pulling the hood over my head.

"Okay," he mumbles as he follows me out of the locker room.

"Avando, North, in here!" Coach calls from his office, and I groan. The man is going to get knocked in the fucking face if he brings up his whore of a daughter right now.

"Hey, Coach," Dixon says as he steps inside, making me want to knock him the fuck out too.

"How's the knee?" Coach asks, concern lining his features.

Don't misconstrue that, he only cares for his game.

"Good. Seb has been helping me with strengthening it."

Coach gives me a surprised look, and I smirk back at the old fuck. I know I'm not much of a team player, but I like sinking my cock into Dixon's ass, and I figure it's a way to give back.

"I'll be lining up the strings next week for some scrimmages, going over new plays to get us into top form."

"Sounds good," Dixon replies, the eagerness to please the man grates on my last nerve.

He's drooling his daddy issues all over the fucking floor.

"Can you give me and Avando a few minutes?" Coach asks Dixon who nods then heads out of the office.

I cross my arms, looking the old man in the eye. "What is it?"

"I need you in the right mindset this season. If you need more time, all you need is to ask."

"I'm good." I turn, ready to leave the office.

"Think about your teammates and what it would mean to lose because you're having a bad day."

"Watch your mouth," I turn to point at him. "I said I'm good. Don't put your lack of preparation on me if we lose. North and I ran circles around your lazy team last season."

He doesn't say another word as I storm from his office. He knows I'm right, and if we lose another season, it's on him.

"That was rude as fuck," Dixon snorts.

He's standing right outside the door, and if he hadn't spoken, I would've run into him.

"He's just lucky he didn't bring up his daughter because then we'd really be fighting," I groan.

"I mean," his fingers stroke his beard, "that kid has more of a chance being yours than mine."

His smirk nearly bowls me over, especially when it's coupled with the heat liquifying those brown eyes. I'm so fucking hard it hurts.

"Watch it," I grunt, covering up as much of the desire that's barreling through me as I can.

While we stretch out on the field, I somehow manage to keep my eyes away from the rookie as he bends over. I won't be losing to temptation out on the damn field we play on.

I start us out at a leisurely jog, and after a few minutes, I hear him scoff beside me.

"You want that knee to heal, right?"

"This is doing nothing. I feel like an old man running this slow," he whines.

"I shouldn't have to remind you how much you've been fucking that knee up." I pick up the pace slightly, no longer wanting to hear the little bitch whine.

Two laps later, he's opening his fucking mouth again.

"You're having headaches. I can tell because you're more of an asshole than usual."

"Mind your business," I roll my eyes.

"Like you're minding yours?"

"I'm fine, baby." I put some heat in my tone. "Is that what you want to hear? This is starting to feel like a relationship, and you're turning into a nagging wife."

"Sorry." He picks up the speed, pulling ahead of me then tossing me a wink. "I didn't hear anything after 'baby.'" He palms his cock through his shorts, biting into his lip.

A haze of want drops over me, and I lose all train of thought as I race after him. I catch up easily enough because he's a fucking cripple now, lifting him right off his feet, tumbling us both down to the ground. I take care not to let him land on his knee, taking the brunt of the fall and having him land on top of me instead.

His face is inches above mine as he laughs, and before I can stop myself, I reach up to run my finger along his bottom lip.

"You're playing a dangerous game with me, Dixon," I warn him as my finger continues back and forth over his velvet skin.

"How dangerous can this really be?" He leans down farther, pressing his cock into my lower stomach. "You forced your dick up my ass not too long ago."

"I'm about to do it again, out here where anyone can watch me make you my bitch," I smirk, and he gives me one back, pushing off me to stand.

We stretch out again, and this time, I sneak a look over at him, nearly coming in my shorts when he's bent over and looking at me from between his legs. He's asking to be fucked again.

I sit on the grass and look out over the field. Everything feels different now.

"Are we heading in?"

"Go ahead," I tell him. "I'll see you inside."

He jogs off back to the locker room, and I smile, knowing this is the first day he hasn't limped off the field. It's progress, even if he is impatient about it. I need some space from him, though because I'm losing focus of the plan I set forth before coming back here.

He's luring me into his web, but I can't be trapped yet, not until I have my wife's murderers six-feet under.

Once I've put myself into a better mindset, I stand to head back inside. Only to find myself face-to-face with Dani.

"Interesting little jog you two had out there." Her hands are on her hips, eyes narrowed.

"Were you watching us?" I get into her face, wrapping my hand around her throat, feeling the pulse flutter beneath my palm.

Her hands come up to wrap around my wrist. "Sebastian."

"Did you see how hard he was for me when he came back in? I had him rubbing his cock all over me." My forehead hits hers with a bump, making her whimper. "You'd be smart to stop talking to me like you have the upper hand."

I release her before I do something really stupid like strangle a pregnant woman, then I walk into the locker room. My anger is burning hot inside of me, and I know it has a lot to do with the fact that I have yet to deal with anything emotionally.

The only way I know how to do that is to aim a bullet to the middle of a motherfucker's forehead.

Dixon is sitting on the bench as he looks up at me, a smile curving his lips. I lose it. I head straight for him, and he must see the rage simmering through my features because he has the common sense to look apprehensive.

I stand in front of him, yank my shorts down to mid-thigh, then grip the top of his head.

"Suck it."

"Sebastian." He tries to pull his head back.

"You do it willingly, or you die with my cock rammed down your throat."

He can act like a bitch who pretends he doesn't like when I force him, but it'd be contradicted by the look in his eyes. He fucking wants me any way he can get me.

"We cannot do this here," he hisses, that delicious lust still swirling in the depths of his irises.

"Then you better hurry the fuck up before someone comes in. I don't care who the fuck sees it, but if you do, start sucking." All of my words are clipped, filled with poison.

He opens his mouth as I line myself up, pushing inside and letting his teeth graze me. The light scrape against my cock has me gritting my teeth to stop myself from fucking exploding in his mouth.

It's been too long, and this mouth was made specifically for my cock.

There's no being gentle, not with my blood boiling the way it is, and certainly not when his mouth has done nothing but run off since I've been back. Rookie needs a little reminding.

I slam into his throat, and his loud gag fills the locker room, making me groan as he constricts around the head of my cock.

"Fuck, yes." I pump a few shallow thrusts into him before I pull out, giving him time to breathe. "Tell me you missed this." I grin down into his watery eyes, my words reminiscent of another time we were in this exact situation.

I don't give him time to answer as I thrust back in, watching as saliva drips from his mouth then runs down into his beard.

"I'm going to come all inside this pretty mouth, North," I grit out as I invade his throat again. "I'm going to teach you not to fucking talk back."

I can't even lie... Between his sopping mouth and watering eyes, I won't be lasting long at all. His eyes widen as they redden from lack of oxygen, then I pull out, enjoying his deep inhale.

"Do you need to say something?" I grin, taunting him as I slip the head of my cock over his tongue. "Or are you about done with the fucking attitude you've been copping?"

My balls tighten as his hands land on my thighs, and he leans forward sucking me deep down his throat, moaning around my girth.

"Fuck," I hiss as he looks up at me with mirth in his eyes. Fucking brat.

He slurps around my length, and his fucking tongue licks along the head, making stars explode as I groan through gritted teeth. The force of my come has me tipping forward, and he swallows nearly everything I give him.

Nearly.

A door slams out in the corridor, and Dixon pulls back, panic flitting across his face. A thick rope of my cum drips from the tip of my cock, hitting his beard. When he looks back up to my face, I shake my head with a tsk.

"You missed some."

My thumb scoops along the string of cum, and I slip it up over his bottom lip, shoving it into his mouth. Defiance settles in his eyes as he cleans off my thumb.

"Looks like the lesson wasn't taught properly," I mumble as I pull up my shorts.

"Someone is out there," he pushes me back to stand. "Do you want someone to catch us?"

"I really don't give a shit."

"Really?" His hands hit his hips, just like a nagging wife. "And if the team sees this shit? Then what? You're good being the gay man on the Buffalo Bills?"

"I'm no homo." I rear back like the bitch slapped me.

"Yeah, you are." He leans forward. "I'm a man, and you just shoved your dick in my mouth."

I have his back to the lockers, my hand around his throat, and my mouth to his ear in seconds.

"I'm not gay. I only want you."

"It doesn't matter, Seb." He pushes me off. "No one can know about this. Stop flirting with fucking danger. This ain't the streets of Rochester."

"No man is sucking my dick in Rochester," I scoff.

"Never mind," he huffs, grabbing his shit out of his locker. "I need to get out of here."

I watch him leave then consider his words. If anyone on the team sees something between us and attempts to fucking say anything, I'll kill them.

My mother is in the living room when I get home, watching her favorite cooking show. I let Seb's words come back to me as I take in her profile. I should spend some time with her.

"Hey, Ma." I walk into the room, and she looks up.

"Is it time for dinner already?" She hurries to get up. "I've let the day get away from me."

"Want to go out for dinner instead?"

Why my stomach quakes with fear is beyond me. It's like my first fucking date, and I don't want her to reject me.

"Oh, I'd love that, son," she nods.

"Cool," I smile. "Do you want to try that new Italian place in the city?"

"Who could ever say no to pasta?"

The restaurant is nice with its white linen tablecloths and red velvet seats. The lighting is low, and with a bit of paper incentive, the waiter put us in the back for some privacy. Daniel will come up this evening, and I don't want the rich folks here hearing about my gangster brother who was shot dead.

"How are the ladies back home?" I ask as we wait for our orders to come out.

"Talking." She begins to pick at the napkin on her lap, a sure tell of her anxiety.

"About Danny?"

"Yes," she nods, her eyes filling with tears. "They know he was killed by the gang, and they said they're hearing things."

"Hearing what things?" I lean forward.

"That he wanted out. He didn't want to initiate, and when he told them that, he was killed."

"I see." I sit back, my mind working to piece it all together. I knew it was something like that, but to hear it makes my stomach turn with regret.

He wanted out.

"Maisie Williams's boy told her Danny was on the run, and he didn't want anyone coming around us, so he hid out instead of coming home."

"Have the cops come back with anything?" I question as her face hardens.

"No, they won't do nothing for a young black man who was killed by the gang he worked for. To them it does the city good to have one of them off the street."

As hard of a pill it is to swallow, it's the truth.

"I'll look in to it, Ma. But we may have to be prepared to hear details we don't want to hear."

We move on to talk about my training, then about the new church she's been attending. It takes a while to get into the groove, but eventually, we're laughing and reminiscing over childhood memories.

"How is Sebastian?"

The sound of his name has my hand tightening around the fork before the metal prongs hit the plate with a loud *clink*.

"You would know better than me, I think." The comment flies from my lips before I can stop it, and the hurt reflecting in my mother's eyes makes me feel instant regret.

"Dixon—"

"I'm jealous," I admit, cutting her off. "I know you and I have never been close like you and Danny were. I always chalked it up to me being busy. Now I know those were just excuses. I should've made the time to spend with you—with Danny—and now I see Sebastian doing it with ease."

Her hand covers mine on the table as she gives me a sad smile. "Son, your ambitions were always something to be admired, and I know how much it took for you to get to where you are today. I'm sorry for not making you see just how much you mean to me."

My throat seals with emotion at her words, and I try my best not to succumb to the burn that's tearing its way through my eyes.

"We may not laugh and joke about everyday things, but look at what you've done for me. You've given me a beautiful home, and I get to spend each day with you. That's something I truly appreciate. One day, you will make someone special feel extremely lucky to have met you.

"I don't want the same relationship I had with Danny with you, it wouldn't feel right. You are both very different boys. I hope you know I love you for exactly who you are, Dixon, no matter what."

A tear slips over my cheek then disappears into the beard at my jaw. "Does he remind you of Danny?"

"Sebastian? Maybe a little," she smiles. "He has that rough exterior that hides his soft insides like Danny did. I can also see a lot of pain in his eyes, and I get the impression he doesn't have many people in his life. He's been through something terrible, and I share that with him."

I see what she means, I know all about the pain she sees in his eyes. Maybe he shows her glimpses of the raw agony, but when he's with me, he covers it all with anger.

"How about we make it a point to do this once a week?" I lean on the table to grab her hand.

"I'd love that."

CHAPTER SEVEN

"I can't talk too much about this shit, North."

Fernando is an old friend of my brother's, running in the same circles. I've been on the phone with him for the past half hour trying to coax some information out of him without getting him killed.

"I know about him wanting out, and I know he went into hiding. I need to know who pulled that trigger."

"What for?" I can hear the frustration in his voice. "Don't no one get justice around here. We make our own, North, you know how it is."

"Maybe I want to make my own," I offer. The silence on the other end is deafening.

"You have money now, huh? You want to throw down racks to retaliate?"

"I want names, that's all." I pinch the bridge of my nose.

"They're already dead, man." He lets out a curse. "Not too long after what happened to Danny."

"Dead? How? Who were they?"

"They came across your brother by luck, apparently. But no one believes that. There's some weird shit going down around here, and it feels different."

"Fernando, I need more than that."

"I only know rumors, bro." He exhales heavily. "The leaders ain't saying shit, it's all talk that's rolling down from the top. Something about some Rochester men rolling in and taking them out. Real gruesome shit too, if it's true."

Rochester. My fucking blood runs cold.

"What else you got on the ones who killed Danny?"

"I didn't know those guys, they ran different shit than I do," he explains.

"What you mean?"

"They were running some of that pure shit, the shit that gets taken from an evidence room, ya feel me?" He's talking about cops.

"How would they get that?" I sit on the couch, my heart tripping in my chest. My brother was in deep with some real fucked up shit.

"Connections. That's all I know, North."

"All right, Fernando. Anything else on the guys from Rochester?" I ask, all the while praying this isn't somehow connected to Seb.

"All I know is retaliation is in the works, and one man's wife had her head blown in. That's all I got."

"It's enough," I nod, my teeth clashing together. "Talk soon."

I hang up the phone as I begin to pace the room. It all makes sense now. If Seb was one of the guys from Rochester, and his wife was killed because of it, I can see why he blames me.

He chose to avenge my baby brother, and his wife lost her life for it.

They're standing with their backs to the SUV and their arms crossed over their chests, looking every inch the football players they are. The heights they stand at is where their similarities end. Jameson's wide stature nearly engulfs Ortiz's, and where Jameson is light, Ortiz is dark. Blue eyes to brown eyes, blond hair to black.

Both are impenetrable.

"Ortiz, Jameson!" I holler as I jog over to them.

Both straighten when they see me, the creases between their brows matching as they watch me with concern. Being that it's nearing midnight and I asked them to meet me in a paid parking garage would be reason enough.

"Why are we here, North?" Jameson gives me a nervous look.

"I need to know everything you know about Avando and what happened to his wife." Straight up and to the point.

"We don't know anything," Ortiz says straight away, his loyalty shining bright in the darkened underground.

"Look," I begin. "I'm not here to take him down. I'm here to help and find out how I can get him out of the trouble he's in."

"Why?" Jameson cuts in. "You're a good guy, North, and I hate what we did to you last year, but with that being said, after what we did to you, why do you want to help him?"

"Valid." I nod. "I owe him one. That's all I can say about it, and that shit that went down was mostly between him and me, although you two deserve a fucking set of broken legs for it."

"We don't know much about Avando's life in Rochester," Jameson gives in. "He's pretty tight-lipped, but we know he runs some shit. He hasn't been the same since he's been back. He says he has some heat following him."

Cops, again.

"You heard about as much as we did on the news. He took out an intruder who came into his home and killed his wife," Ortiz interjects.

"They're staying pretty quiet about the intruder, who he was and such." I scratch at the hair on my chin. "Did he say anything about that?"

"Nah." Jameson shakes his head.

So the only thing I've learned is Sebastian is being trailed by the fucking cops because they need a suspect to apprehend. Obviously, with him being who he is back in his hometown, they're probably salivating at the chance to bring him in.

"Thanks, guys." I bump each of their fists then back up. "One last favor, though." They both look at me with curiosity. "Don't tell Avando we did this."

"Not unless we want you dead," Ortiz snickers.

"And we'll be buried in the same hole in the ground with you." Jameson adds as they climb in the SUV.

I watch them leave the garage as I start my vehicle, letting it idle as I scratch at my chin. If it wasn't for me, he wouldn't have been there when Danny died, and he wouldn't have seen the raw, unfiltered agony I went through.

He wouldn't have felt the need to retaliate, and his wife would still be alive. It's clear he has this connection with me, that he wants to protect me while he pretends to fucking hate me.

But it's clearly the opposite, and I can't let him get into any more trouble. His career is on the line, and he has a daughter who depends on him.

It's going to feel like fucking hell, but I have to let him go. He'll be another person I'll grieve for, but I can't let him take the fall for whatever shit Danny got himself caught up in.

There's only one way to do it.

Sebastian

My world fucking pumps with red then tips on its axis when I walk into the stadium the next morning. It's become fucking routine for Dixon and me to meet here to rehabilitate that knee, so seeing him standing in the corridor with Dani threatens to send me into a spiral.

And no one survives a Seb spiral.

His hand cradles her small stomach, making my breakfast work its way up my throat. What the fuck is going on here? This bitch just had my cock down his throat yesterday, now today he's what…? A father?

Everything freezes as I stumble into the locker room, trying desperately not to cause a scene. What if the results came back? I know you can do DNA this early.

My ass hits the bench as he walks in, whistling with a wide grin on his face.

"What the fuck was that?" I stand, my anger pulling in front of everything else I'm feeling.

"What?" He looks at me with confusion. Did I fall into another dimension?

"That shit with Dani!" I fucking explode, my head pounding in time with my erratic heart.

"We're having a baby, Avando," he huffs.

"Oh, you are, are you?" I purse my lips. "I thought you said that baby was more likely to be mine than yours."

"I was wrong." He throws his bag into the locker. "What are we working on today?"

"Fuck you!" I snarl, grabbing my bag. "Fuck you."

I storm out of the locker room, and luckily for Dani, she's not lingering around. I stride out to the parking lot and get in my Hummer. What could have happened in the last twenty-four hours? If he thinks

I'll just let this go, he has another thing coming.

A voice in the back of my mind pipes up, giving me pause.

Maybe this is my chance to let him go. What he and I have could never last. It's lust at its most potent stage, but when that fades, there'll be nothing left. I stare back at the stadium doors and exhale a heavy breath. I was becoming reckless anyway. Sooner or later, he could become the next target.

As much as I hate this, he's probably safer under that whore's thumb. At least until this blows over, and then I'm coming back for what's mine.

It's early the next morning when I arrive back on my own turf in Rochester. I needed to be away from the man who owns my thoughts, letting me concentrate on what's clearly becoming a problem.

First, I need to smack around Delano for fucking up my number one rule of no condemning phone conversations.

I know he's been feeling the pressure, and the heat on us has stopped a lot of production, but damn, I taught him better than that.

I could go home and let the bitch sleep a little more, but hell, I think a good four in the morning roll call can do a person good. I'll get them kids riled up while I'm at it.

The driveway has his van sitting in the middle, and the street is dark, the only light coming from the slowly rising sun as it casts reds and oranges across the sky. I hit the porch then stop, my eyes flicking to the dull yellow light coming from the window to the far left. It's his office, and that light is the small desk lamp he has in there.

Sure, he could've left it on before bed, but something is nagging at me, telling me he's already awake, and that can only mean there's more trouble. Trouble I can't get too involved with while I have eyes staring at my every move.

With that thought, I look over my shoulder at the darkened

street behind me to find nothing out of the ordinary. That doesn't mean they're not camped out somewhere. Although we're both pristine on the outside, Delano's rap sheet is nearly as long as mine.

It's the only reason I'm risking anything while being here. There's nothing they can get on him at the moment... Certainly nothing that links back to me.

I have a key for his house—I've had it since the day he and his family moved in. It's my name on the deed anyway. So I quietly slip it in the lock and turn it, smiling when it silently opens. If he's dealing with issues, I want to hear it unfiltered, then I can make my decisions based on that, not on the glossed over facts he usually gives me.

He's my boy. I know he's trying to handle the bulk of the work by letting me grieve and play the game I love, but I'm ready. Shit needs dealing with, and I can throw down whatever it costs to get it done.

I creep through the small living room toward the dark hallway that leads to his office and a bathroom. This house has thin walls, creaky floors, and nothing for soundproofing, so I can hear his muffled voice as soon as I step into the hallway. I don't hear a second voice which tells me he's on the phone.

I carefully navigate the hallway, avoiding the particularly bad spots of the floor. I find the office door ajar, and I can feel the tension radiating from inside. Something is going down.

"I'll try, but you know he's tight about that." He groans like someone is asking the impossible of him. "Do not threaten me with that," he suddenly snaps, causing my spine to straighten. "I'll get you what I can."

After a few moments of silence, I assume the call has ended, and I push open the door with my foot. He stands as the hinges creak, his gun pointed at my head with my own pointing at his fucking dick.

"What the fuck was that?"

He falls back down in his seat, sweat dotting his brow and a sick look on his face.

"We have a few runners." He presses a finger to his temple. "They didn't complete the initiation, and I'm worried they'll hit up the cops."

"So we kill them," I shrug, wincing slightly when I think of Daniel North. "Or we find them and question why they suddenly turned on us."

"It's hard, figuring this shit out. Are they plants? Are they from fucking Baltimore?"

I can hear the stress in his voice, the slight tremor telling me he hasn't slept and this is all sitting heavily on his shoulders.

I was wrong when I assumed Delano could handle this while I sat out, keeping my nose clean. Sure, he's my boy, we grew up together, but he's always been the softer one.

"Give me some names, and let me handle it."

"You know you can't do that." He leans forward. "You know the cops could be involved, and then what? Anyway, what are you doing here?"

The worried expression clears from his face as he sits back in his seat.

"Find any more on those cops?" I sit in the chair across from him, watching him closely. "I need to wrap this shit up and move on with my life."

"They weren't just cops," he says, his hand moving back up to rub at that temple of his, a tell he's had since we were kids. "They were Feds. A task force placed three men undercover inside the Baltimore drug scene. You killed one."

"Feds." I drag my finger along my bottom lip while I watch him continue to rub his temple. There's something he's not telling me, and my stomach hardens at the thought of having to pull it out of him.

"Yeah, they've been closing in on us, and we're losing the street cred."

These *Feds* were double agents, pretending to be working a case, but instead, pushing drugs and making a profit. Danny was mixed up in it, and maybe he saw or heard something he felt was wrong. Maybe they knew he saw or heard something.

"I need more information about Daniel North," I tell Delano, watching him roll his eyes. He wants to die.

"We're done with that." He frowns. "We got everything on him."

"There's a reason he wanted out of the family he made for himself. You and I know what it's like to find a home with people who understand you at your worst." I raise a brow, reminding him of a time when we were like Little North. "What would've made us turn?"

"If we were lied to," he admits, his eyes dropping but that hand still there, rubbing his temple.

"I don't like being lied to." I drop my gun on the desk, the loud *thunk* a warning. "I bet he found out something and felt like maybe his new family wasn't what he thought."

"I'll look in to it," he huffs, sounding exhausted.

"Nah," I stand, picking up my piece and pushing it down the back of my waistband. "I got this one. You keep working on the Feds."

CHAPTER EIGHT

Dixon

I didn't go in there with the intention of latching on to Dani, I wanted Seb to pull away if I alluded that the baby could in fact be mine. I wanted him to be so angry he would punch me in the face and leave.

But I got something else entirely.

When I found Dani this morning, I told her I was ready to step up and start going to doctor's appointments, just until the results came back. I'm not heartless. I can see she's going through this alone, and I did have relations with her.

She was relieved, telling me I made the rightecision because Seb told her what he and I were doing.

He fucking told her.

I can see it clear as day… He was jealous about something, then everything spilled from his mouth, giving him some sort of joy to cause her in pain. Without a single thought for the repercussions that could come of it.

Although Dani had no problem filling me in on what *could* happen if such secrets were exposed. I heard her threat loud and clear, though she hadn't needed to make it because I'd already made up my mind to protect him for once.

I don't think anyone has ever protected Sebastian Avando.

There was no future for us anyway. What we were doing was fueled by the allure of being caught, of doing something so taboo and letting lust override all reason.

Even with those thoughts clouding my mind, all I can see is him, envisioning a life beyond football, him there with me. I give myself a shake and clench my fist. He can't know I have this weakness for him because he will sniff it out then bend me to his will again.

He needs to believe that being with Dani is what I want, and by the time the kid is born, hopefully he will have moved on. I know her child isn't mine, but I am really curious as to whose it is. I'm fucking stressed that it's Seb's. There's something nagging me about their prior relationship and how easy it was for him to fuck her on her father's desk.

Could that have happened frequently?

If it's his, I'll still claim it as mine, and I'll commit to Dani if it means she goes along with it. I wouldn't mind a son or daughter to take to football games, and I would love to be the father mine didn't get the chance to be. The thought of one day having a family warms me. I know I could be an amazing father, whether or not the child is biologically mine.

It wouldn't be much sacrifice to ensure our secret stays that way forever.

"First scrimmage of the year," Coach announces as he leans against the locker room wall. "Let's start this year off right and get in proper shape for the coming season."

He eyes me, and I huff slightly, knowing they're all worried about my knee. Coach has also been keeping a close watch on me since that false positive piss test. It was a fucking scary moment. I thought my career was done. It didn't stop me from shooting up my knee, though. Toradol has been a constant companion. It's the only reason I won't be benched this year.

I used my last syringe today, knowing there'd be a scrimmage and not wanting Coach to see how little it's improved. I don't want to be down on second string again, so I need to somehow convince Jameson to get me more.

Without Seb knowing.

My eyes skip to the side, finding him leaning against the lockers with his eyes already on me. The smirk that lines his lips is sinfully delicious, causing me to quickly look away. I have to consciously stop myself from reacting. *I can't react to him.*

"North." Jameson sits beside me as Coach continues to talk about this year's gala and first season game. "How's the knee? Are you strong enough to play?"

"Yeah, only because I used. It was my last one. Are you able to get me more?"

His eyes begin to raise to look at the man who's burning a hole into the back of my head. I growl, effectively making them flicker back to me. "Don't look at him, he'll know. Are you able to get me more?"

"Yeah." He swallows, turning to keep his eye on Coach. "*He'll* find out, though."

"I'll handle Avando."

One hour into our scrimmage, my knee is aching, the whole leg trembling. Every time my eyes land on his amber orbs, they're lined in knowing humor. He knows I'm in pain, and I would bet my life he knows I shot up.

We hit the line of scrimmage, my eyes on Ortiz who was put on second string, and still, I feel that inky darkness under Seb's watchful eye. It's the fourth down, and first string is at thirty yards inside the opposition's side. That end zone has never looked so fucking sweet.

My knee is screaming, literally pulsing beneath my compression pants and sending waves of pain up my groin.

I need to fucking last until the end, and then I need to not limp off the field. Not only is Coach watching closely, but so is Seb. I can't determine who the fuck would be worse.

Zeal calls the play as we run into position, preparing for the hike. At the snap I'm off, my feet digging into the field and my knee screaming. I ignore it as I maneuver around the second string, trying to get to the proper spot.

My hands are up, that sweet pigskin gliding between my fingers, then I grip it tight. Just before I hit that ten yard marker, I see Dex plowing his way toward me, carving a line with determination in his eye.

I can't take a fucking tackle right now, so I run out of bounds, breathing with relief at the sound of the whistle. I'm hoping no one noticed how I didn't push to run by him, that I choked when this time last year I was running circles around Dex.

"North." Zeal runs up, his hand hitting my shoulder and jarring my body. "Everything good, man?"

"Just out of breath. Need to shape up a bit, ya know?"

"Let's get these last ten yards and get our asses home, ya?" He grins. I give him one back, hoping it doesn't look like a grimace.

"I'll take these last ten yards," Seb calls out, and Zeal nods.

"Sounds good, bro. They'll be expecting North."

I could fucking kiss him right now. I know he did it because he sees my fatigue, he notices everything. Nothing gets by Sebastian Avando.

No matter how relieved I am now, I will hear about it later. He likes to say I bitch and nag him, but he's just as bad.

The ball is hiked, then we're off, Seb and I running parallel to each other on the field, our eyes never straying. I can see the second string's defense closing in on me, and I chuckle as Seb catches the ball, his arms bunching with the motion. He sends me a cocky wink as he flies over that white line, giving us the win by a few points.

Then the guys are catcalling and laughing as he does his obnoxious touchdown dance, the motion of fucking a woman from behind then slapping her ass.

My world slows down as I watch him closely. Fuck, for all I know, he could be thinking about fucking me.

I don't join in on the riotous behavior, it wouldn't look right. Even though the team can see we've buried the hatchet, we want them to think it's sitting in a shallow grave.

Just before I reach the locker room, I find Dani waiting for me, her pregnancy making her skin glow. Her yellow blouse wraps snug around her stomach and brightens her tone even more, making her look like a goddess.

Too bad it does nothing for me.

"Hey, baby." She pushes off the wall. "How's the knee?"

"Fine." I give her a closed mouth smile as she stands in front of me, her hands landing on my firm stomach.

"Tonight we're doing dinner at my place." Her hands skim downward just as the corridor erupts with voices at my back. "We can watch Netflix and chill."

"Good luck with that," Seb sneers as he walks by, leaving Dani glowering at the back of his head. She turns back to me with her nose scrunched up, clearly waiting on me to assert myself between them.

"Sounds good, baby." I bend to kiss her mouth, the boys catcalling as they pass us.

The approving look she gives me instantly sours. I don't want to deceive Seb, but I don't see any other way around this. We can't out ourselves because it would change everything, and no matter how progressive the league says they are, it's all a fucking lie.

No one wants to play ball with queers.

Sebastian

Did he call her baby? Did his mouth touch hers?

I stare, transfixed on that red sauna light as all the guys head to the showers. I continue to stare for several minutes, even though I should be heading to the fucking showers.

He was fucking struggling today, and I know he shot his knee up. Obviously, it's not helping him improve, so all I see are fucking problems from here on out. I really thought he was going to fight me on that last play, but when the relief washed over his face, I knew he was at his end. It's not like North to relinquish plays on the field, and he was lucky I fucking cared I could've watched him fuck himself over.

The old me would've relished in doing that.

Not anymore, though.

I'm a fucking pussy for the man which only serves to get me even more heated. I throw off my clothes, not caring when my jersey and pants hit the locker room floor in grass stained heaps, then I wrap a towel around my waist. He's going to face me, then he's going to tell me the fucking truth.

I rip open the sauna door, the steam hitting me in the face, teasing the sweat already coating my skin.

He doesn't flinch, doesn't even move from his spot on the bench with his head tipped back against the wall. His sculpted arms are spread out across the bench, his tats shimmering in the steam's moisture, and his abs flexing with each labored breath he takes.

His knee has ballooned since he took his pants off, the sight of it causing the anger I'm feeling melt away. He's going to make this injury permanent.

"Can you do me a favor?" He doesn't startle at the sound of my voice, telling me he knew it was me the whole time.

"What?" His voice carries a lilt of agony, and I have to steel my spine to keep from running to him.

"Rehab that knee properly, go back to the clinic, and recover properly. Can you do that?"

"I have a specialist coming by the house tomorrow and then coming by three days a week until it's healed." His eyes open, the deep brown pools hitting me like a ton of bricks. "Dani suggested it."

"That's it, then?" I hate the way her name sets me off, it makes me weak. "You and her?"

"Yeah, I told you," he shrugs, making the ink on his shoulders move. "I need to be there for my child."

"Cool." I nod, my insides quaking at the thought of losing him. "Remember this moment when you come running back."

"I won't, Seb." I can see the sincerity in his gaze, hear it in his despondent tone. "It's better this way."

Those words, spoken into the mist-filled space around us, are truer than he realizes. I need to let him go because it keeps him safe, and even though I know Dani will do nothing but pulverize his heart, it's safer to be heartbroken than dead.

Right?

I nod while giving him one final look, a slow sweep of the man who changed me forever. He does the same, and I feel it thundering through me.

This is goodbye.

The door shuts behind me with a click, the finality of it coursing through me. I grit my teeth, forcing myself to swallow the words trying to crawl up my throat. I don't go out quietly, never have.

I haul open the door one last time then stride up to the man whose very heart beats for the both of us. I yank on that beard, pulling him forward. Then my mouth is on his, my tongue gliding along his as I swallow every sound he makes, committing everything my senses absorb to memory.

Our teeth clash, blood stains both of our mouths, and our desperation saturates the air around us, turning the temperature up to fucking scorching.

When I finally pull back, I find his cheeks wet with tears, so

I lean forward to lick each one. If he's crying for me, then the salty fluid belongs to me, just like he does. Eventually, I will consume every molecule of him.

"Bye, North." I step back, watching his plush lower lip tremble, the flesh there swollen from my kisses.

I leave before I do something stupid like beg him to choose me, to give up lying to himself and to let what's happening between us grow. That would only cause more problems in the end.

He's safer this way, at least for now. Especially with what I'm about to dive in to.

CHAPTER NINE

Dixon

"The baby looks healthy, and the growth is on par for what it should be this far into the pregnancy."

It's been three months and one week since I chose Dani and this unborn child. Looking at it on the screen, its arms moving and its little feet kicking out, makes it all worth it.

Mostly.

"Have you guys decided if you want to know the sex?" the technician asks as my eyes find Dani's hazel ones.

"What do you think, baby?"

Baby.

She only ever says it in public to keep up the ruse we're playing, but the word always sends me spiraling back to Seb.

"Sure," I smile, the action easier after months of practicing to make it look genuine.

Even though I know this child isn't mine, there's still a connection, something that makes me want to watch it grow … to protect it and its mother.

"All right," Dani wiggles on the examination table. "Let's do this."

She grabs my hand, and I swallow down the instant need to shrug her off. I only need to think of his face to make the desire to walk away disappear.

"Here is the scrotum," the technician coos, causing Dani to squeal. "It's a boy."

"Daniel," Dani says with reverence. "We're going to name him Daniel."

The overwhelming urge to smack the name out of her mouth has me taking a step back, pulling curious looks from the technician.

"Everything okay there, Daddy?" she smiles as Dani throws me a dirty look.

"He's been hoping for a boy," she lies through her perfect teeth. "He's just shocked."

I am shocked but not about the baby's gender. It's the name she plans on giving him. I can't let that happen.

"I'll leave you to get dressed." The woman smiles as she leaves the room, just as all the pretenses fall.

"Would it be too difficult for you to fucking pretend you're excited?" Dani snaps as she sits up. "Or should I let my father know you enjoy sucking Sebastian's dick in the locker room?"

It's the same threat every time I begin to back away from her and this fucking game we're playing. To be honest, it's getting fucking old.

"Don't ever call your baby Daniel again," I mutter as I hand her a paper towel to wipe off the lubrication from the ultrasound.

"I like the name." She gives me a menacing look. "It's a lot like Danielle."

I don't argue with her further because it'll only make her fixate on the name more, and I have less than three months to put up with her. I can have a DNA test done then figure out my next move after that.

I may have something to hold over her head as much as she holds Seb over mine. What kind of reputation would she have if everyone found out the baby wasn't mine? Especially when I've been playing the dutiful father.

The last three months have gone by in a flash of doctor visits and rehab sessions. My knee is better, but it's only because Jameson has been providing me with the Toroidal I've been needing to play.

My rehab sessions have been going well, but the recovery is still way too slow. I can't be left out of a single game this season, I won't allow it. I'm still the rookie until the next one comes in, and I refuse to be a letdown so early in my career.

The Buffalo Bills did acquire a few new players, and I can't wait to hit that field without the rookie status hanging over my head. I won't lie… If Seb reacts to any of them the way he did with me, there's going to be a problem. The jealousy will coat every fucking move I make on that field. I don't think I could stand it.

I'm supposed to be the only man he's ever wanted.

I blame this sudden bout of insecurity on the fact that I have barely spoken two words to Seb since that day in the sauna. He's stuck to his word and no longer acts like I exist. The only time we interact is out on the field, and I live for those moments. The stolen looks, the excitement and the nearness of him.

I live each day for those few hours when he's once again all I see.

"Are you coming over for dinner tonight?" Dani asks as she hobbles down off the table. "Dad has been asking for you."

"Sure," I mumble, not really wanting to be around her or Coach.

The man has been acting like a proud father, too excited for a grandchild, and asking too many questions about my future with his daughter. I hate that I may have to let him down eventually.

"You should bring your mother, the grandparents should meet each other." She shoots a pointed look at me as my stomach sinks.

She's been pretty insistent lately about having our parents meet and wanting to tell my mother about the child growing in her belly. A child that isn't mine.

"You know the deal, Dani. I won't tell my mother until those results are in my hand."

There's no way I would ever put Ma through the heartbreak of losing someone else. I can't let her know there's a baby coming only to take it all back when those results come in.

"She should know." Dani gives me a knowing look, a threatening look. It's one I've become accustomed to, so it no longer sends shards of fear through my veins.

"One step at a time." I give her a saccharine smile.

"Sebastian has been going back and forth to Rochester often." She smiles, the look anything but sweet. "I wonder what he's been up to."

"He has a daughter," I shrug, trying to look nonchalant.

"He didn't care in the past," she argues.

"Because his wife was alive," I refute, hoping this finally shuts her up.

I hate that she gets information from her father and dangles it in front of me, teasing me with snippets of Seb's life. She wants the constant reminder to be there, letting me know she can destroy us both in the blink of an eye.

We leave the medical building, and I walk behind her, watching her over-exaggerated waddle.

"It's not like he gave an actual shit about his wife," she continues, much to my dismay. "He fucked me many times while he was married, but it all makes sense." She gives me a look over her shoulder. "He doesn't respect women because he's gay."

"The fuck?" My head rears back. "You're saying gay men can't respect women?"

"What are you now? An advocate?"

I ignore her as she gets into my vehicle and we pull out of the parking lot. The sooner I get her home, the sooner I can be away from her.

Ten minutes of blissful silence and then we pull up to her house.

"Look," she reaches over, placing her hand on top of mine. "I'm sorry about what I said back there. My hormones get the best of me sometimes, and when I think about that man, I want to explode."

The touch of her clammy skin on mine makes me close my eyes in disgust. But I accept her apology if only to get her the fuck out of my SUV.

"Be back here in three hours for dinner," she sing-songs, the sound making me want to gag.

The things I'm enduring for the man who raped and tortured me...

Sebastian

I've been working hard, keeping my head down and being an upstanding citizen. That is until I'm back home and driving the streets at night, chasing down rumors of cops who want a piece of the drug trade.

Three names. That's what I've recovered, and Delano was right, they're all Feds.

In my quest to find out what had Little North running from his crew, I've uncovered some shit, and all of it is beginning to make a lot of sense. Veteran federal agents who were either looking to beef up their retirement funds or put their kids through university decided to join the drug scene to make some quick flow.

When I fill my free time with trying to find answers, it saves me from having to think about Dixon and Dani. The cute, new family the team has been oohing and aahing over. I've even turned a blind eye to Jameson dealing Toroidal to Dixon because I don't want to have to talk to him. I want to live in ignorance, like I don't even know he exists.

But when we're both on that field, all our issues fade away, and he's there, making it feel like nothing's changed.

Everything has changed, though.

Every time I walk off that field, I'm hit with that realization, forcing me to start all over again at square one. The more I see of Dani, the more the hatred inside of me grows, and I watch her stomach grow with bated breath. Any day now she's going to be exposed for the blackmailer she is, then hopefully, she fucking disappears.

Until then, I have work to do. Dixon's safe if he stays in the arms of the venomous bitch until everything is sorted. Then, I'm taking back what's mine.

The light turns green as I race through the intersection, my tires squealing as they try to find traction on the rain soaked asphalt. Baltimore reminds me of Rochester at night, so I don't feel out of place. It's comforting knowing Dixon grew up in similar circumstances.

I have a meeting with a kid who was close to Little North, and he wants out of the same gang. He was easy enough to find when I started staking out Little North's old turf, his face kept popping up. I don't know who's training these kids, but they're not as slick as they should be.

I pull into a parking lot, the plaza beside it completely dark, making the grills lining the windows and doors shine under the street lights. Looks like they shut everything down here too, just like in Rochester. No one risks their register drawer staying open twenty-four hours. I grab my gun, tucking it into the inside pocket of my leather jacket. Then I pull my black and white bandana down closer to my eyebrows before slipping on my all black cap, the peak obscuring my eyes.

If I'm recognized by anyone, they'll die tonight.

I step out of the Hummer, giving the area a quick scan. The punk said he'd be here, and I'm giving him another two minutes before I'm out. A Hummer sitting here in the open like this is like a fucking target, but he best not think I'm fucking stupid and try to rob me. That's a sure way to fucking die.

"Psst."

I roll my eyes at the sound coming from the side of the plaza, my teeth clenching as my head moves slowly in its direction. Is he calling a fucking cat? Do I look like a pussy?

"Kid, I ain't coming into no dark alley with you. Get your ass out here, and make it look like you're lining my pockets with the good shit. Ya feel me?"

"Fuck," he hisses and steps out.

He's young, maybe eighteen or nineteen. He's dressed in an oversized jersey that reaches his knees, baggy pants, and a cap pulled to the side of his head. He's average height, and when he steps under the light, I can see his Hispanic features.

"This is dangerous, bro." He looks around, making me tsk loudly.

"Don't look suspicious, and tell me your fucking name before I pop a hole in your forehead."

His eyes widen as he takes a subtle step back. "Fernando."

"Don't do that either." I pull my gun from my jacket to point it at his feet. "You're looking like a runner, and if I'm buying drugs off a kid who's acting flighty, I would shoot them. Comprende?"

"Si." He clears his throat, stepping back up. "I don't usually deal with people like you."

"'People like me?' Who are people like me?"

"Packing heat and threatening to kill me," he scowls as he begins to put his hands in his pockets.

"Don't do that either," I chide, and he lets them hang back at his sides. "Tell me what you know about North, and I will see if I can help you."

"It was the night before he was supposed to be initiated. We were chilling on our regular block, smoking a J and passing back and forth a 40."

I grin because that was the life I had before I played football.

"Then North gets a call. He has some shit to pick up back at the base, and he's excited because it's more of the good shit we'd been running. The cut was hella good."

"What was it?" I lean back against the Hummer but keep my hand inside my jacket.

"Pure coca, bro. Like this shit was so white it looked like actual snow. I don't think it was cut with *anything*."

I know what he means. When the coke was running my streets as a kid, it was nearly cream colored or gray. None of that pure white cartel shit hit my hands, and if it had, I would've been just as excited as those two were. That would mean a bigger price tag.

"Go on."

"So we get back to base, and there're these large bricks sitting in the center of the table. Some guys were already bagging it, but we could see the stamps on the brown plastic wrapping, it said *evidence.*"

Cop shit. I wave him to continue, and he looks around him again.

"North just didn't keep his mouth shut, man. He took one look at that and asked if we robbed the police station. Everyone went silent, except these two guys in the back who started to laugh and didn't look familiar to me. . They came up to North, started asking him about his moms and if she was good in the new house his football star brother bought for her. They knew shit, man."

He starts to shift his weight from foot to foot, his eyes beginning to water.

"North got spooked. No one ever directly threatened his family, not in our crew anyway. You just don't do that, and we could tell by looking at these big *gringos* that they were cops."

I want to correct him and say *Feds,* but right now, they're one in the same. Infiltrators.

"Did you get names?"

He nods, moving his head to look around again. I hiss to make him stop.

"One of those idiots called the other Jones and knew he made a mistake because he looked at us right away. Now we have this name, right? We know they're not a part of our crew, and they look official. *Jefe* comes and starts giving us bags of this shit, but Danny backs away, shaking his head. And I could feel the shift in that warehouse, right here." He hits his stomach. "I tried to give him a look, like take your shit and let's go, but he was spooked, bro."

Jones. Special agent Gregory Jones. He's the one I popped in my kitchen, *puto.*

"Danny said he didn't want to go to jail. He thought these men were cops, and he thought *Jefe* didn't know. He was scared for his mom, he was scared for his brother who just got picked up by the

Buffalo Bills." He smiles, a proud look coming over his face, then it falls just as fast. "So my man booked it, ran from the warehouse like he was legit running from the po-po."

"He probably thought you were all about to be arrested," I mumble, the images clear in my mind. It was like I'd transported back in time, putting my mind frame inside Daniel North. I would've done the same.

"Si, I tried to tell him that, but when I turned to call out to him…" He lifts his shirt to show me a scar running along his ribs. "They capped me, bro. Not enough to kill me, but I wasn't running anywhere. That was when North went into hiding." He drops his shirt and kicks at a stone on the ground. "If I wasn't shot, I could've found him and convinced him to come back. *Jefe* cared about North, he was family."

"Kid," I put a hand on his shoulder. "*Jefe* would've put a bullet in him too. He wouldn't have had a choice. It's not your fault."

"Dixon keeps calling me, asking for information, and it scares me, ya know? Danny did what he did to keep them safe, and I don't want to make his death for nothing."

The kid was loyal, and I liked that, but the fact that Dixon was nosing around made me fucking nervous.

"Don't tell his brother anything, *entiendes*?"

"*Comprendo*," he nods. "I want to run too. I don't got anyone here to protect, but they found North, and I'm scared what they will do if they find me. Danny got off easy. I wouldn't be so lucky as to get a bullet to the head, I'd be fucking tortured."

"I'll get you out." I make him a promise, bumping my fist to his. "Now tell me about the guys who found and killed North."

"They weren't crew. They were sent by those *putos gringos,* and they left him there on that boat like he was fucking nothing. *Jefe* told us if we found him to bring him in, he wanted to speak to him. But those assholes just shot and left him there."

"What happened to the guys?" I know what happened to them, I fucking barbequed them in Delano's basement, but I want to know what this kid knows. Whatever he tells me will be what the word is on the street.

"They got picked up by some out of state crew. Someone said Tri-State, but no one knows for sure. They were killed, *Jefe* got a few videos sent to him." He scratches the light scruff on his face then chews into the skin of his cheek. "I heard one of those guys was related to the *gringos*."

"What you mean?" My forehead crinkles, moving the cap on my head.

"He was the son of one of those *puto* cops."

CHAPTER TEN

This is my second year at the Bills Camp, and I feel both excited and apprehensive. We have two new rookies this year which means my rookie title has been passed on, thank God. We've also acquired a new offensive lineman and a running back, positions we need to beef up our offense.

The locker room is buzzing with voices, and I pick out the new faces instantly. They're standing with Zeal who's doing his thing by making them feel welcomed. Him being quarterback means it's his job to do so.

My eyes scan the place, looking for Sebastian of their own will. When I spot him, he's sitting with Jameson in what looks to be a hushed conversation. My stomach flips with nerves when I see Seb give Jameson a dark look, one that suggests violence if Seb doesn't get what he wants. Sweat begins to gather at the base of my neck as I imagine them talking about the Toroidal I desperately need to actually play this year.

Jameson is my only hookup for it, and I can't start looking for another. I don't trust anyone else.

Jameson gets up to stalk toward the field, giving me a quick nod as he passes by. My eyes don't move from Seb, though as he sits there on that bench, looking at the new rookies. I wait for it. A flash of hatred, a look of interest … anything, but there's nothing.

Relief hits me in the gut, and I hate myself for it. Jealousy is waiting just beneath my calm exterior, searching for the perfect moment to rear its ugly head to out us both in one fell swoop.

I get to my locker and open it up, waiting to feel the dark tendrils of his stare wrap around me, but it doesn't happen. My eyes skip to the side, finding him still watching Zeal as he continues to tell the new guys about the team. He's lucky he looks practically bored because otherwise, I'd have my fucking fist to his cheek.

"Fuck," I hiss, dropping my forehead to the cool metal of the locker. I've become him, toxic and fucking disturbed.

A body hits the metal beside me, driving my head up to look into a pair of warm, honey eyes. "Look who isn't the rookie anymore."

My breath is trapped in my throat as I soak up the sound of his voice, my mind repeating the first few words he's spoken to me in months.

"How's the knee?" I finally pull my eyes away from his mouth, swallowing down the shock still choking my air supply.

"Fine."

"Better be," he sneers as he pushes off the lockers. "You don't want these guys to see you act like a pussy out there. They're at the bottom, and they need to know it takes work to climb up on this team."

"Or you'll force them to know that?" I seethe as images of what he did to force me to understand flash through my mind.

"You're wondering if I'll keep them in their place with my cock?" His words are spoken low, but as soon as he says *cock,* mine perks up. "Does that make you jealous?"

"Fuck off," I groan, but there's no heat behind the words.

"You are," he chuckles. "You sick fuck, North."

My eyes meet his. Instead of the disgust I expect to find behind such words, all I see is unbridled lust, and it nearly knocks me off my fucking feet.

Time has done nothing to change how I feel about him, and guessing by the look in his eyes, it's the same for him. I thought this was a fluke, a one-off, and instead, I'm beginning to realize that this thing between us just might be the real thing. Something most people search their entire lives for yet come up short.

I suddenly have the overwhelming feeling of fear as I continue to stare back at the man who forced his way inside of me, imprinting himself on my heart. I'm settling with Dani because I'm afraid I found the needle in the haystack with Seb, and instead of grasping it firmly in my palm, I kicked it farther away, hoping to never uncover it again.

"Wipe that look off your face, North," he sneers, turning his back. "Your baby is going to be born soon."

Ice water rushes through my veins at his words, shoving me right back into the reality I created for myself. I have no one else to blame, and I can't stand here longing for a man I deliberately turned my back on. I just want to protect him, but I can't do that if Dani isn't kept in her lane.

He wouldn't understand, and even if I did tell him my reasoning, I fear he'd kill her. Pregnant or not. I've seen the manic look he gets in his eyes when he's teetering on the edge of control. I've looked down the barrel of his gun, feeling him shake with the need to press into that trigger. I couldn't have her death on my conscience.

He walks over to the new guys, his swagger pronounced, and when he holds out his hand to shake theirs, I let out a small breath of relief. He never once welcomed me, and look what we've become. Maybe this is his way of assuring me that I'm his one-off too.

My knee is screaming in pain as I struggle to walk back to the locker room. I'm slow and hanging behind as everyone rushes back through the large, metal double doors. An arm wraps around my shoulders, his scent hitting me. I don't even need to look up into his face to know it's the bane of my fucking existence.

"Easy," he literally purrs into my ear. "Lean on me."

I want to ask him why he's helping me now, why he ignored me all these months, yet no words form inside my mouth. I'm in too much pain to even function.

"Put a big smile on your face and make it look like we're celebrating."

I do as he says, hoping to God it doesn't look like I'm cringing because that's what I feel like doing.

"North!" Zeal exclaims as I come inside, and Seb slowly releases me. The sudden weight on my knee has me swallowing back a groan, then when Zeal throws his weight onto me, I nearly scream out. "That was a fucking amazing game. We're going all the way this year, baby!"

It was a good scrimmage today. The new rookies are a great addition, and I ran my fucking ass off to show what I could fucking do, only now I'm paying for it.

He sees my grimace because he backs up, looking down to my knee. "How is it?"

"It gets tender after practices, but it's good."

"You sure?" The crease between his brows deepens as I begin to stress. I can't let him think I can't play.

"Yeah, man. I promise, I'm good."

"I'll get you some ice, and then when that's done, you hop in the sauna. Yeah?"

"Sounds good." I walk back to the bench, keeping my walk steady so any eyes on me won't start to wonder about my condition.

Zeal comes back with an ice pack as I remove my pants, placing the pack on my knee. Everyone heads into the showers except for Seb who's casually leaning against the lockers.

"You need to lay off that shit. I mean it. You're going to do permanent damage, and then what happens to you and your mom?"

"I need to play, the season's beginning soon," I explain, my knee finally starting to numb with the ice.

"This game, this fucking league isn't worth breaking your body for. You're not their workhorse only to be put down when you can no longer produce."

"Are you fucking kidding me? Of course, I am. So are you. So is every other fucking player in this league, but we do it because we're compensated well. This career takes men like you and me off the fucking streets, putting us in mansions on the hill." I can feel the burn of emotion in my eyes because as always, I think of my brother who never made it off the fucking streets.

"No, your talent did that. Don't fucking give anyone else credit for what you trained yourself to do."

"My talent brought me here, but I don't sign my own checks."

He's quiet after that, watching me as I rotate the pack on my knee. The swelling has gone down, but the pain still radiates upward, making me crave the sauna for the relief it'll bring. I just don't want him in there with me.

"That's done now, you need to head into the sauna," he tells me as I look up at him.

"Alone."

"Yeah," he nods, his eyes never straying from the pack. "I won't be in there with you."

I stand with relief, taking off the rest of my clothes then watching as Seb walks to the showers. I wrap a towel around my waist and head to the sauna, hoping to be left in peace.

It's the only peace I have because after this, I'll once again be thrust into the hell I've made for myself.

Sebastian

The sauna light is on when I come back from the showers, and I'm not alone in the locker room. Dani is standing just inside, her hands crossed in front of her and her eyes hungrily roving over my body.

I drop my towel, grinning at her quick intake of breath. I bet Dixon isn't giving her any dick.

"What do you want?" I ask as I begin to dress.

"I'm waiting for Dixon." Her voice is like nails on a fucking chalkboard.

"Same." I shoot her a wink, watching as her face reddens.

"For what?"

"I want to say bye. He had a rough day, his knee and all," I grin.

"He told me his knee is fine." Her hands land on her hips.

"Because he doesn't give enough of a shit to tell you the truth. Tell me, has he fucked you yet?"

Her eyes narrow, and I let loose a thunderous laugh, a feeling of elation gathering in me. I had hoped he wasn't touching her, but I couldn't be too sure, knowing how persuasive the bitch could be.

He's still mine.

I'm pulling up my pants when the sauna door opens, and I hear his groan.

"Dani, you can't be in here. If Coach sees you, you're going to be banned from the stadium," he chastises her.

"He went home." She sounds like a fucking brat.

"Still, wait for me outside. People are changing in here," he demands.

I quickly haul a sweater over my head then look up at the both of them, him with a towel still wrapped firmly around his waist and her eyeing me.

"It's all good, I'm leaving."

I pick up my bag, tossing it over my shoulder, my fingers wrapped around the strap. I stop when I'm in front of Dixon, our chests no more than a few inches apart. I can feel his breath on my cheek, but my eyes stay on Dani.

"I'll see you tomorrow," I say to him, watching as Dani's face reddens.

Then with my other hand, I grab his beard, yanking his face to the side to devour his mouth. He fucking melts into me, helpless to the inferno burning around us, and unable to pull away, regardless of who's watching.

It's been months since I've tasted him, I refuse not to make it worth it. I don't know when the next time will be, if ever. So my tongue snakes into his mouth, tangling with his then swallowing his small mewls of enjoyment.

My eyes stay open as I watch her in my periphery, grinning into Dixon's mouth when hers drops open. I want her to see how he can't help himself. I want her to see how much I affect him, and when she falls asleep tonight, I want this to be the image she sees.

I pull back, dragging my teeth along his bottom lip, and then, just to drive the fucking message home, I grab his hard, throbbing cock through the towel. I give him a quick yank as he groans, the sound carrying around the room.

The moment he catches himself, realizing what just happened, he steps back, but it's too late. Dani looks embarrassed and livid, the red of her cheeks making her look like a child on the verge of a temper tantrum.

"Fuck." He gives me a dirty look as he brushes by, heading for his locker. He can be pissed all he wants, doesn't matter to me. I like him angry.

I head for the exit, stopping in front of Dani to give her a disgusted once over.

"Looks like he'd still fall to his knees and slurp my dick if that's what I wanted." I flick her hair, laughing when she bats my hand out of the way, her eyes shining with unshed tears.

The anger that's swirling around her is so fucking potent, I can almost taste it, so I take a deep breath, inhaling the energy.

"Fuck, you smell like heaven when you're seething like that." I chuckle as I head out to the corridor. "Have a good night, Dani."

It's been another two weeks of silent treatment and avoidance, but it was all worth it. I knew what would happen afterward, but I still wanted it. I'll let him sulk for now, make him feel like he has the upper hand, then when I'm ready for my next taste, I'll fucking take it.

It's the last few days of camp, and today we're hosting a friendly game with the Green Bay Packers. It's good because we have our first game of the season with them in a couple of weeks, so this gives us a chance to feel them out.

Coach said we can have family and friends in the stands tonight, making my fucking heart ache. I wish I could call up Paola and tell her to bring Carla, just to have her watch me at least once in person instead of on a TV screen.

I stand on the edge of the field, watching as a few people come in, taking seats around the field, but there's one in particular who catches my eye. I grin and jog across the field toward the stands when I see her and who else's attention she's caught.

Marian sits with her purse clutched in her hands on her lap, and when Dani waddles her pregnant ass toward Dixon's mother, I see her side eyeing the bitch hard. A chuckle escapes as I get closer, and Dani takes a seat beside Marian, leaning in to say something to her. The older woman doesn't budge, her eyes having found me instead, a small smile working over her mouth.

"Hi, Marian." I stop in front of her, hoisting myself up by the railing then leaning in to kiss her cheek.

Dani is glaring a hole into the side of my head, but I don't bother to acknowledge her.

"Hi, Sebastian." Marian's smile stretches across her face. "How have you been?"

"Sorry I haven't been around much, life has been a bit hectic." I finally look at Dani then back to Marian with my brow raised. "For everyone."

"Yes, well, hopefully things calm down soon."

"When are you due, Dani?" I rest my chin in my hand as I give her my attention, her face working to hide her anger.

"In a few weeks, although the doctor said first babies can sometimes be late." Her hand rests on the top of her stomach.

The silence from both me and Marian sets an uncomfortable air around the three of us, and Dani struggles as she gets up, her hand on her lower back.

"I'm going to go see if Dixon needs anything before the game," she says quietly as she slowly moves back out of the row.

Once she's out of earshot, I turn to look at a fuming Marian. "Are you okay?"

"I don't know why he carries on with her," she shakes her head, clutching her purse tighter.

"She's pregnant—"

"You and I both know that's not his child," she cuts me off then softens her tone. "I'm sorry, I am just so angry with my son over this. He's strapping himself down to a hussy. I know he's careful, and I know she's not carrying my son's baby. He admitted he didn't want to tell me until he had a DNA test, but she wouldn't stop pestering him."

"You and I both. Soon enough, it'll all be cleared up." I give her a wink, holding out my fist.

She bumps it with a chuckle, and I hop back down. "Good luck, Sebastian," she calls out, and I hold up my hand.

These last few weeks have been stressful with lack of sleep, camp, and still trying to run down the men who thought they could kill my wife then get away with it. I've had Fernando running his streets, but all his information is coming back to me, and when I'm ready, I'll be pulling him out to Rochester where I can keep him safe.

The information he's getting me is a lot more valuable than Delano's. If I'm being honest, Delano isn't giving me much because he's always too fucking busy to talk. It's becoming irritating and suspicious. I hate that the trust I have for my childhood friend is waning, but I have never second guessed my gut instincts.

That's a lie.

I have, but only when it comes to what I'm feeling about Dixon North.

Just as I think about him for the umpteenth time this past hour, I find him with his arms crossed in the corridor while he listens to a bitching Dani. He looks bored and over it. When he straightens to head back inside the locker room, I don't miss the devious look she shoots at his back.

She steps back into her father's office, shutting the door behind her, the force of it a little louder than usual. She's pissed about his mother's attitude, and Dixon won't do anything about it. His mom is the only family he has left.

I get inside the locker room to find all the guys quiet, everyone doing what they need to do to get in the zone. Dixon is on the bench, wrapping his knee, and I don't miss the wince he tries to hide. Jameson told me he's been steadily supplying the Toroidal, but right now, it looks like he hasn't taken it. I fucking hope that means he's stopping.

I take the seat beside him, fuming a little when he doesn't even look up. This fucking game we've been playing is getting old. I'm waiting out the time until that kid is born, proving it's not his, but then we're figuring this shit out once and for all.

I'll also have my own shit figured out, ensuring he'll be safe.

"I saw your mom," I tell him.

"So I heard," he grumbles as I struggle to hide the smirk.

"She has every right to feel the way she does, no one believes that's your kid."

"Whatever," he shrugs. "Sometimes the bigger picture is all that matters."

"What the fuck does that mean?" I lean in, making sure to keep my voice hushed. "What's the bigger picture? Why are you doing this?"

"Let it go," he orders as he stands. "Your desperation fucking stinks."

His words are sharp, and their aim is true as they slice through to my very soul. I am desperate for him, but I think I've been pretty controlled during this whole fiasco.

"Fine," I raise my hands. "You got it."

We all finish up getting ready, and the room is deadly silent as we line up to head out to the field. Coach gives us a brief pep talk, telling us to be aware and vigilant, to take more than a win out of this game.

We get it. He wants us to learn the Packers and all their plays.

The locker room doors open, then we walk out in a single file, me ending up behind Dixon. I nearly plow into his back when he stops suddenly, his sight trained to Coach's office. I look over to see Dani giggling with a Packer, her head tipped back.

"That's Dillon James," I tell him once he starts walking again.

"I know who he is," he fumes, and I grin at his bratty attitude.

"Then you know he used to be a Bill."

"And?" he sneers, my hand itching to slap his ass.

"Well, you know how well Dani is at welcoming players to the team." I run by him and out onto the field, letting that statement sink into his mind.

It's time he stops playing house with the team whore and moves on with his life, even if it means I have to constantly remind him about it.

I've always been good at pointing out the little things.

CHAPTER ELEVEN

The shot I took thirty minutes ago is starting to take effect as I step out on the field. This will always be like home to me, the grass under my shoes and the lights shining down onto my shoulders. I just want to enjoy the game I love and not be in constant pain while I do it.

The look Dani gave me inside that corridor while she was talking to Dillon James was unsettling. I don't know why, but it looked fucking devious, especially when her head tipped back in the fakest laugh I have ever heard. She's planning something, and the thought scares the shit out of me.

My eyes find Seb as he stands in front of my mother on the field, making her laugh with his antics, the sight tugging on my heart. She clearly adores him, and that makes me fucking sad because if she knew what he and I were doing, she'd surely dislike him.

I'm adjusting my gloves when the Packers come out to the field. All of them are walking one by one when I hear a snort, making me turn my head. Dillon James is walking beside another player, their heads together with his helmet in his hand. His eyes comb over me slowly, and then they both laugh as they take off for the field.

I look over my shoulder to find Dani leaning against the door, a small smile on her mouth while her hand rubs her extremely swollen stomach. Something works its way through my stomach as I turn back to the field, watching as Dillon James huddles with his team.

It's an overreaction, surely. Why would she do anything to cause her father's team harm? She's full of idle threats and insecurities, hoping they'll keep me in line.

I shake off any lingering doubts then run to my team huddle. Zeal smiles, giving me a clap on the shoulder.

"Let's pound these pussies with our monster cocks, yeah?" Zeal's mouth stretches wide around his mouthguard, making us all laugh. It relieves some of the tension, and we all loosen up as we listen to the first play.

"Dillon James has his eye on you," Seb leans in to murmur in my ear. "I think I need to knock him the fuck out for it."

"Shut up." I side eye him, seeing his taunting grin. I breathe out some relief when I see he's playing, but I still don't like how James is fixated on me.

My gut is telling me something is wrong. Dani must've told him I'm her baby's father, and they all think I'm an idiot for knocking up the team's whore. For the millionth time, I feel disgusted by the decision I made.

"Avando, you ready to take our ball over the line?" Zeal asks as he pulls on his helmet.

"Fuck yeah." Seb crashes his fist to Zeal's as we all walk to the line of scrimmage.

Seb and I hang back a bit. We need to get that ball over into the opposition's side which means we need our defensemen to clear the offense first. Seb being the tight-end and myself as the wide receiver means we need to find a way to position ourselves in their field. Dex stands in front of me, shaking out his arms and flexing his fists. He's a huge motherfucker, and I'm fucking glad it's me he's in front of.

Zeal won the coin toss earlier, so he chose to have the first play, something we rarely do. He likes to defer mostly, but I can see he's wanting to throw the Packers off our game. We're also doing the most commonly known plays, putting ourselves in the i-formation, and not letting the Packers see our more unique plays.

The ball is hiked, and I watch as Seb takes off, his feet blurring with his fucking speed, my chest burning with envy. Our times used to be neck and neck, but now, I couldn't fucking get near his if I tried. Thankfully, Coach doesn't pit us against each other, but I'm sure he notices the difference.

I notice James hot on his tail, and when Seb catches the ball, he's tackled by the big fucker. I'm running toward them before I can even think, worried about Seb's head, flashbacks of his last tackle heavy in my mind.

I rip James off him to find Seb fucking laughing, his arms cradling the fucking ball.

"Don't touch me." James shoves me off him. "Bitch."

His words run off me like water, none of them mattering because Seb is okay. But Seb heard it, and he's not as forgiving.

"Watch your mouth, James." Seb calls out as he gets to his feet. "If you keep running your mouth, I'll fucking smash it."

"I bet you will!" James shouts over his shoulder as he jogs back to his team.

What the fuck was that?

I'm undressing my knee, the pain of it scorching a path of fire up my thigh, and by the looks of it, it's going to be swollen for the next couple of days. We won the game, but it didn't escape me the few times I caught Dillon laughing with a few teammates.

An ice pack lands in my lap as I look up to find Seb with his arms crossed, his face a mask of disdain.

"It's looking worse."

"Nah, it's about the same," I protest, giving him an attitude.

"Did you want me to shove my cock down your throat? Is that why you're testing me with your bratty attitude?"

"Will you shut the fuck up?" I look around him, ensuring the guys are still in the showers.

"How many did you use today?"

"Two." *Three.*

"Stop fucking lying!" he roars, my eyes rising to look up at him in shock. "I can tell by the way you chew into your fucking cheek."

"I'm only going to use on game nights," I try to talk him down from the rage pushing through him.

"It's illegal to use it the way you are, you know that." He bends over to grab my thigh, squeezing it and making me cry out. "This isn't getting better, and you're causing irreversible damage."

He continues to massage the thigh out, but the pain makes my eyes cloud with tears.

I stand, his hand falling away. "I'll rest it for the next few days."

The guys come out of the showers, loud and amped, all of them talking about hitting Sky Lounge.

"You in, North?" Dex asks, his big grin taking over his face.

"Nah," I shake my head. "I need to rest this knee, but count me in next time."

"What about you, Avando?" Zeal cuts in.

"Can't tonight. I got a little FaceTime date with Carla."

The guys all groan but do it with smiles on their faces. It's not often Seb talks about his family, but when he does, he has this shine of pride in his eyes.

I bypass the sauna, heading into the showers, my knee screaming for rest. It never fails… Every time I pass by the stall I was attacked in, I pause to reflect. The agony I felt, both physical and emotional, then to where I stand now with the man who caused it. None of it makes logical sense, but it all feels meant to be.

Fucked, right?

I step into that stall and turn on the water, letting the first rush of cold hit my knee. My hand lands on the tiled wall as my head drops forward, letting the warming spray roll down my back.

The feel of the cool tile under my hand has me pressing my fingers against it, letting images flip through my mind. Jameson and Ortiz held me down as Seb had his way by *keeping me in line.* Then it flips to him standing in his stall, his toned and muscled body flexing as he washed. Me stepping inside then giving him the same treatment, letting out whatever residual animosity I held inside.

My cock hardens as it usually does at the thought of him. My free hand wraps around it, squeezing in irritation.

Will it ever stop?

"I like how we get off in locker room showers." His body presses into my back as his hard cock nestles in my ass cheeks.

"Seb." It's more a moan than a warning while everything around us disappears.

It's been too long, and I've been craving him, fucking dreaming about this.

"Spread your legs for me, baby," he whispers into my ear, sending my heart into overdrive. It's rare Seb is this affectionate. "Let's make this quick."

"The guys—"

"Gone. Now open up."

I spread my legs for him as I continue to stroke my cock, and when his fingers press against my hole, I jerk forward and release a moan.

"Don't move," he warns as a finger works inside me. "I'm going to fuck this tight pussy so fucking hard."

He's always called my asshole a pussy, and suddenly, it dawns on me that maybe this is why he denies he's gay. Maybe he thinks as long as he tells himself it's like a pussy, he can tell himself he's straight.

"It's an asshole," I correct, looking at him over my shoulder.

He pulls apart my ass cheeks then meets my eyes. "You think I don't fucking know that, you little brat?"

"You *are* calling it a pussy, aren't you?" His eyes narrow at my response, telling me I'm working myself into punishable territory. The thought has my cock jerking in my hand.

He drops to his knees, and I startle, frozen in place with shock.

"What are you doing, Seb?"

"Shh, baby." His finger continues to work in and out of my hole, making me moan. "I'm going to show you how well I eat this fucking pussy."

Before I can even absorb his words, his tongue hits the rim of my hole, and I gasp at the contact. He eats it, just like he said he could, and both of my hands slap against the tile as my legs threaten to give out.

His tongue flicks against the circle of muscle, his teeth scrape along the rim, and then to my utter fucking shock, his tongue replaces his finger. He pushes it deep inside of me, his lips pressing around the hole as I bite into my lip to keep from screaming out.

He begins to fuck my asshole with his tongue, quick swipes in and out, each one curling upward while hitting a spot that threatens to make me come all over the wall in front of me. He moans like he's enjoying a decadent meal, and a curse escapes my lips at the sound.

How can this be so wrong when everything about it feels so fucking right?

He withdraws with a chuckle. "How's that, baby?" He pushes two fingers inside of me then spits on my hole to ease the intrusion. "You ready to take me now?"

I nod because I've never been more ready. Just the thought of him pushing his cock inside of me has my own leaking with precum.

"Good boy." He pulls his fingers out and kisses my hole, spitting onto it one more time. "Make sure you keep that pretty mouth shut, we don't want anyone coming in here."

He stands, his chest hitting my back, then his mouth rests on the sensitive spot just under my ear lobe. "It's been a while, baby. I can't go easy."

I can hear the pained restraint in his tone and give him a quick nod, consenting to what I know will leave me sore for days. It doesn't matter because I fucking want it.

He spreads me open, groaning, and I turn to watch his face as he lines himself up. He looks reverent, and when his head pushes against my hole, his eyes come up to meet mine.

"Let out that breath, baby, and let me in."

I do as he asks, and when he pushes in farther, I can see the potent pleasure in his eyes. It does nothing to cover the other emotion lurking around the edges. It makes me catch my breath, and when he's fully seated inside of me, his chest to my back, his mouth hits my ear again.

"You're mine." He pulls out a bit then slams back in, pulling a strangled cry from my throat. "You're done with everyone else, do you understand me?"

"Seb," I whine as he pulls all the way out then thrusts back in, the burn sending pleasure throughout my body.

"Mine, you fucking brat." His hand clenches around the back of my neck, pushing my face to the tile. "Say it."

He begins a punishing rhythm, my mouth falling open as pain and pleasure swirl together in a dance of dominance.

"Dixon." His hand tightens in warning. "Don't make me rip this pretty pussy in two. She's already looking stretched beyond her limits."

Just as he says this, he switches up his angle, and the tip of his cock hits that sweet spot and stretches me wider.

"Yours," I pant, my fist working hard over my cock. "I've always been yours."

"Good boy," he praises, releasing my neck.

He grips both of my ass cheeks as he plows into me, helping me push my cock through my fist. I squeeze it tighter as my balls tighten, and the sensation of flying hits me, sending me into a cloud of euphoria.

"Yes, baby," he groans. "Paint that fucking wall with your cum."

His words send tremors through me, and when I finally come down, he's groaning through his release deep inside of me.

I wait for the shame to hit me, the regret I felt before, and sigh when there's nothing but contentment. He stays inside me, his cock jerking with his forehead on my shoulder.

"You're mine," he murmurs quietly.

"Seb, how?" I croak out as he pulls out of me.

"One day at a time," he assures me, the small smile on his face genuine.

He's mine.

"Can I ask you something?" I turn to face him, letting the water run down my back, washing away his release.

"Yeah." He grabs my waist, hauling me into him, his mouth hitting the corner of my lips.

"If Paola was still alive, would this be happening?"

He pulls back, his eyes flicking back and forth between mine while his mouth turns down in thought. I like that he doesn't answer right away, it means he's taking my question seriously.

"I think so," he nods. "She knew about you before I did."

"What does that mean?" My finger comes up to brush against the cupid bow shape of his lips.

"She knew I found you and what you meant to me before I even figured it out," he whispers as a tear skates down his cheek. "I was ashamed while she was happy for me."

My brows knit together, and he looks up at them, a small smile working around my finger.

"I married her to keep her safe, a promise I made to her brother and one I would've kept forever. But I'm starting to realize, she only wanted me to be happy."

"Are you?"

"Not yet, baby. But I will be soon. Make sure you're ready for me." He slaps my ass cheek and leaves the stall, his ass bunching with each step.

I shut off the water, following him into the locker room where we both get changed into our clothes without uttering a single word. Nothing else needs to be said because our actions have already painted the story. I'm his and he's mine.

We leave the locker room, shutting off the lights behind us. We stop when we find Dani standing by the exit, her face a mask of irritation.

"Took you long enough," she scowls as she watches Seb walk by her, his smile one of taunting victory.

"Goodnight, Dani," he coos sweetly, her clenching in response.

She knows exactly why we're late.

I shake off the thought and walk toward her.

I am his, and he is mine.

"What's up?"

"I need a ride home. Dad had to go out to dinner." She rolls her eyes, and it's my turn to lock my jaw.

She does this whenever she wants to try to coax me inside her house, and it always leaves me uncomfortable. Luckily, I know my mother is home, waiting for me to celebrate our win.

"It'll have to be quick, I'm having dinner with my mother."

"I could join you guys," she suggests from behind me, trying to keep up with my long strides.

"Not tonight, she's cooking for two."

I hear her huff of annoyance, but nothing could rip me down from the cloud I'm on, and it has everything to do with the man who's watching us get into my SUV, a small smile playing on his sexy lips.

Sebastian

The dial tone sounds from the Hummer's speakers as I watch Dixon head for his car, a fuming Dani struggling to keep up behind him. It makes me smile to see he's not coddling her or assisting her up into the seat.

Progress.

He gives me a look before he gets into the driver's side, and it has my cock hardening again, wishing I could walk over there and fuck him against that vehicle. Smug brat.

"*Jefe*," Fernando's voice fills the interior as I watch Dixon leave the parking lot.

"Did you get what I needed?"

"*Si*." He sounds excited, and that makes me fucking excited. I'm ready to have this over with. "Special Agent Dawes. I saw his fucking badge, bro."

So it's confirmed. The two men I'll be hunting are Special Agent Emilio Gomez and Special Agent Paul Dawes.

"Good work. I'll be down to see you this weekend."

"Cool." The click of him hanging up has me smiling to myself in the rear-view.

It's all falling into place, the only thing left to do is figure out where Delano is sitting in all of this. I hate that I've been keeping tabs on him, but something feels off, and after the past few months of him feeding me bullshit, I'm ready to call him out on it.

He's going to be taking a trip with me to visit these *Feds*, helping me see exactly where his mind has been lately. I've been watching every move he makes with our production, but I don't know what the fuck he does behind closed doors at home.

If he's working to overthrow me, best friend or not, he's going to meet his fucking maker.

After a quick video chat with my daughter, I take another shower while I mull over my options for tonight. Sure, I'm a little sore and should rest, but after today, I'm fucking amped with energy. I could go to Sky Lounge and meet up with the others, but I don't think Dixon would appreciate it. Not without him anyway.

The thought has me grinning and makes my decision for me. I'm going to go check in on what's mine.

The lights are on as I pull up, and when I buzz the gate, it automatically opens. He knows I'm here. This feeling of excitement is foreign; I can't remember ever feeling like this about anyone in my life. No woman has ever sent me into a tailspin like this man, and instead of confusing the fuck out of me, it's starting to make sense.

I exist for him alone, and nothing else will ever live up to this explosive bubble that's brewing around us.

He's standing at the top of the driveway as I pull up, his white tee clinging to his chest, and a pair of gray track pants detailing one of my favorite parts of him. I get out, noticing the forlorn look on his face.

"What's up?"

"I fought with my mom." His shoulders curve in with shame.

"About what?"

"Dani." He looks back up at me. "She wants me to stop seeing her."

"I agree," I nod.

"I can't until I have those results. Coach would fucking snap because as of right now, he believes that baby is mine."

"I don't understand why the fuck you did this to begin with." My fingers curl into a fist. "Why you thought entertaining that whore would be a good idea is beyond me."

"I was protecting you," he grits through his teeth as I tip my head to the side.

"From what?" I take a step closer.

I can see the indecision on his face as my stomach clenches with apprehension. What the fuck is he hiding from me?

"Can you just let it be for the next few weeks? Then it will all be over. It's the same thing I promised my mother."

"Dixon." His name shoots out of my mouth like a warning. "What the fuck are you keeping from me?"

His face darkens with anger, then all of a sudden, he's up in my face.

"It's all your fucking fault," he growls, his eyes ablaze. "You told her!"

Maybe it's the fucking headache pounding through my skull, but he's getting in my face, and I don't have a fucking clue what he's talking about. I grab him by the throat, turning us around to trap him between me and the Hummer.

"You looking to get that ass railed out here, brat?"

"Dani." He doesn't even bother to struggle against my hold, his eyes darkening with lust.

I press my hard cock into his, pinning him tighter to the vehicle as I click my tongue against the roof of my mouth.

"Do not say her name when your eyes are begging for my fucking cock."

His hand fists my t-shirt as he pulls me in closer, our mouths brushing together.

"You told Dani about us." I see it then. The fear, the anger, and the betrayal.

"So what?" My head tips. "She probably had her suspicions anyway."

"That's why I'm doing what I'm doing." He releases me. "She's threatened to out us."

"So—"

"Say 'so what' again, and I'll fucking knock you out." He bares his teeth. "The team would treat us differently, our careers would be on the line, and my fucking mom…"

His words die on a choking sob I can feel in my soul. He fears he won't be accepted, and even though it's cowardly, I get it.

"First off," I loosen my hold on his throat. "It would always be her word against ours, no one would believe it. And as soon as that baby is born, you can paint her as the scorned whore she is. As for your mom," I look up at the house. "I think she likes me." I grin at him.

"She has her beliefs." He shakes his head.

"She told you she hates when men fuck?"

"The fuck?" His head rears back. "She doesn't believe in homosexuality."

"That's cool," I shrug. "I'm still not gay, I only want you."

"I'm a man!"

"You're a fucking whiney bitch." I lean in to grab his bottom lip between my teeth. He moans as I grin, knowing I've got him where I want him.

I hear the front door open and step back, watching as Dixon's eyes widen in fear.

"Hi, Sebastian," Marian calls out. "I was wondering why Dixon was out here for so long."

"Hi, Marian." I lift my hand. "I just had a few game details to go over with him, but he's all yours now. I'm sorry for interrupting."

"Won't you come in for dinner?" she asks as I wink at Dixon.

"Told ya." He rolls his eyes, asking for my belt to his ass while I call out to his mother. "I can't tonight, but I'll come back, and we'll have a chat this week. Sounds good?"

"Oh, yes!" She raises her hand. "Take care, honey."

She steps back inside while I smile smugly at the sulking boy with his arms crossed at his chest.

"She called me honey."

"Will you just leave?" He pushes off my Hummer, but I can see the ghost of a smile on his face.

"Not without a kiss first." I grab his shirt.

"You have fucking lost your mi—"

I swallow the rest of his sentence as my mouth attacks his, moaning when he opens for me without a second thought. My hands grab either side of his face, my body presses into his, and my cock strains against the fly of my pants.

"Yeah," I whisper against his lips. "I have."

"I should go inside before she comes looking for me again." He presses another kiss to my mouth.

"I'm heading out for a few days. I'll be back this Friday."

"To see Carla?" My daughter's name on his mouth sounds sweet, making me smile.

"Yeah."

"Okay," he nods. "Will you call me?"

"Maybe," I snicker as I get into my Hummer.

He watches as I leave, his hands in his pockets with a saddened look on his face.

Agent Emilio Gomez was the second man in my home that night, I can tell by the hazel color of his eyes.

I put down my binoculars to cross my arms over the steering wheel, watching as he throws a ball back and forth with his kid on the front lawn. He's a family man by the looks of it, but he still came in my home to terrorize mine. The allure of drug money is strong, I should know, and the need to fill your bank account is something every red-blooded American feels. They don't call it the American Dream for nothing.

A dream is just one aspect short of a nightmare, fear.

Fear makes people act stupid, forget themselves, and training goes out the window. It's when you watch the woman run up the stairs away from her killer instead of out the front door in popular movies, or it's when a deer stands stock still in the middle of the road, watching as your vehicle plows into it.

Nothing will fuck up your life faster than fear, which this man will learn it soon enough.

I'm his walking nightmare.

I'll let him have a few more days with his kid while I go check out his gang infiltrating partner, Paul Dawes. I killed his son in the basement of Delano's house, so I bet he's chomping at the bit to get at me. Life is a bit dangerous at home in Rochester, I probably have a hit on me out there. As soon as I'm alone, I could end up with a bullet in my head.

So I have to be proactive.

I have a daughter to live for. And Dixon.

I'm not calling him my boyfriend, we haven't established any labels, and to be honest, it sounds weird. Not because it's trite, but because it's juvenile. I have a borderline obsession with the man, complete lack of control, and the man I thought I was disappears when he's around.

He's my salvation.

Just two blocks over, I find Paul Dawes's residence. A nice quiet street, two story homes nestled in each lot, a couple trees in the front yards with nice cars sitting in the driveways. Your typical picturesque neighborhood, right down to the white picket fences. This one I know lives alone, inheriting the home from his grandma, and has never been married.

His son was a one-night stand from college. He never raised the kid, but when he came around looking for his deadbeat dad, he found a federal agent instead. Must've been both a relief as well as a slap in the face. Your dad isn't a useless sack of shit, but he did turn away from you when he found out you existed.

Apparently, Paul decided to be the father his son needed and took him in while he attended college. Only the kid dropped out to begin working intel for Daddy. Big fucking mistake.

He ended up being roasted then sent back home, buffet style.

Paul has continued on with his life, his days filled with agent shit then moonlighting as some kingpin drug runner at night. Taking cartel coke from the evidence pen is his specialty while sitting around waiting for kids on the street to sell it is another skill of his.

I drive by his house, seeing his car sitting in the driveway with the first floor curtains open, giving me a clear view into his living room. His TV is on, and I can see the back of his head as he sits on the couch.

I park my Hummer over on the next street to change out of my leather jacket and white tank top. I pull on a black sweater, put on my leather gloves, and wear my black cap, hoping I blend in a little better. I slip my gun into my waistband then take the short walk back to the Dawes's residence. The houses are close together, so I'll have to be mindful of loud noises, and I'll have to keep the torture to a minimum because I need to get back to my hotel to talk with my little girl.

The walk is slow, purposeful, almost relaxing. I see why old folks do it, it's therapeutic.

I walk up his driveway, crossing in front of the window to stand at his front door. I could ring his doorbell, stand out here and wait for him to haul himself off the couch, but I'm willing to bet the cockiness of a Fed will play in my favor.

My hand grips the door handle, meeting no resistance as I push down. This stupid motherfucker is supplying blow to the local gangbangers and therefore, his son found himself charbroiled, coincidently. Yet he keeps his door unlocked.

His balls must be swollen to the point of pain.

I step inside and hear some game show on, sounds like *Wheel of Fortune*. Jandro used to love that shit. I remember how he and Paola used to fight over who would guess the puzzle first. The thought of them both twists my stomach with sadness, but it also hardens my resolve for what I'm about to do.

This is for them.

I stand behind him on the couch, my piece in my hand, watching as the woman on the screen spins the wheel. My head is pounding in tune to the clicking sound, making me clench my teeth against the pain. *Big money* they all chant as I mouth it along with them, watching that little red flag flick along the metal bars.

It lands on a small amount of money, and the woman calls out *Y*. Who the fuck chooses Y?

"That's a bad choice. Y is nearly as bad as X."

Paul startles at my voice, nearly toppling off the couch, but I catch him and pull him upright, the nice guy that I am.

"Who the fuck are you!" he bellows, his eyes blazing with violence.

"My name is Sebastian Avando, and I heard you've been looking for me."

His eyes flash with recognition as I give him a slow nod. "You killed my son." The accusation flies from between his teeth as if he actually gave a fuck about his kid.

"You knew it was a possibility when you placed him in that environment. You're a Fed, you of all people know just how dangerous being a gang member is. In fact…" I grin at him. "I hear you now have firsthand knowledge."

He looks at the gun in my hand, then I watch as his eyes flick to the table by the door where I saw his gun when I strolled in. He's not going to get to it, but I like watching as his mind works to figure out how the fuck he's getting out of here.

"I was sent undercover, supplied with the drugs to give to the gang, and I was supposed to come back with intel on who the leaders were." His eyes flash with defiance. "I did what I had to."

"We all do what we have to survive" I agree. "Tell me about what happened with Daniel North."

"The runner." His mouth turns downward. "You get kids like that, who aren't too intelligent, and they see something they don't understand. Then they tell other people, like maybe their mothers or maybe their big-time football playing brothers."

Who aren't too intelligent. This bitch.

"Are you determining his intelligence by the color of his skin, Dawes?"

He swallows, his eyes roaming over my own brown skin. "No, I'm judging it by his demographic."

"Ah," I nod, "*demographic.* Did you know he was attending a private school? No? That his mother worked two jobs to make sure she could afford it? Do you know what it takes to get into such a school? No? *Intelligence.* They are all tested before admittance. Tell me… What school was your white son attending? And did his pale skin award him straight As?"

"I'll never know now, will I?" His eyes are narrowed in rage and filled with a contempt I know all too well.

"Is that why you sent those men to my house? Because I killed your son? Or was it my demographic?"

He takes that opportunity to try and tackle me over the couch, but he's been living the good life lately, thinking he didn't need to keep up with his training. I punch him with my left hand then swing the gun in my right around to smash into his temple.

He falls to the floor with a groan as the side of his head begins to bleed, blood rolling down his cheek. The sight reminds me of Paola, cementing my reason for being here.

"Gregory Jones killed my wife." I kick him in the ribs. "Blew her fucking brains across my kitchen. Was it because of her demographic?"

"They were only ordered to kill you," he grunts as he works himself up to his hands and knees. "They acted on their own."

"You sent them to my house. What if my fucking daughter had been there?" I grit through my teeth.

"I didn't order them to kill your family." He looks up at me. "And you killed Jones, so what the fuck are you doing here?"

I crouch down, looking him in the eye. "They were in my house on your orders."

He opens his mouth to say something, but I don't give him the chance as I begin to beat his head in with the butt of my gun. Hit after hit, blood sprays, bones splinter, and still I continue until his fucking brains are coating my hands.

One down, one more to go.

I wash off in the laundry room I find at the back of his house, making sure to clean the blood and brains off my gloves.

When I leave his house, it's like a sense of calm rushes over me as I look up to the sky. If Paola is watching, I know she's not happy I took a life. But she knows what happens when someone fucks with mine, and I won't be happy until they're all dead.

CHAPTER TWELVE

Dixon

The team has been resting the last few days while Seb has been away, back in Rochester doing fuck knows what.

He hasn't called.

I know I can call him, but that's not the fucking point. I asked him to call me.

Fuck.

He's right… I do sound like a fucking brat.

I'm fucking irritated because I've been trying to get a hold of Fernando, and he hasn't been picking up, doesn't answer his texts, all my voicemails filling up his inbox. I don't want anything bad to happen to him, but I can't call anyone else to check in. It would alert them to the fact that he's talking to me in the first place, which I'm not wanting to make apparent.

Or he's avoiding me.

That last option is fucking annoying because he would only be avoiding me if he's hiding something. If he is hiding something, it would have to be about Danny because what else would even pertain to me?

I shove up out of my bed and begin to pace. I could take a trip out to Baltimore. I'm not due back to the stadium until the day after tomorrow, and Seb will also be gone that long. I don't have anything better to do around here. Ma is out often, working the soup kitchen lately, cooking for the less fortunate. I could leave her a note.

I pull out my duffle bag and begin to pack some clothes while pulling up the hotel app on my phone. I book a room for one night then make sure to pin my note to the fridge.

I hate lying to my mother, but she can't know I'm going to Baltimore. Instead, I said I was heading out to Seb's place to chill for the next few days. She likes him, so I know she won't worry as much.

The thought of sitting around at home and not doing anything makes me anxious. I want to find out what happened to Danny. It's the only way I'll get any closure.

I wake up to the sun shining in through the hotel room's windows and let out a groan. I got here around midnight, deadass tired and with a raging headache. I check my phone, hoping to see a missed call from Seb or at least a text message, then roll my eyes when I realize I sound like a bitch.

There's something about him that just fucking twists me up inside, and I can't figure out where this is going. Where can we go from here? I sit up in bed, pulling up his contact, deciding to fucking be a man and text him myself.

How's Rochester?

Then I sit there, watching the fucking screen like a schoolgirl waiting for his response. It takes a few minutes, and then those little dots pop up.

Seb: Miss me, baby?

"Fuck," I hiss into my fist. I do look like a bitch right now.

Seb: Don't you dare fucking think of closing this chat without answering me.

I can't help as a smile comes over my mouth. I can practically fucking hear the graveled tone of his voice.

I told you to call me.

Hey, if I'm going with bitch, I'm going all in.

Seb: Yeah, you missed me. Send me a picture of your dick.

I drop my phone to the bed and shake my head, feeling my morning wood jerk in my boxers. Is there ever going to be a day when this man doesn't control me like this?

The phone vibrates again, and I yank it up quickly, reading his words like they're the fucking Bible.

That day is not today.

Seb: Where's my dick? Don't worry about your mom, she's at the shelter this morning.

First of all, him toying with me mixed with the toxicity of what we are doing is fucking addictive. But this obsessive, stalking behavior… It's a little concerning that he knows my mom's schedule.

I'm not at home.

I want him to stew. He's left me to my own devices while he was gone, and I hadn't heard from him. He deserves to wonder where the fuck I am.

Seb: Stadium?

Nah.

Seb: Where the fuck are you, brat?

Is it wrong that I like it when he calls me that? Probably just as wrong as everything else about us.

I'm in Baltimore, chilling with some friends.

Seb: You're where? Is this some joke? I'm your only friend, and that's the way it'll stay.

Again, a smile coats my lips at his possessive behavior. I can't help that I like it, and I feel just as possessive about him. Hence why I'm pissed he didn't call.

I'm in Baltimore, and yes, I have friends. Besides, you're lucky I even told you. All you had to do was call to find out.

Seb: Where are you staying?

Seb: Answer me.

I give him the name of the hotel then throw my phone back on the bed. I need a shower, and then I'm heading out to find Fernando. I know what block he covers because he and my brother worked it together.

After my shower, I get dressed then pick up my phone. Surprisingly, there are no messages, and that kind of pisses me off. Maybe he's pissed I'm here, but he doesn't have the fucking right. He's not my man.

Right?

Or is he?

Am I dating Sebastian Avando?

My palms begin to sweat at the thought as I once again begin to pace the length of the room. Maybe we're not dating, but we're definitely hooking up. I am hooking up with a man.

My internal freak out is interrupted by a banging on the door. I stare at it in confusion as I stride across the room. I didn't fucking order anything.

I open the door to stare into the face of the man who fucking haunts me.

"Seb!" My mouth drops open as he pushes me backward, his hand sealing around my throat. "What are you doing here?" I croak out.

"I should be asking you the same thing right now, but my dick is hard, and I need it inside of you first."

His mouth crashes into mine. Nothing about this kiss is sweet or sensual, it's primal and animalistic, rough and painful. The pain combined with the feral energy makes for a heady combination. I give it as good as I'm getting and when we pull apart, both of our lips are lined in blood. I lick along the surface of my bottom lip, letting the rusty tang burst along my taste buds.

We stand there panting, staring at each other, and then it's like a bell goes off, making us rip the clothes off our bodies. Our hands roam every hardened edge of each other's bodies, my nails scraping along his back while he bites down on my nipple, both of us grunting like fucking animals.

"Get on the bed and spread your legs." He shoves me toward the king-sized bed.

I stumble, my back hitting the mattress. He barely gives me time to breathe as he falls on top of me, grinding his cock against mine. The smooth velvet feel of him is such a contrast to the hardness, the scruff of his beard dragging along my shoulder as he bites into my neck.

"You're in so much trouble." He nips at my ear next as I buck up, searching for him. "Tell me how badly you want me to punish your ass."

"Fuck, Seb." My mind is a jumble of thoughts, but none of them make any fucking sense to say out loud.

His hand wraps around my cock, the callouses rough on my sensitive skin, and when he strokes me, he does it like he owns me. And he fucking does. Sebastian Avando fucking owns me.

He pushes up to his knees, his body still between my spread out legs as he begins to thrust his cock along mine. My balls tighten, my cock fills, and I'm just about to blow my load all over us but grit my teeth to stave it off.

"Spread these wider." His hands grip my thighs, opening my legs farther. The stretch burns its way along my groin, but I don't dare tell him to stop. "Let me see my pussy."

His fucking mouth and the shit he says is so fucking wrong, but I can't be bothered to correct him, not when his fingers find my hole. As soon as one breaches, precum leaks from the tip of my cock, the thick drops hitting my abs.

Seb pulls his finger out to swipe them up, bringing it back to my hole. He rubs my cum around the rim, giving me a devilish smirk as he teases it with the wide head of his cock.

"You better jack yourself off." He pushes against the rim of muscles, forcing himself inside of me. "You're going to want some lube back here."

I begin to pump my dick in my hand, and when he works the head of his cock inside of me, I immediately hiss at the burn. It hurts, but the feeling of him sets me off, and I'm coming, the thick ropes of cum shooting up my torso.

"Good boy," he praises as he pulls out. He scoops up my release, bringing it back down between my legs to smear it all over my hole and his cock.

It's wrong, it's debased, and it's the hottest thing I've ever fucking seen.

He falls over me, his hand hitting the mattress beside my head, the other lining himself up between my legs. His mouth is so close to mine, his eyes boring into me, and when he begins to push in, my lips fall open on a silent scream. I will never get used to this invasive feeling; the way it hurts but feels so fucking amazing is perplexing.

Seb leans down farther to lick his tongue into my open mouth, tasting me. Then he slams himself all the way in, pulling back to watch me scream out at the intrusion.

"Hurts, baby?" His voice is soft, smooth, but his face is mischievous as he lets me adjust around his thick cock.

"So good," I manage to mumble as I lift my hips, trying to make him move.

His hand lands on my lower stomach, forcing me back down to the mattress. He loops his arm under my left leg, hauling it up and pressing it down onto my chest, spreading my hole out more. He presses in even farther, and the feel of him deep inside me has my cock hardening again.

He pulls out only to thrust back in, angling himself to hit that one spot, driving me insane.

"I'm stretching this tight pussy out," he says against my lips. "Tell me how much it hurts."

He picks up the pace, the wet sounds of my cum filling the room as our bodies slap together. I watch his face as he nears his release, the way it fills with awe. His eyes widening in disbelief is something I want to sketch and keep forever locked in my heart.

He slams in one final time, his groan filtering through the room and his eyes rolling back into his head as his cock jerks inside me, his warm cum filling me.

"Mine," he proclaims, the word filled with an angry heat.

He pulls out, falling on the bed beside me, an arm thrown over his face.

"I'm here to find out about Danny." I tell him after a few silent moments.

"I figured," he grunts.

"Why are you here, Seb?"

He looks at me, his eyes roving over my face, and I watch as his softens. "Same reason."

"What? Why?"

He rolls over on the bed, reaching down to his discarded jeans to pull out his wallet, throwing it between us.

"Open it."

I grab the small, square, leather wallet and flip it open, shock coursing through me as I stare down into it.

"I took it when I broke into your house. I saw it in your wallet, and something about him called to me. He reminded me of the young man I used to be. Angry, determined, and fucking impulsive."

"You're still impulsive," I retort as I drag my finger over Danny's face. "You stole his bus pass. I thought I lost it."

"I knew how he was feeling, and I needed to help him. So I asked my boy to look into him for me, to put out some feelers. I told myself it was to have something to hold over your head, to force you to do as I fucking said. But it wasn't. He looked exactly like I did at one time, and I wanted to give him the same push that was given to me."

"You were going to find my brother?"

"I was too fucking late. But I made up for it," he says quietly.

"What do you mean?" I remember what Fernando told me, but I want to hear it from Seb's mouth.

"Danny found out some shit about the guys he was running with. They were in deep with the Feds, and he got spooked. He ran and tried to hide out, not wanting the heat to come back on you or your mother. They found him, though, before I could."

Tears run down the sides of my head as I continue to look at the picture of my brother's defiant face.

"Who found him?"

"Fucking kids working for the Feds. One of them was an agent's son. They killed him then left him there. But I found them, Dixon, and I made them pay. Real gruesome shit too"

I don't want to know the details, but I'm appreciative of what he did.

"They retaliated and killed your wife," The words hit my like a punch to the gut.

"Yeah, the Feds decided to break into my home and kill me. They found my wife and decided she was fair game."

"I'm sorry." I get why he blamed me in the beginning, and I would understand if he still did.

"Nah," he sighs. I turn to look at him, watching as his Adam's apple works to swallow down the emotion I see in his eyes. "It wasn't your fault. I was just angry at everything."

"What are you doing here now?" I ask as his hand finds mine on the bed, interlacing our fingers.

"I'm hunting, baby." His head turns so he can look me in the eye. "But I need you to go back home."

"No." I shake my head, tightening my hold on his hand. "I want to help you."

"I can't lose you, Dixon." His eyes become glassy with the thought. "I can't."

"What does that mean?"

"It means you're mine." His eyes are begging me to understand.

"Like we're together? Are we together?"

"There's no one else." His sexy mouth tips up in one corner.

"For good?"

His grin widens as he leans in to press his mouth to mine. "Are you asking me to be your boyfriend, Rookie?"

It's insane. My one time rapist is here in bed with me, fucking my brains out and making me lose my mind. Yes, I'm asking him to be my boyfriend.

I nod because I don't know how to form words that'll make any sense.

"How will I put up with a little bitch like you, hmm?" he taunts as he rolls on top of me. "How will I keep you in line?"

My cock is hard before he's finished speaking, but my ass is burning, so I can't imagine him taking me again so soon.

But instead of spreading me open, he kisses his way down my chest, paying close attention to my nipples, that devilish tongue of his dipping into all the dips and crevices of my stomach.

I prop myself up on my elbows because if this man—my boyfriend—is about to suck my dick, I don't want to miss a fucking thing.

My cock is pulled up off my stomach, his rough hand giving it a few strokes, the shaft jerking in his palm. I hold my breath as his face lowers, and when his pink tongue slips out from between his lips, I almost die of anticipation.

He doesn't keep me waiting. His tongue flattens then licks over the head of my cock, and the pained groan escaping his throat has me going cross eyed, nearly seeing double.

"You taste good, baby," he mumbles as he sucks me into his heated, blissful mouth, his saliva running down toward my balls.

He hollows out his cheeks, cushioning my cock all around, then he bobs up and down, taking me a bit deeper each time. I fight the urge to pump up into him, only because I don't want him to stop, and I don't know what his limits are.

Then he shocks me in the next second when my cock disappears completely down his throat, the tight, wet channel pulsing around my length as he works to stop his gag reflex.

I lose the fight with my control to pump up into him, making him gag as he looks up at me. His eyes are tearing up, the pools of liquid threatening to tip over the edges of his lash lines.

He releases me with a *pop* then begins to massage my balls with his other hand, quickly propelling me to the edge.

"I'm close, Seb," I moan.

"Yeah?" He releases my cock, sitting up on his feet.

He begins to stroke his own cock while grinning at me, seeing the frustration on my face. I reach for my dick, planning to finish myself off when he slaps my hand away.

"Ask me nicely to finish you off."

"You want me to beg you to suck my cock?" I look at him with shock.

"Yeah, and when you do, I'll choke all over it."

"Please." The words blurt out of my mouth as my hips coast off the bed. "Fucking please suck my cock."

His eyes darken at the sound of my desperation, and he awards me with a, "Good boy."

Then Seb grabs my cock to fuck me with his mouth. Straight up fucking me. Gags and wet choking noises rise mixed with my moans, filling the room with a symphony of sinful melodies.

His eyes water, the tears dripping from his eyes and coursing down his cheeks. They redden with the force of his gagging, and still, he doesn't let up. My balls slap into his chin as he swallows my length, then he gathers his saliva at the base of my cock, moving to smear it over my hole.

"Fuck!" I shout as he shoves two or three fingers inside me. I can't tell because the burn is intense, but he hooks them, hitting the sweet spot he knows will set me off.

Stars dance along my vision, and my back arches off the bed as my throat strains from the scream wrenching out of its depths. I come long and hard into his mouth, tipping my head up to watch him slurp every drop off my cock then lick it completely clean.

He falls down beside me, his arm draping over my stomach as his heavy breathing hits my neck.

"You suck cock like a fucking dream, you homo."

His head comes up and tips to the side, a humorous look in his amber eyes.

"I guess I am gay now, huh, brat?"

Sebastian

He's following me.

The rookie thinks he's fucking slick, but I'm enjoying playing ignorant as I take him on a wild goose chase. We've circled his old hood three times, and I can bet he's fucking fuming in that small car he rented. He's probably folded in there like a Jack-in-the-Box.

I decide to put him out of his misery and pull over into a convenience store parking lot. He must be getting cramped in that fucking clown car.

I park, drumming my fingers on the wheel when he pulls in, then I step out to wait for him. I rest my back against the Hummer to watch him park, his expression one of a petulant child.

He gets out, draping himself over the car door. "I was that obvious, huh?"

"How's your back feeling?" I snicker.

"Like I've been sitting in a cardboard box for an hour."

"Why are you following me, North?" I question, keeping a close eye on his face. If he lies, I'll choke him with my cock until he passes out.

"I don't want you to do something stupid." He closes the car door then comes around the hood, stopping in front of me. "I'm worried. I don't want another phone call like I had last year."

I yank on the front of his shirt, pulling him in against me to run a hand along the front of his sweats, grinning when he hardens instantly. I fucked him one more time in that hotel room, so I know he's fucking sore, but he's still ready to go.

"Go back to the hotel." I kiss his swollen bottom lip, savoring the way his tongue snakes out to flick against my mouth.

"We're out in the open." He gives himself a shake, trying to step back, but I have a firm hold on him.

"I thought you were mine now, rookie." I narrow my eyes playfully. "Or was that just you talking on a dick high?"

"A what?"

"You were coming down from my dick up your ass. Were you just saying shit? Or are you mine?" His eyes skate around the parking lot at my loudly spoken words, and when they land back on me, a small smirk forms on his mouth.

"I'm yours."

"Fuck yeah, you are. Don't make me force you to suck my dick in public to prove it."

His eyes widen like he knows I'm being one hundred with him, then he rolls them like the little shit that he is.

"What are you planning to do today?" he asks as I release his shirt.

"Tie up one final loose end, then we're goin' home."

"I don't want you to do anything to get you in trouble." He shakes his head, fear evident in his eyes.

"He had Danny and Paola killed. There's no way he can continue living. This may not be Rochester, but my rules still remain. You fuck with mine, your ass is getting capped."

"I'm coming with you."

He lost his brother, and he's afraid to lose me, but if he's with me, he's safe.

"You'll stay in the car." I point at him as he nods, already rounding the front of the Hummer to get in the passenger seat.

Special Agent Gomez's house is quiet and completely dark. Anyone driving by would assume no one is home, but I know he's in there. His kids are away at summer camp, and his wife is at a spa. I'm real good at finding shit out, especially since this has been a plan in the making for months. I can't let Dixon fuck things up, this is my only chance.

"What did I tell you?" I ask him as I pull off my leather jacket to slip on another black hoodie.

"Why are you dressing like that?"

I stop what I'm doing to give him a serious look. "What the fuck did I tell you?" I repeat, ignoring his question.

"You want me to stay in the car," he rolls his eyes, then they widen as I pull on my leather gloves, one finger at a time. "Seb—"

"I let you come with me, but I need you to shut the fuck up." I hope my clipped tone silences him, turning my back to him to grab my gun out of the glove compartment.

It took me all day yesterday to clean the fucking thing, but I swear, it still slightly smells like Dawes's brains.

"You're really killing him," he says, his voice filled with trepidation.

"I'm not inviting him over to our house for a gay gathering."

"Sebastian!" he gasps. "This is serious."

I inhale a deep breath, hoping the gesture calms him down, because right now his anxiety is bleeding into me.

"Look, I know what he's done, but is there any other way to bring him down? One where he pays for this his whole life? Doesn't death seem too easy?"

He's so naïve, another piece of proof that Dixon was sheltered even though he lived dead center in the middle of this shit.

"They didn't give Danny that mercy." I remind him of the reasons I'm here. "What about Paola? She had no idea about anything, and she paid for it with her life."

"I know," he murmurs, his eyes skipping to the darkened house in front of us. "But I feel like something bad is going to happen."

"It is." I flex my fingers in the tight leather gloves. "Someone is about to die."

"I can talk to the cop who was investigating Danny's death," he supplies, an earnest look in his eyes. "He was helpful."

"Dixon, this is why I didn't want you here," I groan.

"Why?" he throws up his hands. "So you could've gone in there and possibly died yourself without hearing reason?"

I face forward, my jaw locked with my eyes trained on the house holding the prize I know is sitting inside. After the news of Dawes's murder, he must be expecting me, and I don't want to let him down.

"Seb," Dixon's voice breaks through my thoughts of blood and revenge. "Please, let's go back to Buffalo, and I promise to tell the detective everything. Let them take down one of their own."

"You really think that will happen?" I finally blink out of my stare off to look at him. "A black man ratting out a federal agent? You think they'll believe you over him?"

"Look, the other one was brutally murdered. Right?" His eyes widen like I'm missing the point. "It looked like a gang killing. You didn't steal anything, right?"

"You think you can prove this man's guilt by how the other one died?"

"Yes," he nods emphatically. "It would show they were working together."

He really is naïve, so it looks like there's no other way to show him but to let him live through it himself. These streets are ruthless, no one survives by trusting another, it's all gut instinct. And my gut is screaming at me to go in there and shoot a bullet into that bitch's head.

"Fine." I pull off my gloves, dropping my piece back into the glove compartment. "I have a feeling I will be saying I told you so, North. And when I do, you never interfere in my shit again, understand?"

"Yeah."

"Whatever happens here on out is on you." My brow raises when he remains quiet. "Understand?"

"Okay." I don't miss how his throat works to swallow or his brows crease together.

He needs to feel the weight of his decisions because I can't always intervene to protect him and his choices.

CHAPTER THIRTEEN

Dixon

Tomorrow is our first game of the season against the Green Bay Packers, and it's also Dani's due date, although she doesn't look anywhere near ready to go into labor. She and I have been talking, but there's a distance between us now which is relieving.

Seb and I decided not to make ourselves too public at the stadium because she's impulsive and also because I don't want the team treating us differently. It's none of their business anyway.

My mother is also still very much in the dark about us, and she's been counting down the days until Dani gives birth, knowing that once she lays eyes on the child, she'll know it's not mine.

"I called Sebastian to invite him over for dinner," my mother announces, pulling me from my thoughts.

"You called him? Like you have his number?" I stare at her with shock.

"Yes, we're friends," she shrugs.

My palms are growing slick with anxiety as my heart pounds through my ribcage. How the fuck are we going to be able to act normal in front of my mother? We just came back from Baltimore, and that hotel room was our literal sex den for two days. She'll know, she can read me like a book.

"Is that okay, Dixon?" She places her hand to my forehead. "You look ready to pass out."

See?

"I'm fine. It's fine," I stammer over my words as she gives me a curious look.

"You sound like you're having a seizure."

"Ma!" I stand. "I said I'm fine."

"All right, don't you raise your voice at me." She wags her finger, going back to the stove. "I'm making curry chicken and rice."

"Okay," I fucking squeak then run off to my bedroom. I need to call Seb and tell him to decline. He can tell her he's sick or something.

As soon as my bedroom door is shut behind me, I call him and begin pacing the room.

"Hey." He sounds like sex on two fucking legs.

"Tell her you're sick," I blurt out, my chest beginning to hurt from how hard my heart is pounding.

"I already said I'd bring pie," he chuckles. "I'll have apple pie for dessert with your mom and then your pussy pie later." His voice drops on those last words, and my dick hardens while I groan in frustration.

"Stop that. That's why you can't come over. She'll know." My words are clipped as anxiety takes over my thought process.

"Breathe, baby," he coaxes me back off the ledge. "You need to relax, everything will be fine."

"No, Seb." My throat begins to seal with emotion, and I think I'm about to pass out. "I'm not ready."

"I get it, I respect that. I'm not going to out you to your fucking mother, you brat," he growls into the phone. "Will you sit down and chill?"

I fall back onto my bed to stare at the ceiling, my vision blurring out the longer I don't blink.

"I'm just scared. She's all I have," I whisper.

"Yeah, I know." I can hear clothing rustling through the phone. "I'll be there in a few hours. I could never say no to chicken curry."

The click of the call closing hits my ear as I swallow down any lingering fear. He wouldn't lie to me, he knows how much my mother means to me. Then that nagging little voice inside my head reminds me that he had no problem outing me to Dani.

"Fuck."

"That was amazing, Marian," Seb gushes as he wipes his mouth with a napkin. "The best I've ever had."

My mother reaches over to pat his hand, her face shining with pride. "Thank you, son." *Son.* Then her eyes fall to my still full plate, and she clicks her tongue. "Any reason why you're starving yourself?"

"No," I mumble as I scoop up another spoonful, pushing it into my mouth.

I love my mother's curry, it's one of my favorites, but today it tastes like ash as I watch her converse with my boyfriend. They laugh and joke around, he asks her how the soup kitchen is, and she asks him how his daughter is doing. It's all mundane, but I am literally on the verge of hyperventilating.

"Have you heard anything from *her*?" Ma asks me. *Her* being Dani.

"Nope." I avoid Seb's heated glare.

"I can't wait for this to be over," she sighs, her spoon hitting the bowl.

"Same," Seb growls.

"I know it's not Dixon's child," she continues as I bite into my cheek to stop myself from explaining my situation again for the millionth time.

"I know," Seb agrees, and she gives him a little hum.

"I know why you know," her voice is low.

My head snaps up at her comment, finding her looking at me, her eyes filled with something close to sadness.

"What?" I look between her and Seb. He looks just as confused as I am.

"I'm disappointed you couldn't come to me and tell me how you were feeling," she says as her eyes gather with moisture.

"Ma—"

"I know about you two," she holds up her hand to cut me off.

I push back from the table as my vision tips, threatening to black out altogether. Seb stands and reaches for me, but I slap his hand away, fear coating every inch of my body.

I must've heard her wrong. This is not what it seems.

"Dixon," she says softly, "sit down."

Her voice is muffled as my ears ring with alarm, my stomach lurching in terror.

"North!" Seb's voice booms its way through the static, and I turn to find his concerned face. "Let's talk, sit down."

I shake my head as my hands land on the tabletop, the smooth wood bearing my weight and shame.

"How?" I ask, my mind automatically skipping to Dani. She told her.

"The security camera on the front porch," she replies softly, her hand coming to cover mine. "Last year."

Last year.

When Seb nearly attacked me at my front door. I turn an accusing eye on him, and he has the common sense to look apologetic. He's never cared about our public image nor the consequences of his actions.

"Don't be mad at him, Dixon." My mother grasps onto my hand, trying to gain my attention from the man who's ripped every preconceived belief I've known out from under me. "I'm not mad."

I slowly turn toward her, trying to concentrate on her kind face, on the small smile that dances on her lips.

"I was a bit when I first saw that footage," she admits, then her gaze lands on the bane of my fucking existence. "But I think it was meant to be. I see the way you are with him, Sebastian. I see how fiercely you want to protect him, and I see how much you care. That's all I've ever wanted for my boys."

"Fuck." I fall back into my seat.

"Language." She still manages to chastise me even after learning I'm fucking a man.

"I will always protect him," Seb tells her, his voice the softest I have ever heard it.

"You haven't said anything." My mother tells me just as I watch a tear escape her eye.

"I didn't want to disappoint you," I admit. "I didn't want you to resent the fact that I'm alive and Danny's dead."

"Dixon!" she exclaims. "Why would you ever think that?"

"He's projecting his feelings onto you. He resents his life because Danny lost his." Seb pushes away from the table. "I'm going to clear my head. You two talk."

"You should be here," my mother says to him, but he shakes his head.

"Your son needs to finally understand that no one blames him for Danny's death, and he needs to forgive himself. I've tried to tell him, but I think he'll only believe it if he hears it from you."

He heads out into the backyard, and I breathe out a sigh of relief when I realize he's not leaving.

"Do you love him?" she asks as I continue to stare at the space he was in.

"Yeah, I think so."

"Why would you think I'd feel like that?" her voice breaks.

"Because I know what you believe, Ma." My own mouth trembles with the emotion I am trying desperately to hold in. "I grew up hearing it."

"I know I have not always understood the lifestyles I don't live, but I would accept anything you do. As long as you're happy, I am happy for you."

"You're okay with me being with a man?" A tear rolls down my cheek.

"I am okay with you being with someone you love and who loves you back."

"I doubt he does." A sarcastic chuckle falls from my lips.

"I think you're wrong there as well." She pats my hand. "Now you can go and tell that pregnant hussy—"

"It's not her we're hiding from, she already knows. It's the league."

"Would they kick you off the team?" she gasps.

"No, but they would make it uncomfortable at the very least," I shrug.

"You were wrong about me. Could you also be wrong about them?"

Silence surrounds us as I think over her question, but I always come back to the same conclusion: we would be treated as outcasts.

"Go talk to Sebastian," she stands. "I have a few errands to run." She kisses the top of my head as I swallow down a ball of emotion. "I love you."

"I love you too."

"You are not responsible for Daniel's death. You have to believe that, Dixon. He made his own decisions, and the people who hurt him will find justice. If not in this lifetime then surely on judgment day."

"Okay." The relief I feel is miniscule, knowing it has everything to do with the fact that I need to forgive myself.

I watch as she grabs her jacket and purse, then she gives me one final look before she slips out the door. I get up from my seat, dragging my feet to the backyard where I find Seb sitting in a lawn chair with his head thrown back. His eyes are closed, and now that I really scrutinize him, I can see the large bags underneath them. He's not sleeping well, and I can imagine why. His thoughts are probably consumed by the need for revenge.

My angry avenging angel.

He sits up at the sound of the door opening, his head swinging around to look at me, his eyes relaying how uncertain he's feeling. I step out onto the deck and close the door, slowly making my way to the chair beside him.

"Just spit it out," he snaps. Always so angry.

"I never thought she would accept this." I swing my finger between us. "I kept it all a secret because I don't ever want to hurt her, not after what she endured with Danny."

"I get it." His jaw tics.

"I could see from the very beginning just how much she liked you, but I could never figure out why."

"Thanks." He rolls his eyes, making me smile.

"There's a weight lifted off my shoulders, but it doesn't change anything. The league—"

"Fuck the league." He stands. "Fuck them."

"Seb," I stand to face him. "I worked so hard for this. I neglected my family for this, and it's always been my dream. If I lost that, *everything* would have been for nothing."

"You found me there," he says quietly, the words breaking my heart.

"I'm thankful." I pull on his shirt to bring him into me. "I'm so thankful, but I'm scared."

His hands land on either side of my face as his forehead settles against mine. "Are we okay?" He sounds so vulnerable, so unlike the man I've come to love.

"Yes." My arms wrap around his back as I press my lips to his.

"But nothing can change right now."

"One step at a time," he murmurs as he kisses me again.

Sebastian

"*Jefe.*" Fernando's voice comes through the interior of the Hummer as I drive home.

"Gomez is still there," I tell him, listening as the line goes silent.

"When can you get me out of here then?" I can hear the nervous tone in his voice. "The other one is dead. They're going to know there's a rat."

"Keep your head down, and do as you're told. I'll get you out by the end of next week."

I have to get a hold of Delano and figure out what's going on, then I need him to help me get Fernando out of Baltimore.

"Okay." He doesn't sound convinced, making me feel like shit.

"I promise."

"Okay," he reiterates then hangs up the phone.

If I didn't have the opening game tomorrow, I would be driving there to get him myself. I pull up the contacts on my screen then hit Delano's name, waiting for the shit to pick up.

"'Sup?"

"I need to move someone out of Baltimore ASAP," I spit out.

"Wait, what? Who?" I can hear his desk chair squeaking in the background.

"A kid who has been helping me out with information. Can you do that for me?"

"Yeah, is this about Little North?" His voice drops like someone is listening to our conversation.

"Yeah."

"Okay, I can do that. Send me his details. How soon are we needing to do this?" Now he's starting to sound more like the guy I grew up with.

"Like yesterday."

"Sounds good. Send it all over." The click of the call ending sounds through the Hummer just as I pull onto my driveway.

I text him Fernando's contact information and leave it up to him to get the kid out. No matter my current issues with Delano, he is good at what he does, and I have all the confidence he'll do as I ask.

I text Fernando to give him a head's up about Delano and the strange number that will be contacting him then head inside. I need to rest for tomorrow, and I need to do it without any aid. I used to be able to smoke a joint then end up sleeping like a baby, but ever since I've cut all of that out, sleeping has been difficult.

My body is sluggish, my head is constantly aching, and stress just keeps compounding on my fucking shoulders. I was hoping with the last Fed's death, I would finally find my peace, and Paola's soul would be at rest. Instead, the fucker is still walking around, and Dixon's conscience is clear.

The things I do for that man.

The thought of him brings a smile to my face as I pull up his contact on my phone.

I didn't get any pie.

It takes him a few minutes, but his response makes me laugh.

North: You're sick.

North: My mother lives here too.

She wasn't home.

North: Win the game tomorrow, and even I'll have some pie.

He ends that off with a winky face as I groan, I should've made him come home with me, no matter how much he was complaining about needing sleep.

It's been too long since I've had my cock buried deep in his tight asshole.

This game has been a fucking shitshow.

We are a few points down and heading into the fourth, our exhaustion evident in the shitty way we're playing. Also, something feels off.

The Packers are playing with an aggression they didn't have during our previous game, and their taunts have been constant whenever we line up at the scrimmage.

I've been keeping my eye on Dixon because I can see his leg giving him hell, even though I watched him shoot two syringes into it. I'm constantly scanning the field for 88, but as the game winds down, I can see how hard he's struggling to stay upright.

Zeal calls the play as we all run into position, putting me right across from Dillon James. He's tired, I can see it in the way he pants, but that doesn't dull the smug look in his eye or the smirk on his mouth.

"Let's crush these ass fuckers and get home tonight, boys!" he calls out as his teammates all snicker.

The fuck?

"The fuck you say, James?" I straighten while Dex looks around beside me.

"Avando!" Zeal calls. "In position."

"Listen to your daddy, Avando," James jeers as I begin to vibrate with anger. "Or is it only North you listen to? Does he fuck you into place?"

My body goes rigid, and I feel myself coil, readying to strike. I whip my helmet off just as James does the same, all too ready to throw down, but before I can get a hit in, North is right there.

In the blink of an eye, Dixon has Dillon on the ground, his fists wailing into him. Both teams erupt into madness as we all try to grab our teammate and toss out a few blows to get them apart.

I can hear Coach screaming, whistles are being blown, and the fans are going berserk in the stands. This sort of shit rarely happens, but when it does, it's never this fucking heated.

Security begins to pull us apart as the officials are bringing an end to the game, both of our coaches looking like they're in a heated argument.

What the fuck was that?

Dixon and Dillon are finally pulled apart, and I nearly burst out laughing when I see the proud look in my rookie's eyes. This is the one and only time I'll accept his fucking misbehaving and reward him for it.

Too bad the league is about to come down on all of us, him especially. Dixon jumped his position to attack another player, he threw the first punch, igniting a fucking all out brawl. No official heard what Dillon said, which I'm thankful for, but both teams did.

With that thought in mind, I look around the field as Dixon is being led off and Dillon is being spoken to by security. I find each one of my teammates' eyes on me, some filled with questions, others with annoyance.

This is going to cost us, but I think what Dixon and I will be paying is astronomically more. We were just outed in front of our whole team and another in the league.

"Fuck." It really starts to sink in as I watch my teammates begin to filter off the field.

I run ahead, my mind solely on Dixon, not caring about the looks and whispers happening at my back. Let them fucking talk. I never gave a shit about that, and the only person I have to answer to is by himself. And freaking out too, I'll bet.

"Avando!" I hear Jameson calling at my back. "Wait up!"

His hand hits my shoulder just as I get inside the corridor. "Bro, not right now."

"We didn't say anything," he motions to a confused looking

Ortiz.

"Okay?" I shake my head, completely perplexed about what he's saying.

"You know…?" he leans in. "Last year in the showers."

"I believe you." I clap his shoulder, relieved that's what he's thinking. "It's some stupid shit James made up anyway."

"It's odd," Ortiz says, his face a mask of indifference. "Where would he get that shit from?"

"What happened out there?" Dani's voice floats between us as I turn to look at her over my shoulder.

She doesn't look surprised, actually far from it. She looks self-satisfied and proud. I stare into her eyes as I slowly turn to face her, making her lose the confident look and replacing it with trepidation.

"You were having a nice little talk with him last week." I take a few steps closer. "That baby is supposed to be due any day now, and you know you're about to lose him. All bets are off, huh?"

"No," she stammers as she takes a step back. "I don't know—"

"Tell me real quick that you don't know what I'm talking about."

Her eyes skip over my shoulder, looking at Jameson and Ortiz, pleading with her eyes for help.

"The fuck you looking at them for?"

"Seb—"

"Don't call me that!" I scream at her as she turns to hurry into her father's office, slamming the door shut behind her.

Stupid whore.

Jameson and Ortiz rush by me, heading into the locker room where Dixon and the rest of the team are, but I hang back in the corridor, nervous about what I could be walking into. Will he finally be finished with me? Is this the final straw?

"Avando, what the fuck happened out there?" Coach strides up to me, his face filled with fury. "This cost us our first game."

"Dillon James was running his mouth at me, and North reacted."

"You're being fined twenty-five grand and a two game suspension, and North is being suspended for six games and fined forty-five grand. They're talking about banning him from the playoffs." His fists hit his waist, and I can see the strain on his face. "A few other guys have minor fines, but that was a fucking brawl in the center of the field."

"They can't take the playoffs," I reply, shocked about the extreme punishment. "He's been working hard for it."

"I'll help him appeal it, but I don't know how far it will get us."

I follow him into the locker room, and the sight fucking shocks me for the umpteenth time today. Dixon is sitting on the bench, an ice pack on his knee with a huge smile on his face. Everyone is talking animatedly around him, and when he spots me, his face lights up.

"Avando!" I hate the formal feel of him calling me by my last name. "You were right!"

"Oh, yeah?" I walk into the room, looking around at everyone's faces.

"Yeah," he nods, adjusting the pack on his knee. "It's time to stand up for what's right no matter what the consequences are."

"Is that right?" Coach's voice booms as he walks in. "How do you feel about a six game suspension and possibly missing out on the playoffs?"

I watch Dixon's face, and when he shrugs a shoulder, I almost fall over with shock.

"I stood up for what's right, Coach."

"I know, son," Coach pinches the bridge of his nose. "I don't know what drove that man to say the obscene things he did, but someone needed to stand up to him."

I look at Dixon with my brow raised, trying to relay a big fucking *I told you so* until Jameson pipes up.

"Coach, Dillon shouldn't have been talking that shit, it weirds out the guys. We all have to be here in this locker room showering and shit with each other."

This man assisted me when I raped North, what the fuck is he saying?

"I'll try to appeal the playoffs suspension, but you're stuck with the six games and fine." Coach lays his hand on Dixon's shoulder. "We'll figure it out."

"All right, Coach."

I begin to take off my uniform, my adrenaline slowly leaving me as the wariness of the situation takes over. It feels like North and I switched perspectives. He's acting like none of this matters, while I'm over here freaking the fuck out.

Dillon James is a bitch, but his reaction is what most players will have. Dixon was right to be apprehensive about it. We're going to be treated differently. Hell, I', already noticing the longer stares we're getting from our own teammates.

I change my clothes, deciding to skip the shower, feeling North's eyes on me the entire time. I just want to go home and chase this headache with some sleep. I don't want to talk to anyone else.

I grab my bag and slam my locker shut, heading straight for the exit.

"Seb!" Dixon calls at my back, but I don't turn around. I don't have anything to say to him, and I can't form any thoughts when my emotions are still jumbled up inside of me.

I know I'm that asshole boyfriend right now, but I never claimed to be any different. I need silence and time away from the high energy of this fucking locker room. I make a mental note to text him later, but for now, I need to decompress and try to see what the bigger picture is.

I have a feeling this is just the beginning.

CHAPTER FOURTEEN

Sebastian

It feels like I just fell asleep when there's an obnoxious pounding on my front door. I know who it is, but honestly, it feels like we've switched personalities. I texted him before I crashed, telling him to give me a few days to figure this shit out, but it looks like he has a few ideas of his own.

I get up with a groan, seeing it's still pitch-black out. He didn't even give me a day. I'm not angry about it, though, I'd have done the same, and the thought of him being angry has my cock swelling. I love a good angry fuck.

The front door is shaking under the force of his banging as I start to feel myself grow angry. This brat is skating right into an inferno, and I won't hesitate to drop him over my knee. I'm used to abusing his ass.

I fling open the door to find him there looking frantic and distraught. My heart drops into my stomach when I imagine the worst.

"Where's your mother?"

"What?" His head snaps back, giving it a small shake. "I come here to talk you out of breaking up with me, and you ask for my mother?"

It's my turn to look confused. "Breaking up with you?"

He holds up his phone, my text message there on his screen. "This bullshit."

Dixon pushes past me and into my home, causing the headache already splitting through my head to worsen. I slam the door, the sound echoing around the room, then slowly turn to face him.

"You're being irrational. I needed a few days."

"You're telling me I'm irrational?" He looks at me with shock as I give him a small shrug.

"If we're together, we sort through this shit together. You don't disappear for a few days." I love when he's so fucking needy like this. Even his nagging is fucking turning me on, making me want to force him over my table…

"Drop your pants, and bend over the table," I demand as I stalk toward him.

"What?" His arms drop to his sides.

"I want that pussy spread open," I drop my boxers to stroke my hard as fuck cock, "and that mouth shut. The only thing you can say is how much it hurts."

"Seb." I watch as his track pants tent. "Sex isn't always going to fix our problems."

"We don't have any problems. But *you're* going to if you don't do as I say."

"This feels like a ploy." He pockets his phone and starts to untie his pants.

"Shh." I motion for him to turn around.

He does it because he's just as hungry for me as I am for him. Even if he is angry, he would never turn down my cock.

"We need lube," he mumbles as his pants fall around his ankles. "It's still sore from the last time we did this."

My hand grips the back of his head, and I shove it down to the table, grinning when he grunts with frustration. I bet he is sore, but that only makes me want to hurt him more. It's a claiming of sorts.

I need him to feel me there long after we part. He needs to be reminded of who he belongs to.

With a step back, I spread his cheeks, and he hisses at the movement. My teeth dig into my bottom lip when I look down to find him swollen. It looks painful but so fucking hot because my cock did that.

Doesn't mean I want to injure him further, though.

"Don't move," I demand as the little shit straightens.

"Why?"

"What the fuck did I just say to you?" I grab his stupid, fucking beard. "Put those hands back on the table, and keep your legs spread."

He rolls those fucking eyes again, and I bite into my cheek to keep from lashing his ass. I'm about to fuck him hard anyway.

My bare ass is out as I rush into my kitchen, grabbing the coconut oil from the counter and bringing it back out with me. He can never accuse me of not caring. His eyes widen then immediately glaze over with lust. He's wanting to be fucked so badly.

I open the lid, smearing the white oil onto his asshole, then watching as it melts. I slip a finger into him, spreading it inside, and this time he moans. My cock is next, and I make sure to coat it well, the slick feeling of it pulling a moan from me.

"Bend over." I smack his ass. He grumbles as his face rests against the wood. "Good boy."

My cock touches his tight hole as he presses back, eager for it. I push into him, the oil making everything slick, and from back here, he looks like he's creaming for me.

Just like a pussy would.

"Fuck, baby." I keep feeding him inch after inch as he squirms and holds his breath. "I wish you could see how well you take me."

"Seb." My name is a choked whisper as I bottom out inside him.

He clenches around me, his tight asshole sucking me in farther, and the way he lifts his hips makes me chuckle as he tries to guide me to the one spot I know drives him mad.

"Feels good?" I ask as I slowly pull out then watch as my glistening cock pushes back in.

"Yes," he moans.

That won't do.

I want him to hurt, and I need to hear him cry out from the pain soaked pleasure. My fingers dig into the globes of his ass, creating deep indents in his flesh as my cock pistons in and out of him, making him pant and tremble.

It's not enough of a reaction, I want him screaming, and if he's here in my home, getting fucked by me, he damn well will do as I want. So I thrust a bit harder, the sound of my hips slapping off his ass cheeks beginning to overpower the sounds of my grunts.

I see his knuckles whiten as he tries to gain purchase against the tabletop, his eyes shut, the creases showing how hard he's closing them, and that jaw is tight, hardening with every thrust.

"Still good?" I taunt. His eyes fly open, those dark brown depths searching me out.

I see his mouth tip up in the corner—the little brat—as he bites into his lip. "So good."

It's all good because I was taking it easy up until this point. He was complaining about the state of this sweet hole, and I was feeling some sort of way. Now he's looking smug as I fuck him, and that just won't do.

I begin to slam into him, each thrust punctuated with a grunt, highlighting my effort to make those dark, enticing eyes of his water. I want to watch that chin of his tremble, and I'm ready to watch him walk up out of here with his legs quaking in pain.

"Fuck!" he yells, pulling a chuckle from me as my cock punishes him.

I'm slipping in and out of him with ease, but when I see him reach down in front of himself to jack off, my balls tighten, readying to release everything so deep inside him.

"Seb!" he calls out, his forehead dotted with perspiration.

I can feel my own sweat collecting on my brow while my hands grip his hips, chasing that edge, ready to fly into the oblivion only Dixon can give me.

His hips banging off the edge of the table, the sound of our skin slapping together, and his small cries are culminating into the sweetest melody I have ever heard.

He comes first, his jizz hitting my floor in heavy drops as his groans fill the air around us. I'm right behind him as I slam into him one final time, eliciting that sweet release I've been looking for and coming so hard.

"Did it hurt, baby?" I fall over his back.

"Yeah," murmurs, but the way his ass is moving against me tells a different story. My baby is a fucking masochist.

I pull out of him, suddenly feeling the mess of coconut oil all over us as our skin sticks together.

"Let's go shower." I push myself up and watch him rise slowly, a wince lining his features.

"I came here to save our relationship, to beg you to realize how much I care about you," he says quietly as he reaches for his pants.

"There was no need. We don't need saving," I tell him as I start for my stairs.

"Do you love me?"

His question leaves me stunned and caught off guard. Do I?

"Well?" He presses when the seconds drag on without an answer, his brows beginning to bunch in the center of his forehead.

I open my mouth to tell him *something,* but thankfully, my phone chooses that moment to ring, freeing me from what could only be a disaster. How can I articulate something I know nothing about?

I pull my pants off the floor and reach into the pocket for my phone. "Sorry, I've been expecting a call."

He huffs beside me as he pulls on his pants, cringing when the mess of the oil seeps through the fabric.

Delano's name flashes on the screen, and I head for the

kitchen. "I just need to take this, and then we'll chat."

I seal myself in the kitchen, closing the door then swiping the screen. "What's going on?"

"Just giving you an update on the kid," he says, his voice sounding hushed. "I contacted him and let him know I'd have someone meet him at the bus terminal in a few days. Is he the one who helped you with the Feds?"

"Yeah, he's a good kid."

"Leave him with me. I'll make sure he's good," Delano promises.

"Thanks, man."

I hang up the phone at the same time I hear the front door open and shut. I step out of the kitchen and look around the empty room. Dixon left. I run to the door and throw it open, just catching the tail end of his vehicle turning off my street.

"Shit." I scrub my hand down my face and close the door behind me.

I need to figure out what it is I'm feeling for this man beyond my possessive behavior.

Dixon

I'm a fucking idiot.

Why did I ask him that?

I pull onto my driveway and rest my head against the wheel. I asked because I need to know if my feelings are reciprocated before I jump into the fire for him. I refuse to be burned then bear the scars while he remains unchanged. This is an effort we both need to bend for.

I'm facing a six game suspension, a large fine, and just to add more salt on the wound, they want to pull me during the playoffs. With the appeal coming up, I wanted to make sure I was doing this for the right reasons, that I had him beside me no matter what and everything would make sense in the end. He was supposed to be my purpose for it all, but instead, I'm left alone in this dark abyss.

My whole life has been dedicated to something outside of myself. Schooling to be able to go to top notch colleges for football, football to better my family, and then Buffalo to be able to pull Danny away from Baltimore. Nothing was for me.

Until Sebastian.

I finally had the chance to do something for me, stand up for the love I am feeling, to say fuck you to the people who try to tarnish it with their prejudices. Only the one I love may have that very same prejudice.

He's always been so open about us, seemingly aloof about what we do in public. I thought that was because he was ready to choose me. But I saw the fear in his eyes when I asked him if he loved me, the way they flicked back and forth in a dance of denial.

"Dixon?" Ma's voice calls out as soon as I step in the house.

"Yeah, it's me."

She appears in the foyer, giving me a once over, her brows creasing over her eyes.

"You don't sound right. Are you okay?"

I shrug and slip off my shoes, trying desperately to keep it together in front of her. I have never been in love, never suffered the loss of it, but now I understand why. This shit hurts, and it's tempting to just let it all out to the woman who now knows everything there is to know about me.

"Dixon," her hand slips into mine. "Talk to me."

The feel of her rough hands remind me that this woman worked herself to exhaustion daily to raise me and Danny. She was away often but always made sure she was there if we needed her. Here she is, wholeheartedly accepting me for who I am.

"He doesn't love me." It slips from between my lips, the words whispered through tortured silence.

She's quiet as her hand grips mine tighter.

"I asked him, Ma, right to his face, and he gave me a blank look."

"Dixon, that man loves you, but I fear he doesn't understand what that is. His childhood, heck, even his adulthood has been coated in lies and deceit. You have to give him time."

"Time to what?" The first tear hits my cheek then slowly drags downward. "To break my heart? He never wanted a relationship."

"Time to heal." Her finger swipes away the tear only for it to be replaced by another. "He's broken, and you, my boy, are his salvation. I truly believe that."

She gathers me in her strong arms, her scent enveloping me as my forehead hits her shoulder. I have never leaned on my mother like this. I was always the strong one, trying to be the man of the house. Now I realize what I've been missing.

So I break down.

Everything pours out of me as I think of my father who died working to give us a better life, for my brother who died because he knew no better life, and for my mother who just wants me to live my best life. I sob into her shoulder as she rubs my back, telling me everything will be okay, that no matter what, I will always have her.

"Give him the time he needs to realize you are the one, my boy. Let him miss you, feel your absence, and when he's ready, you will be there."

I straighten to look down at her, her cheeks wet with tears. "What if he realizes he doesn't want me in my absence?"

"Has that man ever succeeded in staying away from you?"

The answer is no, the thought warming my chest. No, Seb has never been able to stay away for too long. He's always found his way back to me.

"Take this time to heal as well. You need to accept that you weren't the reason for Daniel's death, and you need to realize your worth."

"Okay." I wipe the tears from my face.

"Take a shower. You smell like you've just come from a brothel, and you're covered in oil."

My cheeks heat with embarrassment as I head for the stairs, leaving her chuckling behind me.

"It looks like you and Avando are getting the worst of it with game suspensions," Coach says as he drops the paper to his desk. "Six games for you and three for Avando. You have a fine of forty-five thousand and Avando is sitting at sixteen thousand. A few of the other players received fines too. They are adamant about you missing the playoffs as well. It looks like we'll have to appeal to the league and present a case to the league's appeals officers. I will tell, you they sent over a copy of the video, and it doesn't look good." He holds up a thumb drive.

"Does that have audio?"

"It does." His eyes narrow as I stand.

"I think I can work with that. Am I able to take the video home to watch it? I'll need it to prepare for my appeal."

"Of course." He's quieter, more subdued.

If he watched the video, he knows what was said to set me off. I can see the wheels turning in his mind as he tries to piece together my actions. He believes me to be the father of his daughter's child, yet I was called out by another team for being gay.

I bet that's confusing.

"Dani was having some contractions this morning. She thinks they're Braxton Hicks. Has she told you?"

"No." I decide to be honest with him. "She's been quiet lately. The closer we get to her due date, the further she seems to pull away."

"I see." His shoulders hunch as he runs his fingers along his bald head. "She's been pretty quiet lately. I'm not too sure what's going on. I'm fearful she'll be raising this child alone."

"Are you asking if I will be in the picture?"

"I am asking if you're indeed the father," he fires back, causing my stomach to twist.

Then I remember what I'll be fighting for, and Dani's threats no longer scare me.

"No, I don't believe I am. It would be near impossible to have fathered that child with your daughter. But I am honorable, so when she came to me with her predicament, I tried to stand by her side."

He falls back in his chair. The stress he's feeling is clear through the look in his eyes, and I feel bad that my actions have contributed to it.

"I'm sorry, Coach. I did have a short relationship with Dani, but it didn't work out, and when she told me she was pregnant, I knew it couldn't be mine. She was sure, though, and I wasn't raised to disrespect a woman. I will stick by her until the results come in."

"I always prayed for a son," he grumbles, probably more to himself than me. "For this exact reason."

"A son can be just as problematic. A woman can only have one baby a year, a man can father hundreds if he so chooses," I point out.

His mouth curves upward in a small smile. "Good point."

I head for the door, the letter and video in my hand, and prepare myself for what will be the most profound moment in my life. I once thought it would be my recruitment into the NFL, and I can remember the moment like it was yesterday. I was walking up those metal stairs at the drafts, heading toward the green room, waiting for my offer.

I was wrong.

I shut Coach's office door behind me and lean against it. This appeal will be the most profound.

"What's the damage?"

I look up to find Ortiz coming out of the locker room, his hands taped and ready for the weights.

"Six games, a fine, and the playoffs."

"Yikes," he cringes. "I was handed a fifteen thousand dollar fine for punching someone." His eyes roll.

"I'm going to appeal the playoffs part, the rest I'm good with."

"Good with? Why would you be good with it? That fucker accused you of being…" he looks up and down the corridor. "A homo."

"Because I retaliated, and I gave in to the anger the slur provoked." I push off the door, walking toward him. "It wasn't the words that bothered me, it was the menace behind it."

"It's a lie, though."

I shrug as his mouth curls down at the lack of my agreement. I won't hide myself anymore. Even though I don't find most men attractive, I am in fact gay for one.

"Is my father in his office?" Dani's heels hit the tiled floor as she appears out of the stairwell.

Her stomach is protruding now, and I wonder how swollen her ankles must be in those shoes.

"Yeah," I reply quietly, not missing the look she gives Ortiz as she passes.

He drops his eyes from her ass when he catches me watching then hurries off to the weight room.

"How are you feeling?" I ask her as she stops walking, her hand on the door.

"What do you care, Dixon?"

"This is my child, isn't that what you said? Why wouldn't I care about the woman who's carrying it?"

"I know you don't believe it to be your child." She drops her hand from the door, turning to face me, her features twisted into anger. "You've made me a laughingstock of this organization. The father of my child is having an affair with a man."

"Keep your voice down," I order, not wanting Coach to hear her spew words that could change someone's life. It's not her place to do so.

"I have yet to hear you deny a single thing, and to be frank, it's quite concerning for me and your child." Her hand lands on her stomach. "Our child deserves better, and your lack of respect for me is shining through your actions."

I stand shocked, staring at her as she continues to berate me for something she's already been made aware of, realizing she's the only suspect I have for creating the problem I currently find myself in.

"You told Dillon," I accuse, her mouth dropping open as her hand hits her chest.

"I told Dillon what? I don't know what you're talking about."

Someone clears their throat behind me, and I turn to see Jameson quickly leaving the locker room, making my stomach sink. This is not the way I want things to come out.

When I look back at Dani, her mouth is pursed into a smug smile as her eyes shine with triumph. I don't give her the attention she craves as I turn and head for the exit.

"I'll call you when it's time," she yells to my back, but I'm long gone.

There's no mistaking the malice vibrating from that woman, and I can't really blame her. Two men she's tried to claim but failed are instead fucking each other. That had to burn, but now, she'll be the one left to feel ashamed for her actions. Not me.

I plan on letting everything out.

CHAPTER FIFTEEN

Sebastian

I have three weeks off from having to play a game I no longer find interest in. Coach asked me to stick around, to still prepare for the playoffs and practice for the team, but I'd rather see my daughter.

That field is no longer worthy of all my time.

When I told Dixon I needed time to think, I wasn't trying to push him away. My life is on the cusp of changing, and I won't be the only one affected. He's single, no children, and his mother is supportive. I'm happy about that, but I'm not in the same situation. My daughter will have a different life, and the people I surround myself with will not be as accepting.

I knew this already, and I am ready to fight, I just need to make sure my family will be okay first.

Paola's parents live in Manhattan in an upscale building, living off the money their deceased son and I have accumulated for them. They never cared where it came from, only that it pulled them out of poverty, giving them opportunities they never had before.

I respect that, and I respect that they're now raising my daughter while I play football. Again, it's not completely selfless because I pay for everything they could ever need.

The only things I want to assure them of are that I cared about Paola and explain the arrangement she and I had. I don't want them thinking our marriage was a complete sham. I did it to protect her and her unborn child, but later we became best friends who used the cushion of our marriage to protect Paola's reputation and her daughter. I owe them the truth, especially if everything about Dixon and me comes to light.

I nod to the security at the desk as I head for the elevators, excitement racing through me at the thought of seeing my little girl.

When the elevator doors shut behind me, I punch in the code that'll bring me up to their penthouse. I lean against the side of the car. I didn't bring anything for Carla, and I know she's going to be disappointed. We'll have to go out for lunch.

The doors open, and I step into their lavish foyer, the floors decked in gleaming marble and the walls painted with what looks like velvet.

So fucking decadent, but my daughter lives here, and this is the life I want for her.

My shoes hit the marble, the soft squeak echoing around the cavernous place then carrying ahead of me. My father-in-law's head pops out of a room to the left, his face lighting up when he sees me.

"Sebastian!" he booms. "What's brought you here?"

They don't watch my games, football doesn't interest them, therefore they know nothing of my suspension.

"Got some time off and thought I would swing by to see *la reinita.*"

"She's just waking up from her nap with *abuelita*. Do you want me to get them?" He claps me on the shoulder.

"Na, I'll go see them. I was hoping we could all have a chat too."

"I'll order us some food." He disappears into the kitchen as I make my way down the hallway toward Carla's room.

I can hear their soft voices, the small giggles immediately bringing a smile to my face. I knock on the door, hearing Paola's mother call out, expecting her husband. When I open the door and step in, both of them look at me with surprise.

"Papi!" Carla squeals, her raven curls bouncing as she bounds off the bed.

"Hi, *mija*." I pick her up and hold her close, breathing in her innocence, instantly missing her mother.

"Papi," her little hand cups my cheek. "You look sad. Do you miss Mami too?"

"Always," I admit as I look into her bright green eyes. "How about you get dressed and clean this room." I look around us at the toys and clothes on the floor. "Then you and I will go have lunch and do a little shopping."

"Okay!" she squeals again, the sound of her happiness crowding my chest with pride. This is why I pushed myself to achieve the things I did.

"I am going to talk to your grandparents first."

She gives me a nod and kicks her little feet to be put down, eager to get going.

"She's growing." I watch as she runs out of the room to the bathroom.

"Yes," Elisa smiles. "She is right, though. You do look sad."

"I miss your daughter and son in equal measure now."

"You are all we have left, *mijo*." Her words hit me in the gut as I drop my head for a second. I can't look her in the eye.

"We need to talk."

"So you said." She loops her arm with mine. "Let's find Mateo."

Mateo is in the kitchen pouring over food menus when we walk in.

"Don't worry about food. This won't take long, and I need to get Carla to lunch anyway."

"Okay," he nods and sits at the table, smiling when I pull out a chair for his wife. "What is this about?"

"A few things." Elisa grabs my hand, her fingers tightening around mine. "I want to thank you for everything you've done for Carla, it means so much to me to have you in our lives."

"Of course, Sebastian," Mateo nods. "You are our family."

"The things you have sacrificed for us..." Elisa jumps in. "We could never repay you."

"I have made no sacrifices—"

"*Mijo,*" she cuts me off. "Paola told us everything a few months after you were married and asked us to keep it to ourselves. She knew how proud you were, and she didn't want to upset you. We know why you married her." She leans in, her kind eyes boring into my shocked ones. "And we know about Carla."

It's not often I'm left speechless, but as I look back and forth between them, I'm unable to form any words. The fact that they know about Paola and the circumstance of her pregnancy has my stomach bottoming out.

Paola only ever remembered bright green eyes as she tried to fight him off in the back alley of the bar he dragged her into. She never revealed anything else about it, and I never pushed her. Alejandro needed me to take care of her, so I did the only thing I felt was right. I married her then claimed that child to be mine.

Why not get an abortion? I asked her the same thing, but Paola couldn't imagine it, and I never would have forced her. She believed the little life growing inside her was fate.

"It's admirable what you did and what you continue to do. And we are here for you," Mateo adds.

With the shock still thick in my system, I rip the Band-Aid clear off the very thing I'm hiding.

"One day, when Carla comes home to live with me, there may be a man there as well."

My heart is beating through my chest as I wait for their response.

"Like a roommate?" Mateo asks, his brow lifting.

"Like my partner," I clarify as Elisa gasps beside me.

"Like a lover," she murmurs, and I look down to her hand still wrapped in mine, unable to witness their reactions.

"I did not know this." Mateo clears his throat. "Paola never mentioned—"

"She didn't know." My eyes finally lift to his widened ones. "I didn't know … until recently."

"I don't—"

"It changes nothing," Mateo announces, effectively cutting Elisa off. "You are a good man, and I am still proud to call you my son."

I don't realize I'm scared until relief cascades over me. When I turn to look at Elisa, she's nodding emphatically.

"You are our son."

The driveway is empty, the house standing dark against the backdrop of blue sky. Nothing on its pristine surface tells of the horrors that happened inside. The walk up the driveway is slow, and when I turn the key in the lock, my throat seals with sadness.

Paola won't be here to greet me or chat about the gossip of the neighborhood.

Inside the air is stagnant from months of disuse, and when I close the door behind me, I stay rooted to the spot. My eyes are trained on the entranceway to the kitchen. Even though I want to go face the space that changed my life, I'm so fucking terrified to do it alone. Dixon's face floats through my mind, and I take courage from that, knowing I need to let this part of my life go and open up to the possibilities of a new one with him.

As I enter the kitchen, my eyes cloud over, and I see everything that happened in slow motion, letting myself relive it. The room is cleaned, every surface free of blood, almost smelling like a clinic. Now that the police have given the go ahead for it to be released, I'm going to put it on the market.

I can't live here, and I can't expect Carla to either. There are too many memories. Even though I want to keep the ones she has of her mother clear in her mind, I can't move on with the ones that crowd mine.

"You were right," I whisper as I lean against the counter, preparing to converse with my wife's ghost. "There was someone else, and today I confessed everything to your parents."

I wait for a sign that she's here, and when my skin vibrates with a sensation, I nearly collapse with tears.

"I miss you." My voice cracks as my eyes burn. "I wish I could hear you singing while cooking again or yelling at me for being the pig I am. I wish you were here to watch our daughter grow and help me not be too controlling with her.

"I loved you like a sister, and just as much as I loved your brother, I hope you found each other. The time has come for me to let you go, to release the promise I made to your brother and find where I truly belong." I swallow down the sob threatening to tear through me.

"I think I love Dixon, but I'm afraid to admit it. Everyone I've loved has disappeared, and the thought of him leaving me makes me want to fall apart. If you were here, you would know the words to say, and you would tell me what the fuck I should do. How am I going to live this life without you?"

It would be at this point that she would tell me to man up, grow a pair, and do whatever it is that makes me happy. She was a firm believer in fate and always told me my fate didn't lie with her. I never believed her, she was meant to be my wife, and Carla was meant to be my daughter. I would've died an old man, still married to her.

But I think she would've forced me to go. I could see it in her eyes the last conversation we had about who I was seeing, leading me to believe *my* fate lies with Dixon.

"I need to know if this is love," I say into the stillness of the room. "If it is, why is it so scary? And why do I feel so fucking weak?"

No answer, obviously.

My fingers drum along the dark granite of the countertop as I look around the opulent space.

"I have to let this place go, but I hope you will follow me into the next part of my life. It will be like one of your telenovela episodes, filled with drama and secrets." I smile as I look down to the tile at my feet. "It will be all about the love between two men and how hard they make the church ladies grip their pearls."

I straighten to give the space around me one final look as I commit to memory every moment I spent here with my family.

"Don't leave me, Paola," I beg as I let the tears come, soaking my cheeks. "Stay with me and haunt me for the rest of my days."

Then I leave the house for the last time, closing the trauma behind me and taking the unconditional love I experienced inside its walls.

"When is the court date?" Ma asks as she stands beside my chair at the dining room table.

"It's not in a courtroom, Ma," I chuckle.

"But it's an appeal?"

I look up to find her thoroughly confused, and I laugh again. "With the NFL, in the corporate office."

"What have you written so far?"

"Just everything I did to strive to be here, how I sacrificed my family, and I will always stand up for what's right."

"That sounds good." She pats my shoulder. "When is it?"

"Three weeks," I murmur.

She nods and walks away just as my knee begins to throb. The pain has been receding a bit more every day. It's finally healing now that I'm not forcing it to or pumping it with syringes filled with narcotics. It almost feels like this entire situation happened so I could get my shit together.

Fate.

I never really believed in the concept. For me, everything was always about hard work and striving for the things you want in life... If you achieved those things, you'd succeeded. I have never let myself sit back, handing my life over to some unseen force to pull me down an unknown path.

But maybe it's a mixture of both. Maybe fate nudges you, gives you a little foresight, teasing you with what could be, making you work hard for that certain outcome.

Sebastian and I feel like a merciless sort of twisted fate. The way we connected, the things he did to me, and where we are now feels like something out of a horror story, but maybe everything I strived for brought me to him.

Maybe I've changed him as much as he's changed me, and maybe that's what was always meant to happen.

"Dixon!" Ma calls out, her voice a bit frantic.

I get up and rush to find her in the living room, the TV on with the volume high. It's a news report, and the sight of it brings back unwanted memories.

"It's about the agents who were working Sebastian's wife's murder."

"There has been a gruesome discovery made this past week, but first, I would like to put out a warning that this story contains graphic details of murder," the reporter states, her face grim. "Federal Agent Paul Dawes was found in his home, brutally murdered in what can only be described as a fit of rage."

The screen pans out to show the front of a standard looking, two story home with police caution tape and people trampling all over the front lawn.

"Dawes was working undercover to expose some of Baltimore's largest crime syndicates, and his murder is believed to be connected. It has been described as brutal and targeted. He was also one of the agents who provided a statement regarding the death of his former partner, accusing Buffalo Bills football player Sebastian Avando."

"Fuck!" I growl, and for once, Ma doesn't chastise me.

"Avando has been cleared of any criminal charges in that incident, citing it to be self-defense as his home was broken into at the time. More details will be provided once the investigation has concluded. Today," the screen shifts, and I watch as Seb is being led into a police station in Rochester, his face indifferent, but I see the look in his eyes. He's ready to explode. "Avando is being questioned, yet I am being told that as of right now, no charges have been filed."

"Shit, this isn't good." I scrub a hand down my face.

"Son, if he's innocent, it'll be all right."

When I don't answer my mother, she stands to looks up into my face.

"Did he have something to do with that man's death, Dixon?"

I hate lying to her, but she wouldn't understand, and I don't want her involved in any way.

"No, Ma, but they're trying hard to pin something on him considering where he was raised."

"I see." We both look back at the TV.

Sebastian disappears behind a set of double doors, making my heart beat out a rhythm of doom. He promised me this wouldn't come back on him, and I believed him. His twisted sense of revenge has now landed him in hot water, while I can't help but worry about his daughter.

"Ma, I'm going to head out—"

"Yes," She pats my arm. "Go be with him. But Dixon," her eyes bore into mine. "Stay out of trouble."

It took me forever to find the police station when I arrived in Rochester, and when I headed inside to find out where he was, they had already released him.

That's a good sign, right?

My calls and messages have gone unanswered, and I have no idea where he lives, which basically means I'm stranded here. He's literally a needle in a fucking haystack right now.

After booking a hotel room then settling in for the night, I lie in bed and try to figure out how I'm going to find him. It's not like I can walk the streets, asking the homies where their boy is. I'll be shot in an alleyway somewhere.

My eyes gradually close, and I'm just about to drift off when the ringing of my phone has me sitting up. I nearly fumble the thing, and that makes me snort considering my fucking career. When I see his name on the screen, I'm overcome with relief.

"Seb?"

"Are we always going to run after each other, North?" He sounds amused, and it pisses me off.

"Yes," I grind out, clenching my teeth when he chuckles.

"Where are you staying?"

"No!" I roar. "Not this time. You will tell me everything that's going on before I tell you where I am. You like to use that dick between your legs to make me forget."

"When you left my house, I decided it was time to face what it is that I want." When he doesn't argue or demand anything from me, I lie back in surprise. "Before I could tell you anything about how I was feeling, I needed to speak to the only family I have left."

"Your daughter?" My jaw slackens as my eyes widen.

"And Paola's parents. I've never had to answer to anyone before, and I never cared what people thought of me. But that changes now that I'm with you. I don't want to hide, and I'm not going to force you to hide so you can be with me. It's not fair."

"You came out to Paola's parents and your daughter?" I can't fucking believe what I'm hearing.

"Yeah, and now I would like you to tell me where the fuck you are before I have to find your location and fatten another clerk's pocket to get an extra key."

"I always wondered how you got into that hotel room." I think of him back then, angry and holding a gun to my head while Dani slept soundly beside me.

"Address, North." The way his voice deepens as he demands my location has me hardening instantly.

An hour later, a loud banging echoes throughout the room. I smile, knowing who's on the other side of the door. I open it, and I'm immediately wrapped in a strong pair of arms, his face burrowing into my neck.

"I missed you," he admits, sounding the most vulnerable I have ever heard him.

I won't deny, I was expecting him to come in here and rip my clothes off, demanding I spread my legs for him. Instead, I'm holding him close as his body trembles against mine.

"Seb."

He pulls back, gripping my face with his hands. "I love you, Dixon."

My mouth falls open as I look into his amber eyes. "What?"

"I love you, and I want to be with you but first you need to know who I am. From the beginning."

"O-okay," my voice breaks as I try to form the word.

He leads me to the bed and takes off his shoes, dropping his pants next. He removes his jacket, hanging it over the chair, then he gets into bed, his t-shirt and boxers staying on.

I stiffly get in beside him, my body locked with shock as I wait, watching as he struggles to sort out what he wants to say.

"I told you about how I grew up, about my negligent mother and my never knowing who my father was. How I started with the gang I now run and what all of it did to bring me where I am today, but I never told you much about Alejandro and Paola."

His wife and her brother from what I can remember.

"He was one of the first guys in the crew I called a friend, him and Delano. He was a few years older than me, and I looked up to him. He had a good family, and he liked church, but he was a fucking gangbanger." He chuckles as he shakes his head. "I always thought gangsters were all bad guys who didn't had families. When he found out I had a mother who didn't give a shit about me, he started to bring me home. I met Elisa and Mateo—his parents—and his little sister, Paola, who happened to be my age."

He scratches at his chin as his teeth worry into his bottom lip. I can see the tears beginning to nestle against his lids.

" Paola and Jandro became like family to me. Their parents made sure I was clothed and fed, even though they could barely afford to sustain themselves. Jandro, Delano, and I started boosting cars for parts, making big points with the guys who ran the crew, and eventually, we were sent out farther than Rochester. We started fucking boosting cars in Manhattan, Brooklyn. Basically anywhere in the Tri-State area.

"The money we had lining our pockets helped us go places. I was attending a boujee high school and playing football, attracting scouts and shit. Jandro was buying a house for his family and making sure Paola was in the same school as me so I could watch over her. Delano was finally pulling his parents out of poverty, placing them in better neighborhoods.

"But word travels fast, and when a crew is starting to rise, so do their enemies. We were followed by rival gangs, shot at on the streets, robbed and stabbed, left to die."

Hearing the traumatic things he endured only affirms to me why Sebastian is the way he is, and when I compare the man I first met to the one now laying beside me, it's like night and day.

"Delano's house was gunned down. Luckily, no one was killed, but he had to move his family somewhere else. Jandro was threatened constantly, but he liked guns and made sure he made a reputation for himself which preceded him everywhere. He was the gang's executioner, and he took his position seriously. He was the only one who got off unharmed, sort of."

Sort of?

"We all went out one night, celebrating our biggest boost yet, four cars in one night and none of them under a hundred racks. We hit this bar up, it was just before I had to head back for my last year of college. We partied, we fucking destroyed this bar, and we lost Paola. I found her sleeping in the women's bathroom, locked inside a stall. It was clear she'd been crying, but she wouldn't tell me why. I let it go while I led her out of the bathroom because I was a stupid fucking prick who thought all females were emotional."

A tear drops from his lower lid, hitting his cheek.

"The next day, Jandro had a job up in Staten Island, and he made me promise to look after Paola until he got back. He told me she wasn't acting right, and she wouldn't speak to him. I promised him I would always look after his family, no matter what, and that he had my word. He was gunned down later that night inside a boosted Cadillac Escalade."

I link my fingers through his and hold on tight, knowing this story is nowhere near over.

"After that, Paola withdrew even more. A few days later, I found out our crew's leader and his right hand had arranged for Jandro to be murdered, just to keep us in line. They were worried about us trying to take over. So I fucking did, and within a month, that gang was mine and Delano's. I also found out something else…" He runs his fingers under his eyes. "Paola was pregnant. At first, she was prepared to raise it herself without ever giving the father up. I was sure it was because she was fearful I would kill him, but I later learned it was because she didn't know who the fuck he was."

"What?"

"She was raped that night at the bar, and all she could remember was being dragged from the bathroom into the alley. Nothing about him stood out except for his bright green eyes. I told her to get an abortion, that I wouldn't tell a soul and she could continue living live her life as she'd planned. But she was already a few months into the pregnancy, and she said she felt a connection to the baby she couldn't explain."

"Carla?"

He nods, his fingers tightening around mine.

"Paola's family lived in a new, upscale neighborhood, went to church regularly. Having a child out of wedlock would've painted her in a light I didn't want. So I married her and claimed Carla as my own. We could've divorced at any point after that, but I'd made that promise to Jandro, and Paola became my best friend. It was comfortable, and I finally had a family of my own without borrowing someone else's."

The silence crowds around us as I try to process everything I've learned.

"Carla has his eyes, bright emerald-green. So beautiful against the black of her curls," he murmurs as my heart breaks further.

"You'd still be married to her if she was alive," I state out loud the thought that has been running through my mind.

"I don't know." His admission pulls a gasp from my throat. "I stayed married to her because of a promise but also because I didn't want any relationships. The shit I do is fucking dangerous, and I didn't want to bring an outsider into it. Paola knew the risks, she grew up in it. It's why it took me so long to admit how I feel about you. It means I'm weak."

I don't take offense at his words because I know what he means. His feelings for me could be used against him.

He looks at me with his cheeks wet and his eyes clear. He wants me to see his truth. His loves shines through.

"I love you, too, Seb." I lean in to kiss his tear-soaked cheek.

He gathers me in close, scooting us down on the bed before wrapping his arms around me. "Let's sleep because I plan on waking you up with my dick in your ass."

And who the fuck said romance is dead?

CHAPTER SIXTEEN

Sebastian

The ringing of my phone startles me from my sleep as Dixon groans beside me, covering his head with the blankets. I reach for my pants on the floor to grab my phone from the pocket. Seeing Fernando's name on the screen, I sit up quickly, a bad feeling creeping up on me.

"Hello?"

"*Jefe!*" His voice sounds winded and frantic. "They're here!"

"Who's there? Where are you?" I jump out of bed, and Dixon sits up as well, concern lining his features.

"The Feds!"

"Where are you, Fernando?"

"At the bus station, like your boy told me, but they're here." He's whispering, his voice dropping almost too low to hear.

"In Baltimore?"

"Yes." Barely a sound. "They'll kill me."

"Are you hiding?" I motion for Dixon to pass me his phone, and he flies into action, grabbing it off the nightstand.

"I'm out back, but I can see them through the window. It's

Gomez."

My heart drops, and my ears ring as I look into Dixon's confused face.

Don't blame him, Seb. I try to convince myself, but it's so fucking hard.

I dial Delano's number, and it goes to voicemail, so I try again, but this time there's no dial tone before his greeting begins. Did he send me straight to voicemail?

"Fuck!" I hear Fernando's feet start the pavement. "They saw me!"

"Fernando!" I scream into the phone as I dial Delano again, but the line cuts out. "Fuck!"

"What's happening?" Dixon asks, his face looking fearful.

"That Fed you wouldn't let me kill is chasing down your brother's friend right now!"

"Fernando?" he whispers as I try to call Fernando back.

"Yes!" I snap at him, as the line goes to voicemail. "Please, God." I beg the man upstairs to for once hear my pleas.

I quickly get dressed and throw on my jacket, striding toward the door with my phone in my hand.

"Wait!" Dixon calls out. "I'm coming too."

I turn on him so fast, and whatever he sees in my eyes has him taking a step back while he shakes his head.

"Not again, Seb," he chokes out. "Do not blame me for this."

When I don't answer, his shoulders drop, and I yank open the door, leaving him behind once more.

He pulls onto the driveway then gets out of the vehicle. This time he's alone. I watched him earlier as he carted his wife and kids away. Good thing because they shouldn't be here to witness what's going to happen to him.

I watch as he unlocks his door then looks around behind him, his eyes scanning for anything out of the ordinary. He won't see me. I hopped the fence into his neighbor's backyard, and my Hummer is parked far enough out of the way.

He slips into his house as I release a breath. He's looking shady as fuck, like he just did something outside of orders, and I'm about to teach him a lasting lesson.

I still can't get a hold of Fernando. I can only hope he got away, possibly hiding out somewhere. My gut is telling me something different, though, and it's never been wrong.

Ten minutes later, I'm jumping his neighbor's fence into his backyard, my feet sinking into the flowerbed. I take the steps up onto his deck then remove the shoes, not wanting any dirtied footprints all over the house. I'm sure there will be a thorough investigation; the Feds don't mess around when it's about one of their own.

The back door is open—stupid fucking idiot—and I step into the kitchen, listening for any movement. I close it slowly, ensuring the latch doesn't sound throughout the house, revealing my presence before I'm ready.

No, I need to look this fucker in the eye to make sure he sees his end.

I slowly head down the narrow hallway toward the one dull light that's on, shining from a door that stands ajar. I can hear him and the hushed conversation he's having, forcing acid up my throat. It's sickening having to sneak up on my lifelong friend like this.

I should've dealt with this sooner.

I hear him curse followed by a groaned guttural sound that sounds like it crawled up from the deepest pit in his chest. I can hear the torture. Does he know I'm coming? Can he sense the reaper breathing down his neck?

My gloved fingers push open the door as I step into the office, the sudden sight of me has him startling upward, knocking his chair over.

"Seb—"

"Shh." I hold a finger to my mouth. "I will do the talking. Give me your phone."

Delano grabs his cell with shaking hands then drops it into my open palm as he starts to sob. I tighten my jaw to close off the part of me who's loved this man like family for most of my life.

"I was forced—"

"Shh," I cut him off again as I smash his phone down to the floor, watching it shatter.

I pull my piece out from the inside of my jacket to point it at my best friend's head.

"Outside."

I can't trust that this place isn't bugged. Just because he works with the Feds, doesn't mean they trust him. Which means I may not have a lot of time.

We step out into the backyard, then my foot slams into his back, forcing him to topple forward onto the lawn. His grunt of pain echoes around us, then I watch as he gets up to his knees, turning to face me.

"I had no choice."

"Don't even start with that!" I hiss. "We all have choices."

"They were threatening to take the kids, put my wife in jail for helping to cover everything up. I couldn't let that happen."

"You should've come to me."

"I was going to, Seb, I swear. I just needed some time."

"You're a liar," I snarl as he cowers like the pussy he is. "Did you really think I wouldn't find out?"

"They said they wanted the kid, and then I was out." He begins to tremble. "I wanted to get my family away from it all."

"I am your family too. Or was that just one-sided?"

"You are." He nods, snot running down over his lips as he cries. "There was no getting out of it. They had my lines tapped."

Explains why he called me and tried to pull info out of me, setting me up to take a fall.

"You wanted me to rot in a fucking cell, homie?" I step down onto the grass beside him, pressing the barrel of the silencer to his forehead. "Is that why you were digging for information while you had me on the line?"

"I had no choice." He whimpers, the noise making me want to pop a bullet in him, only it's too soon.

"Where's Fernando?"

His eyes drop, and he looks at the ground, my hand curling into a fist.

"Where is he?" I reiterate, nudging him with the gun.

"Dead," he sniffs. "He was a rat, Seb. You know how tha—" My gun slams into his mouth, sending him to the grass, blood pouring from a split in his lip.

"*You're* a rat, Delano," I chuckle. "He wasn't feeding the Feds info, he was talking to me."

"Wait," he gets back up to his knees, and my gun presses to his temple once again. "I was gathering info, getting you everything you would need on the Feds and their dealings with the cartel. It runs deeper than just infiltrating the gangs of Baltimore."

"You think I don't know that?" I growl. "You're not leaving this backyard without a body bag."

"I know." His hands hit the ground in front of him, his head dropping forward. "Why do you think the wife and kids aren't here? I knew you were coming for me."

"Fernando was innocent, and now he's dead because of you. I never would've believed something like that could happen. But most of all, I never would have foreseen you turning on me."

I can feel the emotion working its way up from my chest, and I grit against it, even as my eyes blur from unshed tears.

"We were all that was left." After I kill him, everyone I'd

considered family from my childhood will be dead.

"I know," he nods, looking up at me. "Check my laptop, the folder is named Jackie."

He grabs my gun with both hands, digging it into the skin of his forehead, his tortured eyes staring up at me.

"Do it," he pleads, closing his eyes. "Do it, you fucking puss—"

The force of the bullet knocks him to his back as the hole in the center of his forehead begins to fill and spill over with dark, red blood. I drop my arm to the side, and my chin hits my chest, a sob finally wrenching free.

I pull it together quickly, promising myself time to grieve later, then turn to head back inside. I need his laptop, and then I need to get the fuck out of here. I slip my gun in my pocket to pick up the boots by the door, heading back in toward the office.

His laptop is sitting in the center of his desk with a note stuck to the screen.

The password is Jandro. I'm sorry.

The sight of my brother's name being used for Delano's deceit makes me want to smash everything around me, but I hold back. I close the computer and pick it up, heading back toward the front door.

I drop Delano's boots back to the porch where I found them before, then slip my Jordan's back on. The footprints in the garden and the mud on the boots won't point to me in the slightest. I turn one last time to take a look at my past, committing the house to memory. After I grieve, I'll never think of him again.

The walk back to the Hummer is short, and when I get in, I drop my head to the wheel. This is why I am the way I am. No one can be trusted, not the one you're fucking, and not the ones you call blood. Nobody has your back no matter what, there's always something that can sway them. A weakness or an envy.

My weakness happens to be back in a hotel room right now, wanting to blow our situation wide open and reveal it to people who will exploit that.

I can't let that happen.

Dixon

My bag is packed and sitting on the bed beside me, ready to leave. It's clear he's not coming back here. After trying to reach him all night and the next without answer, I finally have mine.

He's done.

I inserted myself into a part of his life he wanted to keep separate, convincing him to change his plans then forcing him to do things my way. It cost someone their life, and by the sound of it, they didn't deserve it. Not like that Fed did.

I manipulated Seb by using the feelings he had for me, fucking it all up.

I leave behind the hotel where the man who owns my heart professed his love, and I get into my SUV, ready to get back home. It feels like the end, but there's a part of me that hopes the magnetic pull of our need for one another wins out. I don't want to lose him.

An hour later, I'm pulling up to my house, the drive feeling too short. I still haven't figured out how I'm going to apologize and make him believe how much I regret what I did.

Even now, I know I was only trying to keep him from ruining his life, but then I think of Fernando, and shame washes over me again.

My phone rings through the interior of the SUV, and I cringe when I see Dani's name on the dash screen. It's been days since I've spoken to her, and I don't want to right now considering this day has gone to shit.

"Yeah," I answer, not wanting to tolerate any of her shit.

"I'm on my way to the hospital, my water broke."

The words do nothing for me since that kid isn't mine, and I don't even want to step foot into the same room as her.

"Call me when it's ready to be tested," I clip, hanging up the phone.

Then I sit in the driver's seat, looking down at the darkened screen of my phone while letting the guilt inside of me build from the choice of my actions. Just because I'm angry at myself for other reasons, doesn't mean I have the right to take it out on someone else, no matter how deserving of it she is.

Instead of getting out of the car to check in with my mother, I pop it into reverse to back out of my driveway. There's no reason to tell her about the baby coming, she refuses to acknowledge it, and that's her choice to make. I wish I had done the same.

I just couldn't trust that Dani wouldn't have dragged my and Seb's names through the mud for months until she gave birth, she's that spiteful.

The hospital looms ahead as I park in the garage, knowing I'll be paying an astronomical amount for it later. Inside I find the place pretty quiet, and when I walk up to the front desk, a tired nurse gives me a half smile.

"How can I help you?" She sounds tired too.

"I'm looking for a patient who's here to give birth."

After giving her the information, she asks if I'm the father, and I stutter, knowing the only way to get up to her is to say that I am. So I nod, keeping silent in case something slips out, then I head in the direction she tells me.

The last time I was here my knee was busted up so bad, and Seb came to visit me, letting me know I had someone other than Ma looking out for me. The thought of him has my chest seizing and my stomach flipping. Everything reminds me of him. He inserted himself into my life so seamlessly that I don't remember a single moment when he wasn't there in some capacity.

I get to Dani's floor to find Coach there, leaning against the wall. His head is down, and the fluorescent light overhead casts a bright shine along his bald head. He's stressed and looking fucking tired, probably tired from the team and his daughter.

"Coach!" I call out as I draw closer.

"North." He straightens, trying to school the worried look from his features.

"How is she?"

"They're setting her up for an epidural now. They say she's nearly completely dilated because what she thought were Braxton Hicks yesterday was her actually going into labor."

"Damn," I mutter, leaning on the wall beside him. "How long does it usually take?"

"Having a baby?" He looks at me with amusement. "Depends."

A doctor comes out of the room and looks at Coach. "She's resting now. She'll be pushing soon, though."

"Thank you." Coach nods as I peek my head around the doorway.

"I'm going to go talk to her," I murmur as Coach says something about needing coffee.

I head into the room as he walks down the corridor toward the elevators, giving me the time I need with his daughter. When this child is born, everything will come to light so I'm sure she's just as nervous about that as I am about her revealing my relationship with Seb.

If I still have one.

She's laying in the hospital bed with a band wrapped around her stomach and machines resonating a doppler noise throughout the room. I walk over to the screen and watch as the lines jump up and down quickly.

"It's the baby's heartbeat." Dani's wary voice snaps me out of my thoughts.

"It's fast. Is that normal?"

"Yeah, they say he's healthy." Her voice is small, nearly overtaken by the noise of the machine.

"That's good."

"I thought you weren't coming until they could perform the test?"

I sit on the bed beside her and clasp my hands together in my lap. "I didn't want you to be alone, even after everything you've done."

I look up at her, relaying my feelings and hoping she sees my sincerity. "You should have the real father here."

"I can't." Her words are uttered on a broken whisper, and my heart breaks at the sound.

"Yes, you can. You'll have to—"

"I don't know who it is, Dixon."

Her admission shocks me as I stare at her wide-eyed. "So while we were supposedly together…" I can't even finish my sentence.

"We were never really together." She tips her head. "Were we? And no, it was right after the Sebastian incident. I was so angry, and I did something stupid."

"How many times did this *stupidity* occur?"

"Once," She whispers. When she sees the confusion on my face, she presses her head back to look at the ceiling. "With two guys."

"So it comes down to those two men. Couldn't you have just told them?"

"And Sebastian," she shoots me a look of contempt, then her face falls.

"You and I both know what he told you happened after you left that office was true. He didn't get you pregnant that day."

"I know," she admits, fidgeting with a thread on her gown. "It's funny because you're the one who's here, standing by me even though you have many reasons not to, and still, I want to hurt you. I'm so jealous."

"Jealous of what?"

"The looks you get from Sebastian, the looks he gets from you. No one has ever looked at me like that. I did awful things because of this jealousy."

"You told Dillon James," It's not a question because I already know the answer, I just want to hear her say it.

"Yes." Her mouth tips down as tears slip from her eyes. "I knew he would spread it like wildfire, and I wanted whatever it was you two had to end."

"You may have succeeded," I confess, not sure why I'm giving her the time of day but feeling the need to talk to *somebody*.

"I doubt it," she scoffs. "The energy always shifts whenever you are both in the same space. It's thick, and the magnetism is potent. There's no way it's over. That's not to say you both won't face any hardships, you will. This league is filled with machismo men whose masculinity has to pour from their very pores."

She sounds disgusted as I look at her with confusion. "This coming from the woman who treated me like shit after finding out."

"I'm a part of the problem." She gives me an apologetic look. "I was raised in that atmosphere, and a man who loves another man is too far out of the league's realm of masculinity. This is a man's sport, Dixon, and they don't want to hear about any players' questionable sexuality. There's no room for homosexuality in those locker rooms."

"I know all that," I tell her as she shifts uncomfortably on the bed. "I can't help how I feel, though. The longer I suppress it, the worse I feel."

"When did you realize you were gay? And why did you pretend to like me? Was I used as a beard?"

I chuckle and shake my head. "I still consider myself straight, for the most part." I look at her. "Except for him."

"That's different," she murmurs, and I nod because it is different.

She shifts again, discomfort evident on her face. "Are you okay?" I stand and reach for her hand.

"I feel like I need to use the bathroom." She looks puzzled as I press the button to call a nurse. "Where's my dad?"

"He went to get coffee. I can have him paged."

She gives me a nod, and I rush out of the room just as the nurse shows up. "She's feeling like she has to use the bathroom," I inform the woman, and she smiles.

"Sounds like it's time to push."

After telling the nurse's station to call Coach, he comes barreling out of the elevator two minutes later with a frantic look on his face.

"Did I miss it?"

"No, just started." I follow him back to the room.

We walk in to find the nurse between Dani's legs with her hand up inside her nearly to the elbow.

"Holy shit." Coach whirls back around. "I can't watch that."

I look from him to Dani then give myself a shake. I don't want her to go through this alone.

Looks like I'm watching a baby being born.

"One small push, Dani!" the doctor exclaims. His excitement about being bloodied to the elbows and watching her split in two is concerning.

Twenty-three minutes later, the head is out, Dani giving one final push before it's over. Thank God because she looks on the verge of passing out, and honestly, so the fuck am I. My hand is being crushed in hers, the screaming has my head pounding, and the play-by-play commentary from between her legs is alarming.

She'll never be the same again.

She's being destroyed down there, making me wonder how the fuck she'll recover.

A loud squawk sounds as the doctor and nurses whoop in celebration while I freeze to the spot. That's a brand new life. Nothing has touched it or tarnished its innocence, and I can't help but be appreciative that I've had the chance to witness it.

"How is he?" Dani asks me. "Does he have all of his fingers and toes?"

"What?" My heart pounds erratically in my chest. "Of course he does." I look at the doctor as he holds up a baby covered in gunk and blood, *doesn't he?* "Does he have everything?"

"He's perfect!" His smile is wide, and I once again question the man's sanity. "Does the daddy want to cut the cord?"

"Cut the what?"

"No," Dani shakes her head slowly. "He doesn't."

The baby is placed on Dani's chest as they wipe it down, and I take a couple steps back, not wanting to be in the way.

"Is it over?" Coach pops his head in as I breathe a sigh of relief.

"Yeah, I think so."

"All fingers and toes?" he asks, and I turn on him.

"Is that an issue with your family or something?"

He starts to laugh, his eyes quickly tearing up when he hears the baby cry. "I wish her mama was here to see this."

I don't ask because this family is not my concern, and I don't want to get sucked in any further than I already am.

"He's all cleaned up." The nurse approaches us with the baby bundled up in her arms. "He's gorgeous."

Coach holds his hands out, and when she places the baby into them, we both lean in. It's for different reasons, but our reactions are the same.

"Damn," I whisper as I look over my shoulder at Dani.

Looks like I won't be needing that test after all because the kid crying in Coach's arms looks identical to a teammate, and with one look, I see Coach notices it as well.

The locker room is quiet while I sit here, absorbing the stillness as I think over all the shit I need to talk about. My life has felt like a freight train recently, moving at top-speed while barreling toward destruction. I can't fix it if I don't give myself the time and space to be alone.

Luckily, I have the next six weeks to do that, but first, I need to have a conversation.

"North." I look up to find a confused Ortiz stepping into the locker room, his mouth turned down into a frown. "What's so urgent that it couldn't wait until the morning?"

"Where's Jameson?"

"Here," Jameson says as he steps inside the room.

"I just left the hospital," I begin as both men pipe up at the same time.

"Is it your knee?"

"Where's Avando?"

"None of that." I wave them off. "Dani had her kid, a baby boy. I was there for the birth."

I don't miss the nervous looks they give one another, affirming my suspicions.

"Why would you fuck her raw?" I shake my head and stand, walking toward them. "There's no denying the kid's features." My hand lands on Jameson's shoulder. "You're the father."

"Really?" His eyes fill as his mouth tips up, his reaction shocking me. "I've always wanted to be a father."

I hit Ortiz on the arm, making him hiss as he rubs the spot.

"Wrap your dicks up from now on."

Then I leave the locker room a free man... No kid, no sport obligations, and no significant other. It's time I work on myself and get ready for this appeal.

C.A. RENE

CHAPTER SEVENTEEN

Fernando is dead.

Shot in the back as he ran from those dirty Feds.

Five bullets.

He had no family, no one to claim his body, so he sat in that morgue for a day while I hustled my ass to Baltimore. I had to make up an elaborate story, detailing how he was my third cousin, twice removed. Then, after a ten-minute long confusing tale, the cop let me in to identify him.

I didn't know the kid well, but I do know he didn't deserve the end he got. And all I can do is let guilt consume me as I face the consequences of my actions.

I'm paying for his cremation then spilling his ashes over Little North's grave. They struggled to survive, and then they lost their lives to the streets.

He deserves a proper send-off.

Fernando also deserves revenge, and as mad as I am about Dixon interfering, I think I have a better punishment in store for Gomez. Death would be too easy at this point, and I've never been one to choose the easy route.

Delano's laptop is open in front of me, the screen bright

inside the dark vehicle. Today I wired his wife and children enough money to live comfortably for the rest of their lives. I can trust it will never come back to me, she knew the consequences of being married to a gangster.

This 'Jackie' folder is deep, holding over a hundred other files, all of it information on the corrupt Feds. Interspersed he has some information on dirty cops in New York, a lot of it involving the mayor.

All intricate dealings on how to infiltrate the drug scene and make it their own while still wearing a badge. Mobile screen recordings of FaceTime calls, decrypted emails, and video surveillance.

The fucking audacity to name the folder *Jackie*.

It was the code word Jandro made up for us while we were boosting cars. If we texted that, it meant we were compromised or caught. Delano and I both received that message the night Jandro was killed.

He named this folder Jackie because he knew he was going to die, either at the end of my gun or in the back by a Fed.

Does that make me feel bad for what I've done? No. He knew what this life meant, and he knew what the consequences were. Will I miss him? Every day. My heart will remember when my mind tries to block out the images of our childhood or the nights we cried after Jandro's death. All those holidays I spent with him and his family. All of that will stay planted in my heart forever.

The sound of a car door slamming has me looking up from the screen of the laptop and toward a sullen looking Gomez as he heads into his house. Bet he had a long day playing Fed while he planned his evening cutting out coke. It's a tough life.

The urge to kill him still sits inside my gut, coaxing me to slip on my gloves then enter his home, popping a bullet in his head. But I don't. I drop my gaze back down to the screen, pulling up the information Delano has gathered on the police commissioner.

According to the files, Davis Johnson wants to clean the streets and end racial profiling. Sounds like a pipedream to me, but it looks like he's clean even if his aspirations are comical. I've been pulled over twice since I got here, and one of those times, I was told I matched the description of a known assailant. That is until they found out who I really was, then it was autographs and well wishes.

Fucking pigs.

This is who Delano wants me to send this information to, Police Commissioner Johnson, and he believes a stint in the pen will straighten the Feds out. I get it. Most people would scoff and say a few years of good behavior then they'll be back out again. But what they don't realize is, these guys put those criminals behind bars, imagine the field day they'll have when a few Feds walk among them.

Asses will be sore for days.

I prepare the email, making sure I've attached the right documents, and then I send everything to my secure email address, making sure the files are uploaded before I shutdown the laptop. I send a silent salute toward Gomez's house, thanking him for the Wi-Fi, so when the email is traced, it will bring them right here to his doorstep.

I learned a lot of things while watching Jandro hack and boost his way through most of the Tri-State area, the most important being that no Wi-Fi is actually secure.

Gomez's recycling bin sits out in front of his garage, so I trek up his driveway, dumping the laptop inside. This is rather satisfying, but I won't lie: the desire to pump this motherfucker full of lead is overwhelming.

Come tomorrow, he and his buddies will be taking a little ride in the back of an armored vehicle, and I'll be saying goodbye to my friend Fernando.

This can't be right.

I bring my phone closer to my face as I read Ortiz's message again.

Jameson is the father of Dani's baby. Apparently, these two fuckers had a threesome with the slut and managed to knock her up in one night.

I'm fucking pissed, but it's not because my teammates are stupid idiots. It's because Dixon didn't bother telling me himself.

Fucking toxic.

The both of us, we're so fucking dysfunctional, and it's disturbing. Even knowing all that, I still wanted him to chase me. Hunt me down, find me, stake his claim. I would've fucking done that. Hell, I *have* fucking done that.

At the same time, this is for the best because I want him safe. When he's with me, he's not safe, so until this whole thing blows over, I need to keep my distance.

I'm so fucking mad I'm vibrating and yet I love the rookie.

I love Dixon North, and it's coming time we settle this shit once and for all.

Dixon

This stadium has become my sanctuary, and even though I'm on the other side in the corporate offices, it's still home. My meeting will take place with a compliance officer—whose identity won't be known until I am introduced to them and vice versa—via a conference call in one of the large boardrooms. My explanation is ready, my heartfelt plea for understanding is written onto paper, the pen marks deep into the pages, and yet I know I'll be denied.

It's rare that they appeal such a penalty, I know this, and if that's the case, I won't give up here. Sure, I can pull a Brady and go to civil court like he did for 'Deflategate,' but I won't. I have something bigger up my sleeve.

While I wait for my appointment, I pace the length of the office I was led to, reciting line for line what I want to say in my head. My feet are burning a trail along the dull gray carpet as the light fixture above my head flickers slightly every few minutes.

The compliance officer will go over the footage, hear the officials' statements, and then it'll be my turn to speak, giving me the chance to lay it all out for them.

I'm wearing the same suit I wore to the gala I attended last year with Dani. She's here with me today, straightening my tie and bouncing baby James in his car seat. If someone had told me she'd be the one in here with me and Ma today, I would've choked on air, but here she is.

Is everything forgiven? No. Ma still cuts her the side eye every now and then, but she's enjoying baby James too much to protest. He is cute even if he does look like Jameson.

"I don't think I can do this." I swallow down the bile that threatens to force its way up my throat.

"You can and you will," Dani answers, smiling at Ma as she comes to take James out of the car seat. "Besides, you have to be the role model James needs in a godfather."

Yeah, there's that too.

I was there for his birth, and I stuck around for the past three weeks because I genuinely care about the little guy. So Dani asked me to be his godfather, and I accepted.

He's grown over the last few weeks, but the poor kid is looking more and more like Jameson, right down to the unibrow lining his forehead. They have the same pink toned skin, and Dani complains about how ugly the kid's toes are, saying they're looking more and more like his father's. I find it fucking hilarious.

Coach comes into the room and gives me a once over, settling my fears with a nod. "You look good. Are you sure about the path you're choosing to go down?"

"Yes, sir." I move to scratch at the beard that's lined my chin for nearly six months but instead find smooth skin. I decided to shave it all off hoping to look more presentable.

"Then we'll be behind you every step of the way." He clasps my shoulder. His attention is quickly stolen when he hears his grandson gurgling in my mother's lap, heading over to them.

Coach and Ma have been interacting more because of baby James, and it makes me wonder more and more about what happened to Dani's mother.

"North!" Jameson strides into the room, Ortiz right behind

him. "Most of us are here with you, man. Make that fucker do the right thing."

Most of us. I know who's not here.

"Language, young man!" Ma pipes up from the other side of the room. "Your child has functional ears, you know."

Jameson has been a doting father, and even though he and Dani are not together, they've been cordial. I don't get involved because I have enough problems with my own relationship. I don't need anyone else's.

I've never been in any sort of appeal setting before, and nerves are making my stomach bubble with nausea, but I have to do this. I need to make this right, even if it results in my being shunned by my teammates and the league.

Even Coach doesn't know exactly what I'm planning to say. I've noticed the curious looks he's been giving me, and asking me what I have planned is probably on the tip of his tongue. He's been supportive, always ready to answer any questions I have, and when I visit Dani and James, he often offers to read over my statements.

I always refuse.

This isn't his fight, it's mine, and it's not one I necessarily have to win, I just need to obliterate my opponents.

The door to the office opens, and I stare at the secretary who greeted us earlier.

"The appointment will begin in three minutes. I have some water waiting in the boardroom for you." She gives me a tentative smile, and I realize my face is frozen into a mask of fear.

I can't help it. This will rip my life wide open, forcing me to paint a masterpiece for someone who could sit back, only to see blobs of color.

"Son," Ma grabs my arm, turning me to look at her. "I want you to know I am so very proud of the man you've become, and whatever happens here today, it won't change that."

"Thank you." My throat seals as pride shines bright in her dark brown eyes.

"Dixon." Jameson comes over, holding his son in his arms. "You got this."

It's really the opposite, I don't have shit, but the time is here, and there's no turning back. Even if things don't go as I hope today, I still gained some things by being suspended, things that wouldn't have happened if I'd been playing. The Toroidal is done, I no longer use it, and my knee is nearly healed. This suspension gave me the time to relax, letting my knee recoup instead of damaging it more with the weekly games. My relationship with Ma has strengthened. We go out more, we talk freely now, and I make sure she feels appreciated. I have taken this time to self-reflect, learning to love the man I've become.

I guess not all is lost.

Everyone waits back in the office as I make my way down the hallway, heading toward the large boardroom at the end, somehow placing one foot in front of the other. Time moves slowly toward fate. Even though we plan everything accordingly, you can't change what's already destined.

Your only choice is to live through it and try to make it bearable.

I open the door to see the red blinking light on the phone as it sits on the large mahogany table surrounded by cushioned, black leather seats. I choose one, pulling the phone closer before pressing the red light.

"Hello?"

"Hello," A man's loud voice fills the room. "I am compliance officer Gary Wright. I will be taking a look at your case today."

"Dixon North," I reply, swallowing down the trepidation that threatens to consume me.

"I'll be viewing the video first then going over the officials' statements. At the end, I will ask you to give me your reason for appealing. Understand?"

"Yes, sir." I close my eyes as I lean forward, resting my forehead on the table.

I pull strength from the memory of my father and the tenacity of my little brother. They're here with me today.

Chapter Eighteen

Sebastian

When he steps out of the building, I immediately know he lost the appeal. His mouth is turned down—which I can see perfectly now that he's shaved—and he's running his hand along the top of his newly faded hair, a sure sign of defeat.

None of that shocks me. I knew his violent outburst on the field would result in a stiff penalty, and I knew the appeal's officer wouldn't overthrow it. He's out two more games before he can play, only to be teased with the playoffs, having to watch them from the bench. It's a crueler punishment than it sounds.

What does shock me are the people following him out. Dani and her fucking kid, Jameson and Ortiz, then the whole team crowding him in the parking lot, gathering around and patting him on the back.

I've been away for a while, but what fucking alternate dimension have I walked into? I guess that's what happens when I decide to give him space—to give myself time—and spend my suspension with my little girl. I come back to a fucking shitstorm.

Then my fucking jaw hits my chest when I see *my* Marian walking out with her arm through Coach's, and they're fucking laughing. Does Dixon not see what's brewing there? Does he want Dani as his step-sister?

I rub my hand over my mouth, trying to put it back into place as I absorb the chaotic gathering in front of me.

"This is all the way fucked-up."

So because everything is fucked, I pull a J out from the console between the front seats and wet the paper inside my mouth. I need some of the good shit right now or else I may just lose my temper. Besides, it'll help with this raging fucking headache that's been ripping through my skull.

Seeing this shit doesn't help.

I'm jealous, I can admit it. I have the cock and balls to call myself out. I want to get out of this vehicle, walk right up to him and show everyone who he really wants there with him. But the fact of the matter is, I'm not so sure about that.

The way I treated him in that hotel room was wrong, even if I can list all the right reasons for it. It was because he loves me, that's ultimately why Fernando is dead, and even though it's a morbid way of looking at it, it's the truth.

And that's why I've stayed away from him: our love has dire consequences.

There's no need for me to be here, he has people surrounding him, and I'm sure my presence would do nothing but make him feel worse. That's what we do to each other even though we've confessed our love.

Toxic love, all-consuming, poisonous love.

Besides, my presence would be a hazard to him if certain people found out he was my weakness, the people who want to shut me up for good.

I flick open my Zippo to bring the flame to the tip of my J, letting that first long pull settle deep in my lungs. It's been forever since I've taken a hit, let alone smoked one by myself.

My ass slips down into the seat, keeping my eye on the crowd as they console Dixon. I choke on the smoke as I finally exhale then chuckle at the sound. Choking on weed means it's a good hit, and I can't help but enjoy it.

I take another hit as Dixon shakes Coach's hand then breaks

away, Marian following close behind him. His shoulders are tipped forward with the weight of dejection, but when he looks up, I see his eyes narrowed with determination.

This isn't the end, I know him well enough to see that, but it makes me nervous not knowing just how far he's going to take it. He and Marian pull out of the stadium's lot, and I wait for everyone else to follow suit as I finish up my spliff, tossing the roach out the window.

My eyes focus back on the Bills Stadium as I let the effects of the weed slip me out of my worries. I'll be back here tomorrow, playing the first game since my suspension, and I wonder if Dixon will be here to watch.

Throughout practice and the actual game, Dixon never showed, and I kept watch on Coach's face to see if he was pissed. He looked normal. None of it felt right, like something is going on, yet I know nothing about it. Dixon hasn't left the team—Coach would have to make a big announcement—yet he's not here for practices or games.

The guys have all spread out, heading for the showers, leaving me with Zeal in the locker room.

"Good game tonight, Avando," he grins. "We killed those Texans."

"Yeah." I glance around us then cross my arms over my chest. "Where's North?"

"He's spending time at home. After the rejection from the league, he's been keeping a low profile."

"That doesn't piss Coach off?" I shift my weight, leaning back against the lockers.

"Nah," Zeal shakes his head. "He comes to work out in the mornings most days. If you came by, you'd know that."

"I was with Carla."

"I know," he pats my back. "Family is most important."

He's off to the showers just as Jameson comes out, a wide smile climbing his mouth.

"What's so funny?" I give him a once over. He's lost a bit of weight.

"I have a date with my son's mother."

The urge to say something nasty hits the tip of my tongue, but I manage to swallow it back. "How's the kid?"

"He's growing so fast." Pride shines through his eyes. "He's gonna be like his daddy."

"Can I ask you something?"

"Yeah, sure," he shrugs, grabbing his clothes from his locker.

"Have you given him anymore?" He knows what I'm speaking about because he quickly scans the room around him.

"Nah." He swallows thickly. "He says he doesn't need it anymore."

"Cool."

I'm proud of Dixon for fighting the need to pump his knee with drugs to play a game that's currently punishing him for defending himself.

For defending me.

Dixon

Sweat drips from my brow as I increase the weight on the elliptical I purchased for the gym room in my basement. Working out here isn't the same as the stadium because I don't have a fucking sauna, but I can't seem to bring myself to go there, knowing how hard I was let down.

I knew I would most likely be denied, even after I pleaded my case, and technically my secret was out. It doesn't matter anyway. Seeing that stadium will only serve to piss me off, and then to also see a certain honey eyed man in its confines would tip me over the edge.

Once my legs feel like Jell-O, I make my way back upstairs, groaning as my muscles protest the stairs. I walk into the kitchen, and the strong scent of perfume has me looking around in confusion.

"Ma?" I call out to the seemingly empty house.

"Yes?" She saunters into the kitchen, her hands clasping a dangling earring to her lobe, her hair free of its usual bun.

"Are you wearing lipstick?"

"Dixon," she clicks her tongue, looking at me. She *is* wearing lipstick. "I'm going out."

"Where to? And with whom?"

"Dixon North," she chastises, her eyes widening like she's surprised. "Did I question you while you were out doing God knows what with floozies?"

"It was only one floozy," I mumble, straightening up with realization. "Are you going out to do God knows what with someone?"

"I am a grown woman." She gives me a small smile as she pulls on a blue cardigan.

"That's your nice church sweater!" I exclaim. "Do you have a date?"

"Yes." That small smile stays on her mouth. "As a matter of

fact, I do."

"With who?" I feel like my eyes are going to pop out of my skull if they get any wider.

"Gregory."

"Coach?!" My startled shriek resounds around the room, and she has the audacity to roll her eyes. "Ma! He's my coach!"

"He's a sweet man—"

"Do you know what you just said about that sweet man's daughter?" I butt in.

"I think you should call Sebastian. You've been moping around the house, and you could deal with a date yourself."

"Do not change the subject." I wag my finger at her. "You are not dating my coach."

"I've stayed true to your father's ghost for many years, son. I think it's time I move on, and like I said, he's a good man."

"I can't believe this," I grip my neck as she comes and kisses my cheek.

"I love you. Don't wait up."

I groan at her statement as she heads to the front door, chuckling at my obvious discomfort.

"Call me if you need anything," I call out as she opens the door.

She waves then shuts it behind her, the loud click echoing throughout the empty house.

My phone pings, drawing me out of shock as I pull it out of my pocket. I know it's not him, he hasn't tried to contact me at all, so at this point, I know we're done.

Dex: Poker night at Zeal's!

I've been avoiding the stadium, but I haven't been wanting to avoid the guys. So a poker night sounds good. It'll be a much needed distraction from everything I have weighing heavy on my mind. I'm terrible at poker, so it's a sure bet that I'll lose money, but I like how it brings us together.

My mind automatically slips to thoughts of Seb, and I wonder if he'll be there. He hasn't come to the previous ones, but he's back in town, and maybe he'll want to see me. Not that he's given me that indication, and I haven't tried to find out, but I can't help thinking about him.

You don't just wipe out the person you love.

I climb out of my vehicle after parking at the curb, smiling when I hear the music pumping inside Zeal's house, knowing the boys have long started before I got here. Maybe with them drunk, I can manage to win a fucking game.

The vehicles crowding his driveway are all familiar, especially the one sitting at the back. Seeing the Hummer makes me pause, my heart nearly tripping over my ribs and my breaths straining through my nose as I try to control them.

Seb is here.

I don't know how the hell I'm going to be able to stand being in the same room as him and not beg him to let everything go, to take me back. My throat tightens as I decide it's not worth it. I'm not ready to put myself through that torture.

I turn to head back to my SUV when I hear the front door open behind me, music flooding the street.

"North!" Zeal calls out. "I saw you on the cameras while I was getting a beer. Aren't you coming in?"

"Fuck," I mumble, taking a deep breath. "Yeah," I shout back. "Just need to grab my phone."

The door closes as I get back to my SUV, cursing myself for looking like a fucking idiot. Thankfully, it was just Zeal who saw me because he seemed too drunk to notice I already had my phone in my hand.

Or he's letting me have this small lie without calling me out. He's that type of guy.

Once I collect myself, swallowing down the fear coating every inch of me, I head back to the house. I can't be like this forever. We have to work together, so we need to be civil. Regardless of how much my heart will forever long for him.

When I step into the house, my ears are immediately assaulted by the sounds of Dr. Dre and Tupac's "California Love", making me chuckle because this is all Dex.

The ceiling in the foyer is a good thirty feet high, and I stare up at it, the wisping design on its surface nearly hypnotizing me.

"Bro," Ortiz's voice draws me out of my state. "Are you stoned?"

He has a small smirk on his mouth, and one eyebrow inches up toward his black, curling hair.

"Nah." I step forward to clasp his outstretched hand. "Just admiring this man's house."

"Zeal likes his shit fancy," he chuckles then hauls me in for a hug. "We've been missing you."

"Thanks, man" I pat his back. "Now tell me, how drunk is Dex? "California Love" is a sign he's feeling good."

"I think he said "Too Close" by Next is up after this."

"Shit," I shake my head. "We're in for a long night."

"The two new rookies are here too." He juts his chin toward the sounds of grown men whining. "One of them knows how to wipe the table clean. He's been taking everyone's money tonight. Except for Avando's. You know how he gets when he's being challenged."

As soon as the words tumble from his mouth, I watch his eyes widen in horror, realizing what he just said.

"It's all good." I pat his shoulder. "Water under the bridge. I doubt he's doing the same to them. Or is that what all the whining I hear is about?"

I'm proud of the steady tone of my voice, not a hitch or break as I try to keep my insides together at the picture I just painted. I would kill all three of them.

In a heartbeat.

"I'm sorry," Ortiz sputters as I smile.

"We're good."

I head into the dining room where I know I'll find them all crowded around Zeal's twenty seat table. Where I'll keep this smile plastered to my face as I pretend my world isn't imploding.

That's exactly how I find them, Zeal at the head with what looks to be beer funnels on his head, and Seb to his right, his tongue out, wagging at the rookie across from him as he gathers the chips from the center of the table.

I watch him closely and wonder if he's cheating somehow.

"North!" Dex's booming voice calls out, and everyone reacts.

Except the one I want. He doesn't acknowledge me as he stacks his chips, but I don't miss the tight set of his jaw.

"This looks like it's getting expensive," I whistle as they laugh. "I can't afford these stakes. I have a hefty fine to pay."

Show me something.

"You can come sit on Daddy's knee," Dex pats his leg, "and let me show you how it's done."

The murderous glare Seb sends Dex is fucking amusing. I bark out a laugh when no one notices.

"You barely have any chips left in front of you." I continue to laugh. "Why the hell would I learn from you?"

"Does that mean you're not sitting on my lap?"

"Someone get him some water. He's way past his limit," I chuckle as everyone joins in the laughter.

"That's it for me tonight, guys," Seb stands. "I need to get some sleep."

"Ew." Zeal crinkles his nose then shakes his head. "What's

wrong with you?"

"Too sober," Seb grins, making them all laugh.

He fucking lies so effortlessly. He's leaving because I showed up. A part of me rejoices in the fact that I still affect him, but a bigger part caves in, threatening to take me down with it.

"Thanks for paying my rent for the month, though." He points to the rookie at the table as I crash my teeth together. "I will be collecting."

His words are covered in smooth velvet, and I fist my hands at my sides. He's doing it on purpose. Then he shrugs on his jacket and gives everyone a nod. He slips his hands in his pockets and moves by me, careful not to touch any part of my body as he heads for the door.

Everyone goes back to the game. With the noise once again nearly drowning out the music, I follow him. I need answers, and he can't avoid them forever.

I catch up as he opens the front door, his body stiffening like he can sense me behind him.

"Don't," his voice cracks on the word, and I can hear his heartbreak.

"You're leaving because I showed up." It's not a question because I already know the answer.

"How's your mom?" He finally looks at me over his shoulder as I choke on a laugh.

"Are you seriously asking about my mother right now?"

"Have a good night, North."

I watch with shock as he disappears into the night, closing the door behind him.

Oh, fuck no.

I stride forward to yank the door open just as he steps down from the porch, slamming it shut behind me.

"Still a fucking brat," I hear him growl, and it evaporates some of my anger.

"I'm sorry," I blurt out to his back, making him stop mid step then turn to look at me with confusion. "I've caused you a lot of trouble when all you've ever done is try to protect me and my family."

"Dixon, go back inside."

"I need to say this in case you never speak to me again." I hold up my hand to stop him from cutting me off. "Thank you for what you did for Daniel."

His eyes soften before he looks to his feet, pulling his wallet out of his back pocket. He flips it open to pull out a card that looks all too familiar, and I work not to choke on a sob.

"This is yours." He steps forward to hand me the card.

I look down into my baby brother's face and see everything I ever worked for shining in his angry eyes.

"So that's it, then?" I cringe at the sulking sound of my voice.

He goes to the Hummer and opens the door, giving me one final look. "I'll see you at the stadium."

And that's it. That's all I needed to hear to know this is over. He only wants to see me when we're playing football, and suddenly, it's the last thing I want to do.

CHAPTER NINETEEN

Dixon

The date is set for the night after my first game back with the Bills. That's next Sunday, six days away. The thought of how much my life will change after that scares me, but at the same time, I want to make sure every player knows the consequences of letting their mouths speak before their brain can process the words.

This league is no longer the most important thing in my life. My family is, and I don't care if I lose my position on the team. It'd be worth it.

The front door opens, and I see her outline from the porch light, the sight making me bite into my cheek. Her hair is messy, not the same coiffed curls she left here with, and is her blouse undone at the top?

I flick on the lamp beside me, watching her startle, her hand flying to her chest.

"You scared me!" Ma exclaims.

"Do you realize what time it is?" My voice is even with just a hint of disappointment. I learned it from her.

"Dixon North." She puts her hands to her hips. "I am a grown woman."

"Do you know what it looks like when you come home at nearly eleven at night, and you look like that?" I point to her blouse then nearly lose it, laughing hysterically when she gasps at her open shirt.

"I was enjoying time with a gentleman." She drops her purse, walking over to where I'm sitting. "Get over it."

"I'll kill him if he hurts you," I vow as she slaps the side of my head.

"Don't say things like that."

I grab her hand to give it a squeeze. Internally, I'm glad that she's so happy. Then I get up and follow her up the stairs. She turns to the right and heads down the hallway to her room, humming a tune as she goes. I turn to the left and stifle a yawn into my hand. She's worse than a teenager.

It's Halloween, and we're up against the Dolphins tonight, one of the teams I've idolized since I was a kid. But I can't even enjoy it because I'm too focused on what's happening afterward.

Coach knows, and he's about to let everyone else in on it while we sit here in the locker room, waiting for the start of the game.

We're all back together as a team, and I can feel the excitement around me, but I just can't bring myself to feel the same. I'm nervous about what comes since it will determine where my career goes.

"All right, everyone," Coach calls out, waiting to have all of our attention. "Tonight we're up against the Dolphins, and we're a full team once again."

Dex claps me on the back as a few of the other guys give me nods.

"Dixon has more than the game to worry about tonight as he's decided to hold a press conference here afterward. As you know, his appeal for the playoff suspension was denied, and he feels there are a few things he needs to get off his chest. He has my full support in doing so."

I can feel that familiar, inky gaze and turn to find Seb watching me with curiosity. If he hadn't been avoiding me, he would know all about it.

"Are we allowed to attend the press conference?" Zeal asks.

"Any of you who want to be there for Dixon can do so at the back of the room. We have a few big sports networks coming in, and I want him to be the focal point, not the whole team."

Once Coach signals that he's done, we all gather in a huddle, and we listen as Zeal gives us a pep talk, telling us that no matter what happens out there, we are always family in here. Then we're heading out of the room, slapping each other's helmets and running out onto the field amidst the roar of the fans.

This feeling of being loved and appreciated for what we do is the only part of the game I still crave, it feeds into my ego.

"What's this press conference about?" His gravelly voice comes up beside me, and I turn to find Seb's worried eyes on me.

"Have a good game." I slap his helmet then run toward Zeal.

He doesn't get to dictate when and how we talk to each other, it's time he realized that. I have accepted this thing between us has fizzled out, and I no longer crumble at his feet when he speaks, but it feels like the ache in my heart will never completely dissipate.

The Dolphins have the first ball, so we pop Dex right up at the front, depending on him to carve out the path to it.

"Simple defense, boys," Zeal tells us. "Push them back, and don't let them penetrate."

Jameson and Dex bang their helmets together since this is their play. Our biggest guys are ready to plow through some bodies. This is my favorite part of the game, watching them use their brute strength to ward off the offense and get us back the ball.

The play is called, and I watch as our boys go into action, keeping back the Dolphins with ease. They don't make it past the ten-yard line, making me exhale a long, relieved breath. The next play is called, and I chuckle when I see Dex Carver clap his hands to his thighs. He's on his game tonight.

The crowd is chanting for us, their energy is potent like a crack of lightning, and they never fail to hype us up. The Buffalo Bills have some of the greatest fans, calling themselves the Bills Mafia, and they're definitely here tonight.

The ball is hiked, then the Dolphins QB throws it to the wide receiver who fumbles it. We all gasp a bated breath, screaming in triumph when Jameson lands on it, claiming it for us.

Now it's time to really take this shit home.

It's the fourth period, and my knee is starting to act up, but that's not all… Seb is looking a bit off. He's been running slower than usual, his feet stumbling a few times to catch up with Zeal's throws. I could boil it down to exhaustion, we're all there with him, but it's not like him at all.

I worry about drugs, maybe the lure of feeling nothing won over his need to stay clean. Maybe it's the concussions… That worries me even more.

"Zeal." I grab his arm, signaling to Coach for a timeout.

"What's up, North?" he pants with his hands at his waist.

"Seb isn't looking too hot."

His eyes trail over my shoulder, squinting with scrutiny. "He is a bit pale."

"His speed is off too. I'm worried about his head."

His eyes come back to mine, and I see the questions in their depths, but luckily, he keeps his thoughts to himself as he nods. "All right, let me ask Coach to bench him for the rest of the game."

"Subtly, though? Please?"

His hand hits the back of my helmet, and he gives me a quick nod, running over to Coach. With time dwindling down, I begin to pace, my shoes digging into the green grass of the field. If I look at him right now, he'll know this was my doing, and I don't want to have to deal with an irate Seb. Not before this press conference. My nerves are frayed enough as it is.

"All right, guys!" Zeal comes back, gathering in the first string. "We've got this game in the bag."

We do. Every point on that board belongs to us, and it's a sure win.

"I want to keep them at zero. Think we can do it?"

The guys roar around me as my eyes find Seb who rips off his helmet as he strides back to the locker room, not even sticking around to watch us finish this off. I return my focus to the team and to the field. It's the last play before my whole life changes.

Seb isn't my main focus.

For once.

Sebastian

The guys come running back to the locker room, rowdy and full of energy. Having won a game without letting the opposing team put a single point on the board will do that.

It would've been nice to be there, but Zeal called me out for exhaustion. I guess I should be lucky that was all, my head hasn't been right for the past few days. The nausea and vertigo have worsened. It's gotten so bad that I may need to tell Coach.

"Avando!" Dex booms, the sound feeling like a mallet connecting with my skull. "We fucking did it, bro!"

I try my best to give him a smile, but the pain is quickly working itself down to the base of my skull, radiating thick waves of torture.

"Seb." Dixon's voice pulls me out of my internal agony. I look up to see him staring at me in concern. "Headache?"

I want to shrug him off, to tell him to get the fuck away from me, but my mouth doesn't comply with my brain. I fucking miss him.

"Yeah." My face drops down into my hands. "I'm okay."

"You should get home—"

"Yeah," I cut him off, not wanting to hear his concern. Not wanting to feel any hope.

There is none, not until this shit clears up, and there doesn't seem to be a chance of that happening any time soon.

He backs off after that, and I understand why… He's in his own head about the press conference he called. Everything about it is giving me bad vibes, so I'm concerned for him too. I can't go home yet because I need to see what it's about.

I don't know how much more stress I can take, to be honest. I'm already teetering on the edge of sanity, and my head is in a constant state of torture, making me feel more irrational with each passing day.

There was a brief article in the Rochester Sentinel about Delano's death. A small column detailing a murder and possible break in, leaving out anything of real importance. The Feds are for sure running that case since he was one of their own.

Reading it only served to bring me back into the feelings I was trying to suppress. That was when my current headache started. At first, it was nothing too terrible, just a nuisance, until a few hours later when I was throwing up everything I ate.

Days of nausea, lack of sleep, and constant pain has brought me to the point of extreme fatigue and hallucinations. I zone out constantly, and I'm right back there, in Delano's backyard. My gun is cocked and pressed to his forehead, the unsteady shake of my hand relaying my internal battle.

Or I watch as Paola's head snaps back, blood hitting our pristine white surfaces, the crimson color stark as it drips to the floor.

It's hard enough to deal with those images, but then there's the ones of Dixon and me. In my house after the last concussion, on the bus ride home from Cincinnati, and always ending with him inside that hotel bathroom with my cock in his hand.

Those memories hurt the most because he's right there in front of me, ready to be claimed, yet I can't do a single thing about it.

Dixon heads to the showers, his chin to his chest with his shoulders bent forward, all signs of a heavy mind. It only adds to my worry about what he plans to announce tonight. Could he be retiring after a year of playing for the league? I wouldn't blame him. In this single year, he's endured more than some seasoned players.

"What do you think it's about?" Ortiz sits beside me.

"I don't know, man." I begin to shake my head, hissing through a bout of vertigo.

"Are you okay?" He looks into my face, worry etched through his features. "Is it your head?"

"Just tired." I avoid his eyes as I scan the locker room. It looks like the whole team is going to stay behind to hear what Dixon has to say and to show their support.

Which makes me fucking nervous.

He's made it no secret to me how he feels about this career. It was always meant to be for his family, regardless of the talent he possesses. His hard work and determination were based on pulling his family out of the rough streets of Baltimore, to give them a life he felt they deserved.

Now that Daniel is dead, he's changed. I can see it in the way his laser focus has deteriorated. The Dixon North I knew last year would never have jumped the scrimmage line to beat the shit out of someone for using a homophobic slur. He had too much at stake then.

"Coach seems nervous," Ortiz mumbles. I look up to find Coach pacing the locker room, his hand wrapped around his chin.

"Yeah, a bit." My stomach flips with nerves, and I'm happy I didn't eat today for fear of it coming back up out on the field.

Seeing Coach like that—more than a bit nervous—is sending my heart into a quick drumming beat, the sound pounding throughout my ears.

"This conference is about something big. Do you know

anything about it?" Ortiz continues to speak, the sound of his words crashing through my head like cymbals.

"Why the fuck would I know anything?" I stand, heading to my locker.

"Because you two seem close," he shrugs.

I grab the back of his neck, bending down next to his ear. "Watch it."

He's suggesting something, and by the way he stiffens, he knows I'm catching on. I release him then head to the showers, my aching body and throbbing head needing the relief of the hot water.

It would be a few hours later when I found myself sitting in hot water again.

CHAPTER TWENTY

Dixon

Coach is sitting beside me at the long table along with a few of his assistant coaches and our publicity manager. I twirl the water bottle in front of me and question for the millionth time today if I'm doing the right thing. It feels right, and that's all I'm riding on right now… Gut instinct.

If I don't do this, nothing will change in the league. Hell, maybe after today nothing will change, but at least I'll have said my part. I will never go to bed regretting not stepping up to the plate. This is my chance to say everything I need to before finding the best way for me and my family to move on.

Coach is nervous, I can see the perspiration along his brow and the rigid set of his lips. I give him a once over and try to see what it is my mother finds so attractive. Maybe it's the dark color of his eyes or the way his nose turns up slightly at the end.

I don't see it, but there's something there that has her coming home at all hours of the damn night. I want to call him out on it but figure I'll wait until this is out of the way. Less chance of him suffering a heart attack from stress. Ma would kill me right after.

Are they in love?

Fucking gross.

Coach clears his throat into the mic as all the reporters take their seats. A few of my teammates line the back wall, but I refuse to look at them. I will lose my nerve if I see them watching me.

"Tonight we are here at the request of Dixon North. He's asked me to start by giving you all a brief overview of what has transpired during and after his suspension by the league."

Murmurs rise throughout the room, and the back of my neck grows hot with fear. Am I doing the right thing?

"He served part of his penalty with ease and understanding. Six games and the fine felt like a proper sentence for the actions he showcased on the field. As most of you know, that wasn't all of his penalty. He also has to sit out for this season's playoffs. That's where he feels like maybe the punishment exceeds the severity of his actions."

He clears his throat again, looking around at the faces of the reporters as some begin to raise their hands.

"We will take questions after Dixon has spoken."

The weight of everyone's stare and the heat of the lights set up around the room make me feel like I may pass out. My heart is pounding as my hand presses against my rolling stomach, taking a deep breath.

"My lifelong ambition was to make it to the NFL and to be the best player I could possibly be. I had a family I wanted to succeed for, so I worked hard to pull us out of an impoverished area of Baltimore. My mother raised me well and instilled morals that I have carried with me right up to this moment as I sit in front of you."

I take a drink of the water in front of me, using the time to articulate everything I want to say. It has taken me weeks to memorize it, and I had it down word for word. Yet in this moment, my mind is drawing blanks. It's only when I take a deep breath and stop overthinking that the words suddenly flow unencumbered.

"Respect was something my brother and I learned at an early age. We were taught to respect our elders, our friends, our family, and coworkers. That's how I see every player in this league, they are my coworkers. I forgot about respect during our game against the Packers, so I felt like a six game suspension and the fine were suitable consequences. The only part of my penalty that felt like a kick in the stomach were those playoff games I would have to be benched for. It was almost like an extra bit of punishment for sticking up for what I believed was wrong."

The room fades out as I release a breath, willing my heart to calm as I clasp my hands together to keep them from trembling.

"Any slur used on the field is a direct violation of the Code of Conduct, and it should be treated as unsportsman-like behavior. My coworker, Dillon James, was in violation that day when he repeatedly taunted a teammate with a homophobic slur. It was loud and boisterous, there's no way an official didn't hear it, yet it was ignored. It proved to me that certain slurs are upheld under the violation list, while being a homophobe and taunting others with those biases is okay."

The room once again erupts with gasps and murmured conversations. It's been no secret that taunting was the cause of the fight that day, but the league has been careful not to let too much information slip. They don't want their valuable players labeled as racist or homophobes which wouldn't be good for profits.

"I was also raised to protect those who can't protect themselves. To use any platform I acquire to bring awareness to causes worthy of our attention. So that's why I'm here in front of you today, to tell you and everyone watching that sexuality does not determine a player's worth on the field. It's not an attribute or characteristic that can be suppressed or modified. No one should feel afraid to be who they were born to be."

Pens begin to furiously write onto papers, and recording devices position a bit closer as I draw to the end of my speech.

"I'm not doing this in hopes of overturning my appeal decision. I understand it's final, and I will not be participating in this season's playoffs. I'm doing this because someone had to. I'm not making this grand speech to accuse anyone in this league of not doing enough, I understand all too well the fear of losing your position because you pissed off the wrong person."

Gasps ring out, and I feel Coach's eyes boring into the side of my face. The NFL commissioner will not be happy to hear that.

"I don't want my sexuality or the sexuality of my teammates to determine the type of respect we deserve or which parts of the Code of Conduct apply to us. We all deserve to be treated equally and fairly, and sexuality has no place inside our locker rooms. We're adults, let's begin to act like it."

People stand and applaud, some more enthusiastically than others. My teammates stand there, cheering me on, but I'm not paying attention to any of that. It's the movement at the back of the room catches my attention, Seb's disappearing form through the door crushing the elation I was feeling.

Once everyone settles back down, I lay both hands on the table and lean in closer to my mic.

"I am doing this solely of my own volition, and no one knew the reasons for my calling this press conference beforehand. I know the foundation of this league is strongly built on the masculinity of a man and how skillful he is on the field. I'm just hoping I can start the right conversations to end all phobias while playing the game we love."

I sit back in my seat as everyone claps again, then Coach leans forward, his skin a bit paler. This is new territory for the league, I understand his fear. I feel it too. "Questions will be limited, and this should go without saying… Any questions deemed unsuitable will be ignored."

The stares are intense. I can feel them from my teammates as we crowd around inside the locker room. I turn while lifting my duffle bag over my shoulder to give them all a tentative smile.

"You have questions?" I ask, watching as a few of them shift on their feet. "You want to know if I'm gay?"

They look at one another, and it's no surprise when Zeal steps forward. "No. I mean," his hand swipes over the top of his hair. "I don't care about your sexuality. I want to know if we as a team are doing the things you asked out there. Is there something I can do to make it better?"

"We're good," I nod, my eyes skipping over to Jameson and Ortiz. "We're good."

They're forgiven, they've long been forgiven. How can I hold a grudge against them when my hatred for Seb dissipated?

I leave the stadium with adrenaline coursing through me. My teammates are accepting of more, and I am elated to be the catalyst of that. Maybe I'll have a target on my back now, but it was worth it, even if all it serves is to relieve the burden I'd felt weighing on my chest.

When I get home, I find my mother standing at the top of our driveway, her face stretched wide with a smile. The pride I see radiating from her eyes makes it all worth it too.

I get out just as she barrels into me, her face pressed to my chest and her shoulders shaking with emotion.

"I am so proud of you, son." She hugs me tighter.

"You watched it?" I ask as she pulls away.

"Oh, yes. Every second of it. You were so well-spoken, and you looked enlightened up there."

"Thanks, Ma." I drape my arm over her shoulders as we walk inside.

"Was he there?"

I know who she means by *he*. "In the beginning."

"Come in." She closes the door behind us. "I made us dinner."

A few hours later, after my shower, I fall onto my bed and stare up at the ceiling. None of what I've started has fully hit me yet. When I go back over the conference, it feels like a dream. I'm proud of what I've done, I can rest a bit easier.

I hear the gate open at the end of the driveway, and I get up from bed to see who it is. Of course, it's my mother, slipping out into the night for a secret rendezvous with my coach.

"Fuck," I groan as I scrub my hand down my face. This is something I'm going to have to get used to. She's obviously into the guy.

I think it also gives her a fix, providing her with the grandchild she's been wanting. Baby James has become a gurgling, drooling kid, and she doesn't stop talking about him. I don't know what my future holds, so reassuring her about grandchildren is impossible.

My eyes drift close, and I can feel myself giving into sleep.

What sounds like my front door opening and shutting has me startling awake. I grab my phone to squint at the time. It's only been an hour since Ma left. It couldn't be her, but there's no mistaking the sounds of someone making their way up my stairs.

I roll out of bed, creep toward my bedroom door, and peek out around the wooden slab, coming face to face with Seb.

"The fuck?" He gives me an amused look when I startle.

"How you just gonna walk up into someone's house without ringing the doorbell? How the fuck did you get by the gate?" I fire off questions as he pushes by me into my room.

"Oh, the gate that was left open by your mother when she sped out of here."

Fuck.

She's been leaving it open too often lately and I was too tired to double check it this evening.

"What are you doing here?" I ask as I drop back to the bed, my eyes heavy with exhaustion. "I don't have the energy to fight or whatever it is you're here to do."

Sebastian

He's a sight for sore eyes, and the longer I stand here watching him, the harder it is to stay away. I knew I shouldn't have come.

"Seb," He groans.

It's always been a weakness, the way he says my name, but tonight is different, like no matter how long we've been apart, the familiarity is still there.

"Do you feel better?" I ask him the question that's been bogging my mind. "Do you feel like you've accomplished something?"

He quickly straightens at my questions then narrows his eyes at me.

"Don't do that," I point at his face. "These are legit questions. Tell me, are you completely prepared for the shit that's about to rain down on you?"

"Sure." The brat fucking *shrugs* like this isn't a big deal.

"Dixon—"

"Seb, I knew what the consequences were, okay? I still did it. And yes, I feel better." His palm slaps his chest as his eyes begin to pool. "I no longer want to waste my energy on pretending to be something I'm not."

"So what?" I snicker. "You're about to come out of the closet?"

"No!" he balks. "I'm not in a closet, Seb. That's the whole point. I am who I am."

"And what's that?" I taunt him, stepping closer. "What are you?"

"Whatever the fuck I want to be whenever the fuck I want to be it."

The strength and determination bursting from his eyes has me swallowing down my sarcastic reply. I don't want to burst his bubble just yet, I'd rather he soaks in what he feels is a victory for a bit longer.

"What are you doing here?" he asks again, making my jaw clamp shut.

I round his bed, walking over to the sliding door which leads to the balcony attached. I want to tell him exactly why I'm here, but I'm fearful of his reaction. I step outside and breathe in the fresh air.

Today a sting operation brought down some heavy hitters in the Federal Bureau of Investigations. Men and women who were tied to large drug distribution rings, and not just in the Tri-State area. I've been cleared of all suspicions, and the final man standing in the death of my wife is now behind bars. I've been breathing a bit easier today, but my nerves have been building when I think about Dixon.

But any relief I felt was short lived as something more pressing hinders it. I've scheduled an appointment with a specialist about the severity of my headaches. Knowing something is wrong is all that's holding me back from what I want now.

That has always been Dixon North.

Am I too late? Does he still love me?

"Seb, you're kind of freaking me out." His soft voice hits the back of my neck as he steps out onto the balcony behind me.

I turn to lean back against the railing, raking my gaze over his face and body. With dark scruff lining his cheeks, he looks older. The dark brown of his eyes are glistening under the moonlight which is illuminating his skin and making my heart flip with so much fucking emotion.

The most emotion I've ever felt.

The most *love* I've ever felt.

"What does that look mean, Seb?" He motions to my face, and the way his voice cracks with unease makes me feel like a fucking piece of shit. "The last time you looked at me like that, you told me you loved me, and then you left me."

I deserve that, and I open my mouth to say it when he raises his hand.

"I can't keep doing this." His mouth trembles as a tear slips from those dark eyes. "I don't know how many times I can let you break my heart."

"I'm sorr—"

"Is this all we'll ever be? Hidden behind closed doors and pretending like nothing is going on while in public?"

He steps into me, our chests brushing with each breath, his fingers tracing along my jaw.

"I don't know," I answer him honestly because I'm all out of lies.

"Then make this count, Avando. It'll be the last time."

Before I can protest, he's grabbing my face and dragging me into him. Our mouths collide in a frantic kiss, our teeth clashing and our tongues lapping into each other's mouths. He tastes like home.

He pulls me back into his room and breaks our kiss just long enough to rip his shirt over his head, motioning for me to undress.

"Dixon."

"Not now, Seb." He works on the string of his track pants. "Shut up and fuck me or get out."

My dick jumps to attention at the harsh sound of his words. This must be how he feels when I rip into him. Which I literally plan to do. If this is the last time he'll have me, then I'm not leaving until I've ruined him for anyone else.

I pull the lube out of my pocket and toss it on the bed behind him, his eyes trailing the small tube. "You came prepared."

"Fuck yeah, I did." I drop my pants around my ankles then kick them aside. "I plan on owning that ass multiple times."

"Not before I own yours." His brows jump up as I stop and stare at him. "That's right, Seb. Tonight, I'm fucking you too."

My cock is painfully hard and throbbing at his words, but my asshole squeezes with hesitation. He's had me before, in the same shower stall I forced myself on him in the locker room, and it was rough. Unyielding. It hurt, but it was the most exquisite pain I've ever endured.

"Scared?" he taunts as his hand wraps around the thick girth of his cock. The sight of it makes my mouth water, so far on the other side of the spectrum from fear.

Two steps bring our chests together, and as he leans forward to kiss me, I drop to my knees. There's no way I'm leaving here tonight without the taste of him lingering on my tongue. If this is truly it, I want it all.

I push his hand away and wrap my own around his length, giving him a rough stroke. I look up in time to see his mouth open and his head tipped back as a blissful sigh escapes him. The column of his throat works as I jerk him from base to tip again, and I grin, knowing it'll be choking on my cock very soon.

I don't hesitate with tentative licks, I devour him swiftly down my throat, gagging around him, needing to feel the punishment.

"Fuck," he hisses as he looks down at me gagging with each pull.

I release him, leaving the tip sitting against my bottom lip. "Is that all you got, North?" I tease. "Little mewls?"

His eyes narrow with determination as he grabs the sides of my head. "You asked for it."

I open my mouth wide, giving him the room he needs to fuck my throat, then he does exactly that. Long, quick thrusts have the head of his cock jamming against the back of my throat, the sounds of my gagging loud in the confines of his room.

"Like this?" he continues to goad. "Is this how you like it?"

I nod up at him as tears course down my cheeks. My lungs scream for a breath, and my throat is sore from the force of my gags. But yes, this is exactly what I wanted.

He moans, the sound I know so well, signaling he's close to his end, but he quickly pulls out. I take in a choking breath and look up at him, wondering why he stopped.

"I don't want to come in your throat," he explains as he grabs the lube. "I told you, I'll be having your ass first."

I stand on shaking legs, my heart beating a mile a minute as I pull off my boxers, standing in front of him fully naked.

"On the bed, Seb. All fours."

This is a first, to have myself completely open and spread for him, letting him fuck me in a way I've always thought was wrong. I'm the man, I do the fucking. But clearly, I was the one who was wrong.

My hands grip his bedsheets as I fall forward, preparing to crawl up onto the bed when I hear his sharp intake of breath.

"Actually, just stay there." His voice sounds filled with awe.

His hand lands between my shoulder blades, prompting me forward until my chest hits the bed, and my ass is perked up into the air. My heart climbs up into my throat as I wait for the first touch.

It's the lube I feel first as he squeezes the cool liquid on my hole, the shock of it making me lock my knees.

"Relax," he coos. "Show me this pretty pussy."

With a snort, I bury my face into the bed, groaning into the fabric when his finger pushes inside me.

"She's tight."

"Dixon," I growl, popping my head up to look over my shoulder at him. "Stop playing, you brat."

"Okay, Daddy." He gives me a grin as I hear him applying lube to his cock, the slick noises crowding around us.

"I swear to God—"

My breath is knocked from my lungs as my words get cut off by the feel of him pushing inside of me. He doesn't relent, just keeps forcing my asshole to eat his length, inch by agonizing inch.

It's painful, so fucking uncomfortable, but to be connected to him like this makes up for all of it. Feeling him inside me, working my hole wider, makes me clench around him, forcing a hiss from my mouth.

"Hurts?" He throws my favorite taunt back at me.

"So good," I groan as he bottoms out, his cock throbbing inside of me, and I feel every single inch of him.

His fingers grab my ass cheeks, and he spreads me open,

probably looking down to where we're connected. It's what I love to do when the roles are reversed. The sight must spur him on because he begins to really fuck me, the force of his thrusts sending my head into the mattress.

"This is better than pussy," he grunts, making me fucking preen at his words. "Tighter, warmer, and the slight hint of blood makes it look like I'm taking a virgin."

Blood?

I don't have much time to ponder further because he's ramming in full strength without apology, claiming what he wants and making sure it's something to remember.

I clench the sheets as pain mixed with pleasure courses through me, not wanting him to stop for the life of me.

"I'm about to fill this tight asshole," he declares.

Two thrusts more have him slamming it home, gripping the globes of my ass with intensity as he shouts my name. I feel every hot spurt, every jerk of his cock, and I commit it all to memory.

Nothing will ever top this moment.

He pulls out, leaving me feeling empty. I stand slowly and wince as pain radiates from behind me.

"Don't clean it," he demands. "I want you to feel it drip out of you as you fuck me."

Where the fuck did this man come from? This filthy little brat.

He lies back on the bed, opening his legs and giving me a devilish look. He opens the tube of lube, squeezing some out onto his fingertips before reaching between his legs to smear it over his asshole. The glistening hole holds my rapt attention, and when he slips a finger inside, my cock strains painfully.

I fall over him, running my nose along the length of his, then I grip his chin to pull his mouth open, licking my way inside. He moans around my tongue and props his feet on the lower part of my back, opening himself wider, trying to guide my cock where he wants it.

I push myself up to look at the space between us, the head of my cock nestled just under his balls. I grab them, massaging the smooth skin, then line myself up. Any other time I would ram myself inside of him, ensuring his scream of pain. I don't do that right now. Instead, I slowly feed him my cock, watching closely as his eyes widen.

Once I'm all the way in, I fall back over him and claim his mouth in a slow, sensual kiss. My tongue languidly tangles with his as my hips begin to pump a slow, deep rhythm, making sure to hit as far as I can go.

"Seb." He pulls away from my mouth, his voice hitching. "Don't, please." His begging gets choked by the sob that escapes him. "Don't make love to me. Fuck me, please."

My lips tremble at the sound of his agony, and I bury my face in his neck as my own tears break free. I continue the smooth caress of my cock in and out of him, savoring this. I let my tears soak his neck as his hands wrap around my back, and his nails dig into me.

He continues to beg me with pain-soaked cries right up to the very end when I spill everything inside of him. Then I stay there, nestled in the warmth of him, fearing the moment when I'm forced to leave him.

CHAPTER TWENTY-ONE

Sebastian

It's been two months since I've had him, and it's no easier each time I lay eyes on him. He's been cordial, laughing whenever I crack a joke in the locker room or joining in on conversations I'm a part of. But it's like what we had never existed.

Like he never loved me.

His eyes no longer smolder when I step into a room. He doesn't seek me out with those amber eyes when *he* steps into a room, we're nothing more than teammates. It doesn't keep me from taking his mother out to lunch once a week, which I know pisses him off.

It can't be helped… Marian is my homie.

I nearly choked on pasta when she showed me a large diamond glittering on her finger, proclaiming her engagement to Coach. We don't speak of Dixon. I think she knows how raw it still is for me, avoiding the subject of him altogether. Doesn't stop me from wondering how he feels about the whole thing.

There's still a large, gaping wound in my chest that festers more the longer we're apart.

He's been getting closer with Dani, and if she wasn't in a solid relationship with Jameson, I'd fear for her safety. I couldn't handle him dating anyone, so thankfully, there hasn't been anyone.

I know this because I still follow him. I rarely sleep in my bed at home, my Hummer has become my new bedroom, although that will have to change soon. The nights are getting too cold. I don't know what I'll do then.

Today we are going up against the Jets, the final game before the playoffs and Dixon's final game of the season. He doesn't seem down about it as I watch him running laps around the field. I'm proud of him for what he's accomplished, and his knee has completely healed.

The playoffs will be near impossible to win without him, but the team has decided to dedicate all our power toward making it happen in his name.

My life has been busy outside of this stadium. Beyond following around the man who's always been my obsession, I've been seeing a flurry of doctors and specialists. My injuries over the years— beginning in middle school—have resulted in early onset of Chronic Traumatic Encephalopathy, or CTE.

The headaches still come, and sometimes they're debilitating, but with some holistic treatments, they've been easier to handle. As of right now, there is no cure for what's beginning to happen, so I need to be proactive, starting with the decision about my future.

"I gotta tell you guys something." Jameson strides into the quiet locker room a half an hour later, disrupting our focused states.

We all look up and wait for him to spit it out, watching as he practically vibrates with excitement.

"Dani is pregnant again."

The guys go crazy as they cheer him on, and I nearly scoff, wanting to ask if it's his. But I'm turning over a new leaf, keeping my mouth shut and shit. I don't miss the surprised look Dixon shoots me, like he's thinking the same thing as we both break out in laughter.

"I'm going to ask her to marry me," Jameson beams.

"Congrats, bro." I step forward to haul him in for a hug. "That's amazing news. You two will be providing a whole roster for the Bills to choose from in twenty years."

"Hell yeah, we are." He bumps knuckles with me.

I really hope Dani is serious about him because I'd hate to see him heartbroken, especially with children involved.

I'll be the first to admit she's different, but I also know a cheetah rarely changes its spots, and all of this could be a fucking act. She's getting what she's always wanted: a rich athlete as a husband so she doesn't have to do a single thing but pop out kids for the rest of her life.

I'm obviously still not a fan of the bitch.

"Tonight is the last night we have Dixon running that ball into the end zone, and that means we need to send him out on a high note. I want us to bury them in the dirt." Zeal's speech starts, but today it feels different than all the others. It's loaded with emotion so thick, it hangs around our heads. "Let's go out there tonight and play like it's our last game, giving it our all."

The boys all cheer around me, but I'm staring at the man who's consumed me from the very first day he stepped on the field. It truly is a fine line between love and hate. His eyes meet mine, and the corner of his mouth perks up. But his eyes look sad. No. Not sad. Nostalgic.

Maybe he's thinking the same thing I am.

The urge to walk across the room and kiss that mouth is overwhelming. The energy coursing through me nearly makes me do it, but at the last second I stop myself. He'd probably knock me the fuck out anyway.

My feet are digging into the field, shooting divots of dirt in my path. My hands are outstretched and my fingers taut as I anticipate the ball. I don't slow down. I trust my teammates to cover my back, my eye staying trained on that stippled pigskin as it soars toward me.

Zeal's the league's MVP for good reason, his arm is like no other.

The ball lands right there in the sweet spot between my fingers. I tighten my grip just as Jameson takes out a defensemen on the opposite team in front of me. I try to correct my path but end up jumping over them both as the ball slips from my fingers, rushing toward the field as a free agent.

My teeth clamp around the mouth guard as I get over Jameson and the defensemen, but the ball bounces once, then twice, right out of my path.

Then he's there, as he always is when I need him. Dixon scoops it up just as two Jets plow into him, taking him down in one fell swoop. My breath catches in my throat as I hear Jameson yell, "Does he have it?" from behind me.

That's not what I'm worried about. I don't give a fuck who has the ball, I'm scared for his knee. It takes forever for the official to blow the fucking whistle, and when he does, I'm grabbing jerseys to haul these assholes off my man.

Once they get up, I find him there, curled around the ball secured in his arms and laughing like a fucking hyena.

"Get up." I slap his helmet then grab his hand, pulling him to his feet.

"We still have possession, Avando." His smile is wide around the mouthguard.

All I hear is *Avando,* and my heart sinks further. I've lost him, our love has nearly dissipated. Panic rises in my chest as he runs back to our team, all of them slapping him on the back for not letting my fumble fuck us over while I stand frozen to my spot, letting anxiety rip through me.

I'm losing him.

"Avando!" Zeal waves me over. "One more play! We've got this!" he exclaims as I join the huddle.

I nod, and he goes through the final play of the game, calling for Dixon to carry the ball into the end zone through the final twenty yards. It's a simple play, one we've done countless times. We could all do it with our eyes shut, but mine are wide open. I'm staring at him, yet he's oblivious to it, like he's wiped me clean from his slate.

My heart doesn't stop thrashing, my head is joining in the symphony of pain, and soon, everything around me pulses along with it. I'm losing him, and I'm losing myself too.

My hand grips my chest guard as I try to breathe in slowly, filling my lungs to capacity, hoping it slows the erratic thumping.

Zeal calls the play, and we get into position as my stomach swirls with something akin to fear. This will be the last game we play together for a while, and even though we'll still be teammates, everything that draws us together is coming to an end.

When the next season comes around, we'll be nothing more than the strangers we were when he first started. The thought is driving me further into my head as the ball is hiked.

How the fuck will I move on?

Soon I won't be able to sit outside his house anymore, and the lunches with Marian will slowly dwindle because she will always be loyal to her son.

Toxicity thrives inside of me, and knowing that, he's much better off without me. But he's changing me, he *has* changed me. I want a better life, to provide a secure future for my daughter and give her a stable family. I don't want to be Sebastian Avando the gangbanger. I want to be Sebastian Avando, the football player who loves Dixon North.

I want that so fucking bad.

We take off, running into the field, but my eye is on Dixon, watching as he catches the ball with ease, his eyes straight ahead on that thick white line.

Dixon

I will miss this.

The breeze rushes against my face as I run, the ball tucked in the crook of my arm with the roar of the fans screaming my name in the stands. *"North! North! North!"* There's nothing like it.

Despite the energy pulsing through me, I'm ready to take a break. I want to focus on me, and I want to spend time with my mother before she's out of the house and married to Coach.

It's so fucking weird, but she's happy.

I need the time to get over Sebastian too. He's all I think about, no matter the cool façade I wear whenever he's around. I need to come to terms with the fact that I've missed my one opportunity at true love.

The league wanted to reinstate me back for the playoffs, calling it an apology for their failure to act accordingly, but I refused the offer. Instead, I asked them to create a program to educate all players on the importance of acceptance, to practice inclusivity. *That* I would consider a heartfelt apology, so I was glad when they agreed.

I'll be okay in time. I have the support of my team, and I've been working hard to change things.

Another grunt sounds behind me as Dex takes down a Jet player, and it's like music to my ears, giving me the extra burst I need to pump my legs toward that end zone. My vision tunnels as I zone out, ready to fucking fly. Then I dig in harder, driving myself to my top speed.

The crowd goes insane, and as soon as my toe hits the white paint, I jump off the ground and sail over it, a scream ripping from my throat.

I land back on the ground, well inside the end zone, feeling the sudden pang of pain shooting through my knee that will never fully go away, but it's tolerable. I turn around to see my teammates screaming along with me, their arms in the air.

The playoffs were always a sure thing, this win just solidifies it.

And this time, when I sink to my knees, yanking the helmet off my head, sweat and tears coursing over my cheeks, I tip my head back and scream my brother's name.

"Daniel North!"

I fall forward, and suddenly, a pair of shoes are in front of me, a pair I know very well. I look up into his amber eyes as he hauls me up, and I see something in their depths that spikes both my desire and my fear.

His love is shining unencumbered by fear or rejection. It's pure as it radiates from the depths of his irises, and my heart drops, realizing what he's about to do.

Out here.

On live broadcast.

In front of thousands of people.

He grabs my face to pull me in, his mouth hovering over mine, making everything around us slip away.

"Seb?" my voice wavers, watching as his heat.

"I love when you call me Seb. I always have."

Then his mouth is scorching over mine, hot flesh devouring me and forcing my lips open with his inferno tongue. I have no will to stop him, to consider the statement we're making and just how wide a platform we're standing on.

None of it matters.

My arms are around his back, dragging him in closer and letting it be known that this is the man I love. Judgment be damned.

Suddenly, we're surrounded by arms and bodies as our teammates collide around us, forcing us to break the kiss and laugh. All of their faces shine with pride and happiness, the acceptance from them pouring forth.

"I fucking knew it!" Dex screams.

"You guys look sexy as fuck!" Ortiz exclaims.

"That was fucking hot!" Zeal chimes in.

The noise of the crowd filters back in, and I'm taken aback by their loud cheering, louder than I've ever heard it. It makes me feel ashamed that I ever doubted the reception we'd receive.

Seb leans back in to press a sweet kiss to my mouth, prompting the guys to oooh and aaah.

"I love you," He mouths, those lips tipping up into that mischievous smirk I love.

"I love you," I mouth back.

EPILOGUE

Sebastian

"Daddy!" Carla bellows as she slides along the tile of the kitchen floor. "I want to wear my yellow dress today."

Dixon crouches down in front of her as I lean against the doorway, watching them.

"What did Papi say?" he asks as he twirls one of her curls around his finger.

"He said it's not cleaned yet." Her arms cross over her chest. "But he said that yesterday!"

"I will clean it for you tonight, but that can't be the only dress you wear to school. You have others that are just as pretty." He gives her nose a small tap.

"It's my favorite dress, Daddy." She gives him those eyes she knows melts his resolve, and sure enough, he deflates right in front of her.

"Okay, baby."

Her arms wrap around his neck with a squeal, and I watch as he buries his nose in her curls, inhaling her. I've never seen a love so pure.

"Ahem," I clear my throat. "Did you just give Daddy more work, *mija*?"

"No, Papi." She turns to glare at me, looking so much like her mother it makes my chest ache. "Daddy loves me."

"Come on." I roll my eyes exaggeratedly as I grab her school bag. "Let's get you in the car."

She plants a kiss on Dixon's cheek then runs to the door to slip on her shoes. I pull him in next, claiming his mouth in a short, brutal kiss.

"I haven't forgotten that shit you did last night, rookie," I murmur against his mouth. "You'll be punished later."

"Okay, *Papi*."

I try my damnedest to maintain the stern look on my face, but it all crumbles when he gives me a kiss.

"I love you," he says, a small smile playing around his lips.

"I love you too."

The drive to Carla's school is silent as she pops her earphones in and listens to the music coming from the Spotify app on my phone. Everything has changed in the past year; nothing of my life resembles what it used to be.

I no longer have any affiliates back in Rochester. The day I killed Delano, I wiped my hands clean of that place forever, all ties having been severed.

We didn't win the playoffs last year, but the Bills did go the furthest we ever have, and this year, they plan on bringing it home. Yes, *they*, not me. I'm retiring due to CTE. Even though I am in the earliest stages, my head couldn't withstand another hit. I've learned so much, and it explains a lot about my mood swings and impulsive behavior. I want to live long enough to see my daughter married with a family of her own, so I need to retire.

Carla belts out a Mariah Carrey song, making me chuckle and shake my head. The older she gets, the more of Paola I see in her. It warms my heart to know I will forever have a piece of her with me. I know she's been watching us and is proud of how far I've come.

I'm so proud of how far I've come.

The ring sitting on my finger twinkles in the sunlight that filters in from the driver's side window. I married the man as soon as he would let me, beating Coach and Marian to the altar. There was no way I was giving him time to change his mind. I know I'm a fucking handful.

Paola's parents came, their presence was like a balm, soothing my nerves. They've been so supportive of Dixon and me.

I may have hated Dixon the second I saw him, but he was put there to save me. He saved my life. He believes he was meant to pull his family out of generational poverty, that that's why he's a Bill, but I know different.

God knew I needed an angel.

"Ma!" I groan as I open the door to the frustrating woman with yet another casserole in her hands. "We still have the other one you dropped off yesterday."

"Are you boys not eating? And what about my grandchild? Do you think she can grow on only air and happiness?" she grumbles as she pushes her way into the house.

"Can't you just make Coach eat all these?"

"Gregory loves my cooking." She bats her lashes.

"*Gregory*," I mock Coach's name, making her swat my arm.

"What time are you dropping Carla off tonight? Maybe I should feed her dinner?"

"Ma!" I exclaim. "The last time we dropped her off, she told us you gave her chocolate before bed."

"She needs some meat on her bones." She clicks her tongue as she puts the casserole in the fridge, right next to the one from the day before.

"We'll drop her off around eight this evening," I tell her as I lean on the counter.

Whenever we have early morning practices, Carla spends the night with Ma and Coach, saves us from having to wake her up so early in the morning.

Ma brushes by me, giving me a quick pat to the cheek while securing the strap of her purse over her shoulder. "I'll have dinner ready tonight for when you drop her off."

"Ma!" I yell again. "You just dropped off a casserole!"

"That'll be for your lunch tomorrow." She opens the front door. "I love you."

She disappears as quickly as she appeared as I wearily slump to the counter. It's been a long year, and even though the league has facilitated a lot of changes, there are still many more needed. I've been helping with that, and so has Seb. We're trying to create a fair playing ground, so to speak.

Our life here at home has been amazing. Seb and Carla moved into the house with me, while Ma moved in with Coach. Not only have I gained an amazing husband, but also a beautiful daughter. One my mother and Coach clearly adore. We could never replace Daniel, but it's helped my mother let go of some of the pain she carried around with her daily.

Seb and I exchanged vows before Coach and Ma, who have been inseparable this whole year. I can admit he's really good to her, even if it still grosses me out. They're planning a wedding after the playoffs because Coach can't handle having any more on his plate until they're over.

Not to mention we won't have Seb to see us through to the end. He's retiring after the final season game. As much as it pains me to lose him as my teammate, it ensures I keep him forever as my husband. That's what's most important to me.

Dani and Jameson were married a few months ago, and she's currently pregnant with kid number three. She's hoping for a girl while Jameson wants another boy. Even I'm praying for a girl because the two boys they already have are a fucking handful.

We hang out every so often, but Seb still isn't pro-Dani,

making it awfully awkward when he's around. Most of the time, I pop in with gifts, play with the boys, then head back out.

The door opens and shuts with a bang, the force of it jarring me out of my thoughts and making me roll my eyes. He'll never completely soften, and I'm more than okay with that.

"Pants off, brat!" he hollers as he comes into the kitchen. "You better hope there's lube in this kitchen somewhere."

He strides in, his shirt ripping over his head and tattoos on full display. And as always, I'm hard at the drop of a hat.

He stops, giving me a heated once over. "You're still clothed."

"My mother was just here, bringing food. What if she comes back?" I smirk as he steps closer.

His hand seals around my throat, backing me up to the counter and invading my space. "Then you'd better stop talking and get naked."

My arms wrap around his waist as I tug him in closer, holding him tight to me.

"Thank you," I murmur into the skin of his chest.

"For what?" He releases my throat.

"For fighting for me, for not letting me slip away. For giving me a happiness greater than I've ever known."

"You did all that, baby." His arms encircle my shoulders, his head hitting the top of mine. "You saved me."

Seb believes I came to him at the perfect time and slowly saved him from the life he was sure would kill him. But I know better.

He was sent to me during a time I almost let it all go, when my life seemed like a complete waste … like I was a complete waste. He proved me wrong with the love he forced on me. Regardless of how toxic it was, it was ours.

Our very own Hail Mary play.

ALSO BY C.A. RENE

The Whitsborough Chronicles

Through the Pain

Into Darkness

Finding the Light

To Redemption

The Whitsborough Progenies

Ivy's Venom

Carmelo's Malice

Saxon's Distortion

Gabriel's Deception

Desecrated Duet

Desecrated Flesh

Desecrated Essence

The Reaped Series

The Reaper Incarnate

Hunting the Reaper

Claiming the Reaper

Hail Mary Duet

Blue 42

Red Zone

Sacrificial Lambs

Sing Me a Song

Song of Tenebrae

A Verse for Caelum

Festum Mors
Mimic

For all book updates and social platforms, check out my website

ABOUT THE AUTHOR

C.A. Rene lives in Toronto, Canada with her family, where most of the year varies from chilly to frigid. Most days you'll find her wrapped in her many blankets in bed while reading or writing her next dark, twisted story.
Her stories boast of inclusivity and refusal to be conformed in any small box. Writing across genres is a hobby and drinking wine is a must… Or coffee … with a splash of Baileys.

www.ingramcontent.com/pod-product-compliance
Lightning Source LLC
Chambersburg PA
CBHW051135190726
48290CB00006B/1855